LYING
IN
BED

Also by Mark Harris

Novels
Killing Everybody
The Goy
Wake Up, Stupid
Something About a Soldier
City of Discontent
Trumpet to the World

Novels in the Henry Wiggen manner
It Looked Like For Ever
A Ticket for a Seamstitch
Bang the Drum Slowly
The Southpaw

Autobiography
Best Father Ever Invented
Twentyone Twice
Mark the Glove Boy

Biography
Saul Bellow: Drumlin Woodchuck

Collection
Short Work of It

Play
Friedman & Son

Screenplay
Bang the Drum Slowly
Boswell for the Defence

Television film
The Man That Corrupted Hadleyburg

Editor
The Heart of Boswell: Highlights from the Journal of James Boswell

LYING
IN
BED

Mark Harris

A NOVEL

McGraw-Hill Book Company
New York   St. Louis   San Francisco
Hamburg   Mexico   Toronto

1 2 3 4 5 6 7 8 9 D O C D O C 8 7 6 5 4

ISBN 0-07-026844-4

LIBRARY OF CONGRESS CATALOGING IN PUBLICATION DATA

Harris, Mark, 1922–
Lying in bed.
I. Title.
PS3515.A757L9 1984   813'.54   83-25621

Book design by Nancy Dale Muldoon

For Josephine

LYING
IN
BED

February 1

Dear Dr. Youngdahl:

I want to thank you so much for the glorious lunch at Monti's La Casa Vieja and for giving me Mr. Klang's address. I have awarded this some thought and I think I will send him my manuscript as soon as I am back from the ski lodge. Until you put the idea into my head I could not picture myself as being the kind of writer who sends something to an agent in crass New York, but I will follow your advice anyhow, because it comes from you. I hope to think of an appropriate title soon, and perhaps at the same time I will arrive at a final decision on how to spell my name. Not that anyone is going to print it. (Please forgive me for the phrase "final decision." I recognize its redundance. I know I should not offend you who so relentlessly wars against redundance.)

I look forward to further comments you will be making on my manuscript. I recently learned that the abbreviation for "manuscript" is "ms.," which I consider prophetic because those are my own initials. I had thought "ms." referred only to the form of address for a woman, and to the magazine of that name.

I was relieved that you did not find my manuscript objectionable, and I was reassured to hear you say you did not in any way interpret the subject matter therein as autobiographical; understanding that that is not my life at all but the lives of characters I have invented: pure fiction out of the whole cloth. I understand now why authors like to print up in front of their books, "All the characters herein are purely fictional and any resemblance to real or living persons is purely coincidental."

I am hoping my parents will look on the matter in the same way, recognizing, as you do, the processes of fictional invention. However, that is a great deal to ask of people who have never given one moment's thought to the processes of anything except making money, fattening beef, grinding down children, and campaigning against the teaching of Darwinism in the schools of Arizona.

I suppose I should have known your attitude would be liberal and understanding. I know you don't like us to use superlatives, but you are the most sophisticated man I have ever met. As you can guess, most of the men I meet are boys. I feel so stupid about the wine in the restaurant, and I laugh with utmost admiration for your cosmopolitan wit when I remember your saying, "We should have ordered white wine with a white tablecloth." You amazed me. You never for a single instant looked at the wine; you just stood the glass up and placed a napkin over the scarlet pool and never took your eyes from mine. You are truly sophisticated. It was the nicest thing that has happened to me in a long time. You have told us time and again never to use the expression, "I have no words to express . . ." because a writer should *find* the words to express whatever thoughts she wishes to express. Nevertheless, with many apologies for my error I must say, "I have no words to express my thrill of our luncheon."

You have given me self-confidence without which I could not have gone on. Last semester I was on the verge of leaving, feeling so victimized and put upon by so many people in this so-called institution, when one day you said to me, "O well, that's what we writers have to put up with." You were saying that I, too, was a writer. Nobody has ever said such a thing to me before. As far as I knew (know; I see that my tenses have fallen into inconsistency here) I was the only person in the world who viewed myself as a writer. I could not possibly have gone on without you. You opened every window for me.

Please consider the following thought: Would you consider me as a likely candidate to write your biography? Perhaps I should switch from fiction to non-fiction. Having told my story as a novel perhaps I am ready to undertake a huge, extensive work, such as your biography, which might take me a year to do. You need not answer right away. My plan would be to write down everything you say on every subject in your classroom, in your conferences with students, and at whatever social occasions I could manage to worm my way into. The things you say are so profound and so witty and so freighted with clarity that I should hate to see them wasted on the desert air.

Full many a gem of purest ray serene,
The dark unfathomed caves of ocean bear:
Full many a flower is born to blush unseen,
And waste its sweetness on the desert air.

—*lines 53–56, Elegy Written in a*
Country Church-Yard, Thomas Gray
(1716–1771)

I am flying up again for a long weekend skiing in Colorado. I don't know why. I hate skiing, I hate the people I go with, and I always get a headache from the fireplace smoke in the lodge. The Snow Devil Ski Club leaves me cold. I stay in the lodge all day and write while everybody else is out skiing until the fireplace smoke drives me out. I am allergic to burning wood. Once outdoors I'll ski to keep from freezing to death. I cannot go into my private room because there are no doors on the rooms (therefore they are not even private, are they?) and one sleeps in the smoke all night if one sleeps at all. With no doors on the un-private rooms the mountain night echoes with the sounds of room-crashing by athletic or highly amorous young men similar to my descriptions in the corresponding chapter of my as-yet-untitled novel. But it's an opportunity for me to park my baby with friends here and there in Sin City and we get a chance to get away from each other.

This letter is the hardest writing I have ever done—more superlatives. It doesn't sound the least bit like the me I know and love. I could write ten pages of hyperactive rolling-along fiction in the time it has taken me to write this letter.

Please, please enjoy every minute of your life rich in the love of your numerous family and your many friends, as you deserve. You are the best man I have ever met. You deserve everything good, everything the best, all possible superlatives.

Your very respectful student,

TO: Lucien Youngdahl, physician, Mineral del Monte Indian Preserve, Mexico, and to All Points: Bernice, Bernique, Earl, Glenna, Tetsey, Thornton. Enclosure: "Calling Card Number 40."

February 1

Dear Lucien,

I have been taking these zinc tablets and taking them in large quantities, too, just gobbling them down like mad without anything happening as far as I can detect. What do you propose? More of the same? Won't I become a zinc-head? Why am I laughing? They seem to affect my stomach unfavorably, too. However, I'll stay with them until I hear further from you.

I enclose a copy of my new Calling Card just printed up.

I went to a urologist recommended by Wally Drew. I didn't like him and I won't go back. He didn't like me, either. He seemed to object to my asking or verifying the meanings of certain words contained in the questions he asked, as if I were a petty bother. He acted as if I should answer his questions whether or not I knew the meanings of the words he was using—such a busy man couldn't waste his time explaining things to the ignorant likes of me.

The whole subject is rather embarrassing. I so much envy people with broken legs and sprained shoulders and other afflictions so much more discussable than mine. I am told that seventy percent of all men over sixty years old suffer the same thing, but apparently most men accept it and shrug it off, saying, "O. K., so I'm growing older, it's over, my wife doesn't care for it anyway," but I don't feel that way about it at all, and neither does my wife, I'm not surrendering, I plan to go on, I don't plan to quit, I have no intention of hanging up the old libido.

Soon mother flies off to you on the first leg of her tour, carrying with her all sorts of goodies to compensate you for the difficulties of your isolation, exotic things you asked for or she divined you'd like—liquid ink, shoelaces, popcorn, dog biscuits, and genuine United States toothpaste. If she weren't loaded down with things for you she might not go. She does not wish to leave me alone. She feels that she is failing me by leaving me home all alone with my impotence. But she can accomplish nothing by staying home. Not to be too specific about it—she has tried and nothing has happened. And it's not as if I'm sick in bed requiring daily care and feeding and assistance to and from the bathroom.

She is off and on angry with me. She thinks I have surrendered. But I have not surrendered—I've said that. O. K., so I said it again. She goes for hours without talking to me except to say, "Did you feed the animals?" and after I feed the animals she says, "You overfed the animals." She used to tell me I overfed children. She threatens not to go on her tour. But if she doesn't go how can we ever again face the Travel Agency. It was a lot of logistics, you may be sure. "If I don't cure you," she says, "somebody else will." She has that fear. I reassure her, saying, "No. Only two possibilities exist: Time will cure me or Nothing will cure me." No Somebody Else exists.

Whatever you do, enjoy your life where you are even without so many of the practical things you learned to become accustomed to when you were a boy in the house of your rich and affluent North American father. We all admire your doing it who wouldn't do it ourselves. I am an armchair Christian. Even so, I often wish I were doing something more useful than the things I seem to be doing. These doubts always beset me when I try to confront some sort of new writing project. Every time I get the least flickering wavering glimmer of an idea I lean back and ask myself whether, among all the things the world requires, it truly requires another book from me.

The other day on campus was International Hunger Day, or something of the sort. A student organization had lined a stretch of the Mall with photographs showing children all over the world suffering terrible diseases. In this age of audio-visual aids one of the student exhibits showed moving pictures of children in Africa actually dying. In the film people stood around watching the child as people might watch a child doing some cute little trick. Children dying before people's eyes is an everyday thing there (he says, nibbling from a bowl of fresh fruit, shining red grapes, luscious squares of melon prepared in silence by your angry mother). Why don't I go out and *do* something? Not five miles from where I sit people are starving. I complain that the media do not call these things to my attention, but as a matter of fact within fifteen minutes after I saw the African film I had quite forgotten it and didn't think of it again until today. I went to the bank. I carry more money in the left-side pocket of my trousers than ninety-three percent of the world earn in a year. Statistics invented, but the principle is accurate.

So I write about it in a letter to you, instead of putting on my Tolstoyan boots and going out to fight poverty. Then I'll write about it in a letter to somebody else, or I'll write it up in notes to myself, providing myself with the feeling that now that I've written it up in a number of places I've more or less solved the problem.

Then I'll get into writing an actual book and I'll put the whole world out of my mind for two years. I don't expect to be blocked forever. Mother says she definitely would not go if I had writing going. She has gone away before when I've been blocked, and when she returned home I had smashed my way out of it. But it's hard for me between things.

Some days ago mother said bitterly about her going, "Look upon it as a warm-up for when you're a widower." I started to write a story about a man whose fantasies of his wife's death lead him to some definite thoughts: whom will he marry, where will he live with his new wife, how will he alter his will? When the man found himself actually on the way to his lawyer's office he knew he had fantasized too far. And when I got that far in my story I stopped, too, and for the same reason—I was making things come true. I have always been afraid that my writing made things happen I hadn't meant to make happen. Mine is the art life is always imitating. So that stops me, too.

Well, I'll stay with the zinc as long as you still zinc it might do me some good. Please tell me what you think a next step might be. This damn urologist got me down. He in turn has recommended a specialist in Los Angeles. To whom shall I go and what shall I do? If you weren't so healthy in your mind you'd be succumbing to all sorts of Freudian fits over this: the mechanism which produced you has failed; the apparatus has gone down (only for the moment, we hope). My dear boy, you got in just under

6/

the wire. Another thirty-five years and you'd have been out in the cold, you'd have been a negative existence, a man without a life.

Mother will kiss you and embrace you for me when she arrives, and I in the meantime by advance mail send you as always all my love and affection and devotion and admiration.

THE LIST OF MY BOOKS

The Hard Puncher
The Utah Manner
Boswell's Manhattan Journal (play)
Speed Speed and More Speed
Dreams
The Life of John Lockhart (biography)
The Duck Who Fed People in the Park (children's book)
A Snow Job
The Telephone Tree
Robert Burns's Indiscretions (biography)
When Your Bicycle Tires
Boswell's Manhattan Journal (screenplay)
Sixty-Nine Shockingly Dirty Stories and Jokes (with Abner Klang)
Why Am I in the English Department?
The Man Who Loved Women Who Write

All the works above except *Boswell's Manhattan Journal* (screenplay) were published by Apthorp House. Many of them were kept a top secret by that businesslike house but may be obtained by a campaign of harassment directed at Francine and Frank Apthorp, proprietors.

—*Lee Youngdahl*

February 2
James Joyce's Birthday

Dear Virgilia,

I have had several brilliant ideas in mind lately and they have all come to nothing. I get very hot on them and they go very cold on me. They are ideas I have carried around with me for years and years, and I think to myself, "Ah, yes, this is the idea whose time has come for me at last," but when I sit down and start to compose it it's just not there. Where it went I never know. Under the desk? The dogs ate it? The cats played tug-of-war with it until it came apart at the middle? I am suffering from a deficiency of inventiveness. I am suffering (according to a book on sexual health which I have been reading, for reasons I shall no doubt come to by the end of this letter) from "fantasy failure": my power of fantasy has allegedly been diminished by time in the way our sheer physical powers diminish. Do you believe such a thing is possible? Can fantasy be quantified like blood and made visible and packaged and carried around in emergency vehicles marked *Bloodmobile* which dart into empty parking spaces just as you yourself were about to dart into them? If so, where can I go for a fantasy transfusion to start up my circulation again?

The next day. It's all so universal. I feel so irreversibly universal. Everything that's happened to me has happened, I'm sure, to everybody in my comparable situation in every generation. I'm sure this period of dryness I'm going through has tormented and plagued every writer in every age who ever traveled this distance in his career. I seem to notice the fear of nothingness in many biographical passages I read these days; writers looking back over their shoulders. I had a letter awhile back from Dick Stern in Chicago, my fellow whistler in the dark this past quarter-century or more. Dick wrote, "I'm trying hard now and think I have something—though it seriously occurs to me that something in me may have broken & that I'll never finish another long narrative." This after many excellent and complex books. He goes on with a hopeful view of himself which reminds me of me: "Yet I will be found—I imagine—breathing my last at the ole electric."

As a matter of fact Alan Swallow (you met him in the old days) fell dead over *his* ole electric. Mae Swallow found him in the morning, head on machine, machine humming. The idea of confronting another long work is appalling and forbidding. It used to be I wondered how I did it, but that was after it was done, and I was glad I hadn't known in the beginning how arduous it was going to be. I see this by Updike in *Bech is Back*: " 'Another?' The thought sickened him. A whole new set of names to invent, a theme to nurture within like a tumor, a texture to maintain page after page." Bill Gibson wrote me from Stockbridge recently: "I would like nothing more than to interest myself in writing another novel now, but don't know if I can. . . . Styron said after completing *Sophie's Choice* that writing a novel is like crawling on your knees from Vladivostok to Gibraltar, and I think it does take more old-fashioned *character* in the writer. More patience, more thoughtfulness, more independence of the world and its responses. And certainly more time, which is running out."

And then when you're through crawling all that distance and using up all the little character you had what have you got besides money and fame and pride and satisfaction and a totally new understanding and comprehension of your own life and times? Not a goddam thing. And after a few months even that wears off and you feel as stupid as ever.

You certainly haven't got the love and respect of your colleagues. A week ago I went to the funeral of a colleague who represents for me for all time the epitome of the stupid, ignorant, deluded critic or scholar or whatever he thought he was, who at least at one moment of his life had the decency to be stricken with guilt, which came about in the following way:

When I first came here I knew he was here but I made no effort to meet him. We were introduced, we shook hands, I seldom saw him about. He cared very little to be where students might find him. His retreat was his library carrel—more a room really— where he had spent years and years writing criticism of fiction and pounding the shit out of every writer of fiction who dared to appear with a book, and arranging and ranking all writers in categories according to a system of his own devising, at which he had arrived sitting in his own stink in his little library room. I mean this—his stink. His stink was genuine. But I didn't know that right off.

He was always announcing to the world that this writer or that writer was through, worthless. So And So had nothing more to tell us, killing off writers left and right, killing them off young, or if they got away from him young he killed them off old.

Now and then I encountered him. He scowled at me. He had opposed my coming in the first place, and now that I was here he apparently viewed me as some sort of irritating necessity, the fellow the University was forced to hire to deal with those unruly students who thought of themselves as writers. I was the "creative" professor assigned to leash the "creative" students: those students too lazy or demented or irresponsible to undertake the real labor of literary life, which was not to create stories or poems but to assassinate people who do. We were his target practice. Once when I passed his room in the library I poked my head inside to greet him, not more than how do you d- —when I choked, suffocated, was felled and routed by the most awful stench ever was smelled from a library nook or anywhere else between Heaven and earth. People laughed when I told them. This critic was famous for sitting in his own stink. He was a pathological farter. It wasn't so bad in the morning but after lunch it was awful.

I never went near him again—but once. And here I relate to you an experience as instructive as any experience I have ever had or will. I was passing through the library one day when all of a sudden there he was, looming ahead of me, blocking my way, the World-Famous Critic And God's Own Living Fart himself. He was standing in a state of stupefaction, dazed, slugged by something, smiling at me. He had never smiled at me. He thrust his hand forward to shake mine. Not since the day we had met had he acknowledged me in this way or any other. It was as if he was congratulating me. What had I done? Had something come in on the radio about me? Had my name appeared in *Time*? He went absolutely hysterical about such things, endlessly mentioning the conspiracy of such things, endlessly adoring it and wishing he were in on it.

Let me tell you why he was all a-tremble to shake my hand. It was his finest moment. It may have been his only moment. He was prepared to shake my hand because he had just attempted for the first time in his life to write a bit of fiction. He who for years and years had been writing criticism of fiction and whipping to death anyone daring to try the art of story-telling had now, for the first time, *actually tried to write a bit of fiction.* He asked me if I'd read it. He gave me a copy. I took it home overnight. It was dreadful. I told him so. He said, "Good enough, I'll show it to somebody else." It was five pages long, about an elderly professor buying a cemetery plot. From a humane point of view everything in it should have moved me sympathetically. I tried. Nothing less than the imminence of his own death had finally inspired him to try to practice the art he had spent his lifetime so bloodily and wantonly dissecting. But though I tried I could find not a single phrase to commend. It was simply pitiful. Had he not made his life's work the condemnation of all writers I might have been able at least to pat him on the shoulder, squeeze his arm. Did I weep at his grave? Not hardly. Beth is fond of his wife or we wouldn't have gone in the first place.

The third day. I send you herewith my newest Calling Card. I know this Card has made you angry from time to time in the past. You once sent it back to me shredded. I know your reaction depends on whether you're working well, and since I know you're working well at the moment I send it to you without fear. I'm never sure what season you are in—whether you're loving me or hating me. Either way I wouldn't blame you. Abner says you've got a good book going, so I expect you'll be cordial to me.

All right, forward as promised to the question of sexual health. A couple of days ago I re-read *Doctor's Out* because so much of my life these days seems taken up with doctors. I tell you again what a sterling book it is in every respect. How did you do it? How did we all do it? Where did all our energy come from? I don't know. In those days I could write all night and I could write in any position on any surface and I could write hungry or troubled. I could tend children and teach school and repair my automobile and shop for groceries and read several books a week and in my spare time play softball squash handball tennis and box in the gymn. My eye falls now and again on my shelf of my very own books still shining with color in their jackets as new as the day they arrived in the mail, and their photographs revealing, from jacket to jacket and book to book and year to year, Yours Truly maturing from work to work until maturing becomes aging, one might say (there, I've said it myself, haven't I?). That rash young man with the smoothest cheek in the world has become that seasoned, weathered, grizzled veteran of the literary storms of these last forty years.

Now, however, I have become impotent.

Have you known men to whom this impotence has happened? And what did they do about it? Write or wire.

This has been almost two months now. Beth has reassured me and has encouraged me and done everything (so to speak) to assist me. She has been on the phone and she has slyly or shyly taken some books from the library to read up and find out what it is that makes this thing work that had worked without flaws (by and large) for almost forty years. In spite of her earnest efforts things have gone from bad to worse, from merely embarrassing failure to absolute rock-bottom impotence; nothingness; a deadness like death; utter limpness.

Fearing now that it's not something that's just going to go away like a head cold I mounted my bicycle at last and visited a urologist recommended to me by my physician—Wally Drew, my old Utah boyhood chum, of whom you have heard me speak, I am sure. Wally told me that this urologist was very "relaxed." Yes, he was very relaxed, indeed, especially on medical subjects, in which he appeared to have no interest. His true, tense interest was real estate. Believe me, you caught this contemptible man once and for all in *Doctor's Out*—the doctor who was building the high-rise.

His chief nurse or office manager began by scolding me for being late for my appointment. I had not been late. Oh, that's right, "you're Mr. Youngdahl, it's Mr. Jones that's late, your names are so much alike." What difference did it make?—the doctor wasn't there yet and would not appear for some time. We patients were backed up in his waiting-room, which was plastic Victorian, sturdy plush chairs with graceful, curving ebony wooden legs; the windows were heavily draped; thus the interior lighting was bad, as if we were in the early days of electricity. Some "antiqued" oils were on the wall—bad new American Western landscapes rubbed up to look old, but they were so obscure in the semi-darkness I thought at first What a clever idea, chalkboards for messages for people to write things like "George, don't wait for me." In moments of stress my critical senses fail.

In all this subdued light with its suggestion of an age gone by every imaginable modern gadget was nevertheless sounding off, bells were ringing, buzzers were buzzing. Lights were flashing. The chief nurse and her assistants worked busily out of a bullpen surrounded by the waiting room and examining rooms. Neither nurse nor patient nor anyone else could move from one area to another except by someone's causing doors to be unlocked and locked, locked and unlocked, one door at a time for maximum security, accompanied by bells and buzzers and warning flashers and by agile nurses *leaping* to reach the gate ahead before it locked itself against them—visions of whiteness flying through murky space.

Why all this? I supposed that the security was related to keeping patients' records safe and confidential. But the chief nurse explained it in another way: "We got money and drugs back here." This was not a patient-oriented office. She quite agreed: "We keep 'em moving," said she.

At length she escorted me through gates locking and unlocking fore and aft into a little room-with-toilet where I was to provide her with specimens of my urine to be deposited in "bottles" (plastic cups), after which I might wash my hands with—handing me—this "towelette" (square of paper towel). I performed these assigned tasks. I was sheep-like, docile. But this was not why I had come. I had gone to this doctor to talk, to explore, to inquire. Handing me a white gown the chief nurse said, "Remove your outer clothing." What did she mean by "outer"?

"Everything," she said. "Doctor will be with you," she added.

"When?"

"Shortly."

14/

But I knew he wouldn't. He wasn't even in the house. Where was he? Was he in surgery? Was he attending an emergency? (Was he one of that new breed of Good Samaritan young doctors pledged to help people fallen on the street? What a laugh!) No, he was off with an "associate" negotiating real estate. That much I soon understood. "I wonder what you mean by *shortly*," I said.

"You might as well remove your outer clothing," she said, losing a little patience. "Doctor's charge for a consultation is the same as his charge for an examination. It will cost you just as much no matter what you do."

"I'm not really thinking about cost," I told the nurse.

If I were thinking about cost I'd stay impotent. Think of the thousands and thousands of dollars I have spent on women! Think of the *time* I've spent on women! If I had devoted to writing the time I have devoted to chasing women around five of the seven continents I'd have written two more books, one hundred more stories, and one thousand sonnets. How much food and beverage have I bought for women? How many telephone calls have I placed to women in all corners of the universe? How many letters have I written to women around the globe, each letter post-paid in full so it wouldn't bounce back? (Even then, some came back, arousing Beth's anger.) How many fine gifts have I bought for how many fine women?

The doctor arrived at the clinic at last, or so I assumed because I could now hear from the direction of the bull-pen an extraordinarily deep male voice issuing commands to the nurses, and soon talking on the telephone. But it was not medicine he was talking on the telephone. Indeed not. He was talking real estate. He and his "associate" had apparently just departed from a real-estate conference with a third party or parties and were caucusing by phone while I—now changed into the discomfort and indignity of my white gown—sat listening neither patiently nor sympathetically.

Whether his "associate" was a medical associate or a real-estate associate I had no way of knowing. Apparently they were negotiating to buy a building in Phoenix to be partly occupied by thriving tenants already committed to the idea, and partly by "one of the other groups." Doctor was expressing confidence that they could now "close things" by phone as soon as "you know who" produced certain papers proving clear title to certain property "you know where." During this conversation and others to follow I soon learned the deal not only in its general terms but in many of its particulars, and by a process of deductive reasoning was soon able to identify with confidence who was "you know who" and where was "you know where." So simple is real estate that it may be understood by one untrained man sitting behind a closed door in scanty flapping gown listening to only one side of a guarded telephone conversation.

Doctor talked excitedly, his voice rising and becoming clearer and clearer to me as he advanced upon solutions. The scent of a satisfying deal lightened his head. Now and again (at the warning, I think, of his chief nurse, cautioning him that he could be heard all over the joint by patients growing less patient) he lowered his voice, although as often as he lowered it it rose again.

Of these impatient patients I was one, largest and angriest, so that it was apparently me he came to first when he had, for the moment at least, concluded his land speculations. He was taking me first, he said, "even though you were late." He appeared to have studied my chart a bit while he was on the phone. Chief nurse had written "take number 1" and around "Occupation" had drawn a meaningful circle: "professor."

He was young, perhaps twelve years old, sandy-haired and beardless and so slight of build I had a hard time squaring him with that mighty real-estate voice of high command which had shivered the timbers of this jerry-built structure. I could see why such a small fellow might prefer to "close things" by telephone rather than in person: he was much more impressive heard than seen. In his deep subterranean voice he asked me (of all sentences my least favorite), "What can I do for you, Professor Youngdahl?"

"You can rescue me from impotence," I cried.

"Impotency," he said. Perhaps he was correcting me. "We'll try," he said, reading my clipboard, stalling, and then again: "You were late."

Not as late as you, my child.

Balancing my clipboard on his thigh, he began by asking me routine questions about my general condition and health and background and occupation (it was enough that I was a professor; he did not ask my subject), soon moving to the specific nature of

16/

my complaint. But he interrupted his own thought—if that's what it was—every time he heard a phone call to the bull-pen which might have been that real-estate call for which he was waiting with a great deal more interest than he was taking in my sexual efficiency. Soon, quite without a word to me of apology or farewell (I don't know what signal came to him), he sprang from his little chair and dashed from the room and spoke in his deep bass voice on the telephone to one of his real-estate associates. I groaned to realize that this was not one of the associates to whom he had been speaking: this was an altogether new voice or ear, as I detected by the fact of the doctor's now repeating aspects of the deal with which anyone but a rank newcomer would have been familiar.

I decided to dress. I did dress. He eventually returned, not even with an apology, picking up his abandoned clipboard and resuming his questioning at the point he vaguely remembered having left off.

Except that he was mighty confused! For he had been following a line of questioning suitable to a gowned patient, and here I was fully dressed. He could have *sworn* I'd been gowned. Was he losing his senses? Was his head *that* muddled with the facts of real estate?

He asked me if I had any "neurological" problems. I said I was not certain because I was not certain of the meaning of the word "neurological." I asked if he might define it for me, to which he took a clear objection, darting at me a look of real suspicion, and observing with a glance at his clipboard the nurse's notation ("take number 1") reminding him that I had not only arrived late (which was untrue) but I was a quibbler besides.

He seemed to feel that I was challenging him. "Why are you hesitant to answer my question?" he inquired.

"I'm not hesitant at all," I replied. "On the contrary, I want to give you every bit of information about me as accurately as I can. That's why I want to know what the word means before I try to answer the question."

Turns out he didn't need the answer after all. He crossed over into the sexual area.

When was my most recent ejaculation?

At least two months ago.

Do I masturbate?

No.

Do I try to masturbate?

No.

Was my problem hormonal?

I had no idea—barely knew what hormones were. I was timid about asking, having done so badly on "neurological."

Do I have any blood problems such as poor circulation or high sugar level?

Not that I know of.

Impotence could be a problem of the blood, he said, we'd check into that.

But I began to know that he and I would probably not be checking into anything together because we weren't making it together. He had really rather begun to smirk at me. He was a little boy enjoying a silly triumph over a larger boy. His questions took on an accusative sound. I felt that I should seize him by the armpits and hold him helpless kicking his legs in the air.

How were my relations with my wife?

Perfect.

How were my *sexual* relations with my wife?

Perfect until my impotence set in.

"Why did that happen?" he asked.

"I don't know," I said. "That's why I've come to you. I just died and I want to be resurrected."

"When was the last time you had sexual relations with your wife?" he inquired.

"About two months ago."

"About the time of your last ejaculation," he said.

"To the minute," I said.

Have I had any ejaculations since?

No.

Can I remember my last erection?

Yes.

This also was with your wife?

No.

"Ah hum," said he, "are we getting somewhere now?"

"Let's probe and see," I said.

"In whose presence did you enjoy your last erection?"

"With a young woman I was riding on my bicycle."

"How long ago was that?"

"December tenth," I said.

"You're very precise," he said. "Tell me this, do you get a hard-on when you see a *pretty* girl?"

"Never just seeing," I said. "I don't know what pretty means anyhow, frankly. But just the visual sight of women, no. It'd have to be a much more intimate situation, it'd have to be where there was a *possibility* of intimacy."

"Was there a possibility of intimacy with the girl on the bicycle?"

"We'd have had to get off the bicycle," I said.

"That girl seems to have had an effect on you. Why not see her again? Usually all a man needs is a few excitements. That's what we call pump-priming."

"I see her often," I said.

"She's a student of yours," he divined. "Why don't you ask her to go to bed with you and see if that primes your pump?"

"I don't think she's ready to go to bed with me," I said. "She needs to be educated up to it."

"How old is she?"

"Twenty-two."

"Is she a pretty girl?" he irrelevantly asked.

"She's not a girl," I said. "She's a woman, a senior in her last semester, the daughter of a fascist rancher."

"Forgetting the girl for the moment," he said, "how did your problem call itself to your attention?"

"I'm not getting erections in situations I've been getting erections in since I was thirteen, fourteen, fifteen . . ."

"Could it be that you're losing interest in your wife?"

"Not to my knowledge," I said.

"You know," he said, basically dismissing my problem as if it were of no importance, "nobody ever died from not being able to get a hard-on."

I winced. "I didn't come to you for street talk," I said. "It's not dying I'm afraid of at the moment. I know I won't die of impotence. But the end of sexual existence is an ending of sorts, and I want to avoid it." And here I struck the blow that severed us. "Nobody ever died, either," said I, "from not being able to swing a real-estate deal."

"So that's what's been bugging you," he smilingly said.

"Among other things," I replied.

"Maybe your problem is," he said, no longer smiling, "too many things are going on in your mind. Maybe your impotency is because your mind is over-loaded. Is your work going well? Are you in trouble on the job over there? Are you suffering financial setbacks? I'm not looking for answers to these questions. I'm just making suggestions. I get men in here with impotency every day and it's seldom physical. I can't do anything for you, although I can give you the name of a very fine super-specialist and you can go and see him for a further opinion." He wrote the name of the super-specialist.

"You're already my second opinion," I said.

"Here's the best man in the world," he said, handing me a piece of paper. "He's in Los Angeles. Take a little trip when you have the time."

"I'll do it instantly," I said.

"When you have time," he said. "It's no emergency," and then again, perhaps forgetting that he had already said it, "nobody ever died from not being able to get a hard-on," and I went out as I had come, through the Arizona Victorian waiting-room crowded with patients dimly seen in the semi-darkness, into the blazing sunshine, onto my bicycle.

Well, all right, end of medical scene in doctor's office, a poor thing but mine own. I don't ever expect to write medical scenes like the scenes in *Doctor's Out*, but this at least is my own little eternal record of my own little visit to this little urologist whom I shall never visit again. And if it's nothing else it's at least a letter to you, my dear Virgilia, from whom I seek all the advice you can give me. You who know many men can tell me what I can't know, who have known only myself and no other. You must have some ideas how I can get started again.

Assist me and rescue me. Help me out. Speak right up. You always have. Don't be shy. You never were.

Yours as affectionately as ever,

February 4

Dear Children,

   Just a quick All Points to tell you mother flew off this morning
on her tour beginning with Lucien. As I understand it, the long
hard part of her journey to Lucien will occur over the last fifty
miles where it all slows down from jet planes to donkeys and
burros and mules or whatever. I know there's a difference among
a donkey and a burro and a mule but I don't know what the
difference is. Lucky I'm none of them. If this were a novel I'd look
it up.

   After I put mother on the plane I went down the concourse
to another airline and flew to Los Angeles to see a "super-specialist"
recommended to me by the urologist recommended to me by Wally
Drew for a second (actually third) opinion of my so-called impotence. It was the briefest visit on record. The doctor said "surgery"
and called for his knives and I left. So I don't know any more
tonight than I knew this morning except that mother is out of the
country.

   Mother always likes to look in the cockpits of airplanes to
see who's flying this thing. She hopes to see weathered, grizzled,
gray-muzzled pilots. This morning she observed that pilots these
days are looking suddenly terribly young. We talked to this point
with one who confirmed our suspicion. "Yes," he said, with a
certain young satisfaction, "there are now *no* more pilots flying
commercial airlines who received their training during World War
Two."

   Writers still flying, yes. Pilots no. Writers are supposed to
last, and I'm sure they do, and I will, but I have been flying through
very bad air this past year and can't seem to climb up over it or
through it. But I won't turn back and I don't intend to go down.

   For the past few weeks I've been reading around in my own
books, not with too much conscious purpose. Understandably it

was then an awful shock of recognition on the airplane to read the following in a reminiscence of Edgar Lee Masters (a poet early this century) in a book by his son, Hilary: "Sometimes, I would see him read one of his own poems or pieces of prose over and over, as if to discover how they had been written."

I arrived home and fed the animals and dined alone feeling sorry for myself. Tomorrow I'll put the same piece of paper back in the typewriter and look at it all day.

An incident occurred. A graduate student in Scottsdale phoned me about an hour ago to tell me his son had run off. It was a child of twelve or so. Whom should he call? What should he do? He reviewed the circumstances of the dispute preceding flight. I said, "Look in your automobile." He looked in his automobile and there the child was fast asleep, "You're a genius," he said to me.

Nah, it's only my memory. I remember once when Lucien threatened to run away if his non-negotiable demands were not met, and when I failed to meet them he filled his pocket with change from the ceramic bank he smashed and disappeared, never to return, slamming every door as he went. Smash! Bang! Well, of course, children *do* run away, and the night is filled with danger. I decided at length to cruise up and down streets a little, assuming I would find him pouring out his abused soul to a friend beneath the streetlights. I drove a few blocks when suddenly I heard a short snort or a snore in the back seat, and there was Lucien sleeping. I was enormously pleased.

Would that I had a house full of children here to engage with this night. Instead I am alone, I and my three cats and two dogs. I send each of you my love, and wherever appropriate to your spouses and your children and your friends.

Forever and ever,

February 5

Dear Abner,

I send you about fifty new Calling Cards hot off the.

Beth flew off yesterday on the first leg of a tour of the children, and for that reason or some other I am in a very low state tonight and would jump out of the window if this weren't a ranch house all on one floor. Ranch boasts three head of cat and two head of dog.

I hope you are well. I am having some sort of internal physical plumbing problem and went to my doctor who sent me to another doctor who sent me to yet another doctor in Los Angeles for a second opinion. I'll keep you posted in this matter as it develops. It's nothing fatal.

I thank you many times over for the sack of silver birthday dollars, which the brute from the United Parcel Service catapulted over the fence into the swimming pool and which I fished out with my trusty pool-cleaning net. If it had been something breakable the UPS man wouldn't have thrown it into the pool but onto the deck so's to be sure to smash it. With some of the silver dollars I took a lady and her baby to lunch. The lady is twenty-two and her baby is two. She is eleven times older than her baby and I am thirty times older than her baby and more worldly besides. I am 2.72727272 times as old as the lady, according to my Texas Instruments calculator. Her baby threw a silver dollar at a glass of wine and knocked it over.

This lady, I must tell you, is someone special. You may by now have heard from her. Her name is Mariolena Sunwall. She was my student last semester and sat quietly and said nothing and wrote nothing for my class and spoke very little and smiled very little. All the while, however, she had been writing a novel the first sentence of which proved to be, "Earnestly they conversed together as they lied in bed." This semester we have been reading it in class.

The rest of the work has proved to be as striking as her first sentence. A great deal of it takes place in bed or in nearby locations in a district adjoining the University, known as "Sin City." I assume this is a local play on "Sun City," which is a retirement community on the other side of Phoenix.

None of the sins committed by the people in Ms. Sunwall's Sin City are unique or unprecedented—nothing you haven't heard of—but the book is put together in a fresh way, and I found it sufficiently funny and amusing to want to urge her to send it to you. She has no title yet. I think she may have hurried the ending, rushed along too fast when she began to smell success, but you will easily forgive her that if you like the rest of the book. You always urge me to err in the direction of sending work to you rather than withholding it, and so I do. (Speaking of works I sent to you from my classroom, I enjoyed myself immensely all day Sunday re-reading *Doctor's Out.* I see that you recently sold it as a paperback. I'm glad for that. I'm sure she can use the money.)

Ms. Sunwall's book lunges and plunges forward so hectically and so wildly I've got to say that if she's a young genius she is definitely an undisciplined one. Here's a bit of what it's about: a young woman is constantly besieged by would-be violators in these little boxed apartments in Sin City and up in the mountains with the Mountain Devils or at boating resorts with the Water Devils, skiing with the Snow Devils, *etc.* She fights them off virtuously.

In some way or another, however, at some time or another, every young man for miles around seems to have obtained a key to her apartment. This is too much of a good thing. As well as she can she sets about re-capturing key after key and has caused a locksmith to etch on them *Do Not Duplicate*, but the locksmith himself retains several keys for himself and for sale to various young men. At one point the locksmith arrives at her door "tugging at his bathrobe ropes." How it happened that he took his bathrobe with him I don't know, it sounds dreadfully wrong but it's perfectly right. Mariolena explains everything. As soon as anyone criticizes any aspect of her manuscript she writes a corrective passage—

never going back, always forward. When a student asked why the heroine couldn't have a dead-bolt for her door Mariolena created a landlord obsessed by the dangers of dead-bolts. The bathrobe "ropes" were simply a typographical error she grew stubborn about. She elevates errors to pinnacles of principle. Didn't she mean "Earnestly together" *etc.* they *lay* in bed? Oh no, not at all, they were untruthful people, fibbers, prevaricators, speakers with forked tongues, "that's the whole point of it," she said, and so went on to *make* it the whole point, rather than confess error.

Or when the heroine gives birth to an illegitimate baby and takes the baby home she sets it afloat in a little basket in the swimming pool of her wealthy fascist ranching parents. This is comparable to the Egyptian princess's discovery of Moses in the "bull rushes." No, say I, bulrushes. Wrong again, says Mariolena, bull rushes, these are ranching people and their bulls are rushing around all over the place, and so they do by virtue of Mariolena's cleverly integrating rushing bulls where you'd least expect them.

The baby appears and disappears at the whim of the author. He is passed about from person to person and party to party in Sin City. Frequently the heroine forgets where she has left her baby. She says, "I wonder where my baby is tonight," and begins calling people on the telephone. When the heroine is set upon by University officials for breaking residence rules the baby eloquently addresses her tormentors, although he is so young he has "hardly been born."

I'm sure Frank and Francine will enjoy this book, but whether they'll think it can be profitable to publish I don't know. Mariolena (the author) herself was astonished when I suggested she send it to you, for she has the western child's fear and loathing of New York; she thinks you are vulgar and materialistic, and she doubts that she has the talent to be published there, which her heart desires.

Like so many bold writing women we have known she's herself amazingly shy, demure, and hidden. She does not outwardly appear to be a demonstrative or responsive person, so that when her book came to me my expectations were shattered. You can't tell a writer by her cover. I expected from her a neat, correct manuscript. She handed me instead a headlong book full of pas-

sionate locksmiths and wild insane ranching parents and precocious Nature-defying babies, and subsequently, as she improved
her manuscript, rushing bulls and lying liars lying in bed.

Her manuscript was so gay (in the old meaning of that word)
and so free-spirited I knew the class would be amused by it. I
thought I'd read aloud a chapter to give us a taste of it. I never
expected the reaction I received. They fell off their chairs laughing,
they soaked their handkerchiefs wiping their eyes from laughing,
they positively and absolutely demanded I continue beyond Chapter One. We were soon engaged in a marathon reading, and in
the end we read it all the way through—a rare procedure in my
class.

During the course of the reading Mariolena almost never re-
acted. Now and again I saw her smile slightly; she knew she had
hit a target. Most of the time she gazed out of the window as if
this were just one more boring class, or she casually, almost
surreptitiously, made a little note to herself in her Spiral Binder.
I suspect that her cool distance from it all was a measure of her
commitment, and as a matter of fact she said so at lunch, yes, "I
was in a vulnerable sweat every second of the time," she said.

If I hadn't known she was the adventurous author of that
manuscript I could have been persuaded she was a churchy fun-
damentalist or maybe Mormon child counting up the f-words with
the intention of reporting the obscene statistics to her parents
and her minister, from whom we might soon expect letters to the
editor condemning public education.

At one point in her manuscript an arsonist is running loose
in Sin City setting fire to the toilets. It was at this point I said to
myself, "This is a book Abner will sell." The class was helpless
with laughter, as if someone had bombarded us with chemistry.
Mariolena, it turned out, hadn't meant "toilets" quite as it was
taken by the other students. She meant bathrooms, which you
probably can set afire, though burning bathrooms may not be as
funny to the mind's eye as burning toilets. "Mariolena"—she was
asked—"how can anybody set a toilet on fire?"

With a match, she said.

All right, look for her manuscript. She writes it up in a Spiral
Binder to begin with, and gives it to a friend to type—a young

man, she says, "who's into me for plenty and owes me as much."
Maybe he's the father of her baby. I never see her with any young
men, only with her baby. Never see her with any young women,
either, for that matter. She's a loner. Aren't we all?

Believe me, I wish I were doing as well with my writing as
I'm doing taking young ladies and babies to lunch. I sit in front
of this machine day and night waiting for it to turn itself on and
develop ideas and write them up effectively and artistically and
dramatically and creatively without any help from me. When it
doesn't switch itself on I switch it on myself and it just hums,
and after awhile I turn it off and ride my bicycle and sweep my
pool.

I have lately aborted many manuscripts. You will remember
my mentioning one or another of them with high hopes—a novel
about all the houses we have lived in; a novel about a writer to
whom a mysterious lady leaves two-and-a-half million dollars; a
novel about a man who tries to telephone everybody he has ever
known—soon reduced to a man who tries to telephone all his
relations wherever they may be; eventually reduced to a story
about a man dropping in one day on a lover he hadn't seen in
thirty years, which you said was unsaleable commercially and you
were right. I am circulating it now among literary quarterlies while
contemplating my shelf bearing the weight of seven hundred pages
of unsold beginnings and middles with never an end in sight. I
saw a passage in Graham Greene the other day which struck me
close to home: "As one grows older the writing of a novel does
not become more easy, and it seemed to me when I wrote the
last words [of *A Burnt-Out Case*] that I had reached an age when
another full-length novel was probably beyond my powers."

I really want to do some serious work to elevate the world.
I suppose I should know better. If I want to help the world a book
is not the way to do it: I should break out of this bourgeois prison
and associate myself with some downtrodden church or the Salvation Army or a commune of lepers I was reading about the other
day, but I can't move, and the first thing I think when I think of
abandoning cake for crumbs is, "Who will feed our animals?" So
I look for the little book in which we keep local numbers, to call

/27

our neighbor boy and have him feed our animals while Beth's away and I am saving poor people, but I cannot find the little book and so my plan for human rescue founders.

I am absolutely at a spiritual standstill or sitstill. Nothing happens. Therefore, let me present a plan to you for a procedure to which I have never consented, much less suggested:

A commissioned novel. Tell Frank and Francine the fix I am in. Tell them I have come to the time of my life that I need motivation I have never needed before—outside motivation; mere money. For $20,000 I will whip up a novel to their specifications. Tell me who the people are and what the popular objectives of such people are these days (example: a 28-year-old white Protestant couple who want to own their own computer), where they live, how much they earn doing what, and I will write for the prototypical supertypical bookbuyer a book with him and her at the center.

You know, I just might not have any stamina any more. I might just be empty, drained of all fluids, in a heap at the end of the line. I who always had before me mountains of notes for mountains of ideas now have before me exactly one piece of plain paper. I have mined my journals and my letters. I have written out my passion these forty years of punching these silly rows of keys. Show Frank and Francine this money-back guarantee: if I don't come through with a novel they specify I'll pay back the $20,000. I know that that will make me finish the work they commission because I know how much I hate to pay back money to anybody for anything.

I know that this plan will work. I can go in any direction once I get started. It will turn into literature once I get my battery charged. All I need is my pump primed. All I need is a tugboat to tug me out of this desert into deep water. All my rocketry needs is a lift-off. I can go, you see, by land, by sea, by air, by space. Anything's better than this.

Yours in solitary,

February 5

Dear Mariolena,

I was perfectly delighted to receive your letter because you
mean a good deal to me. I hope you managed to get a lot of writing
done up in the ski lodge in spite of your aversion to smoke and
in spite of the open-door policy permitting young men to dash
freely in and out of young ladies' doorless bedrooms, quite as it
happened from time to time in your novel. May I suggest a title
for your book? *The Fire in the Toilet. A Fire in the Toilet. Fire in
the Toilet.*

I hadn't expected to be answering your letter because I was
expecting to see you in class this week, but you haven't been,
and we miss you. I at least miss you. Every year one student
becomes special for me for one reason or another, usually because
he or she possesses an extraordinary talent for writing. Some of
my students over the years have become my close friends. You've
heard me mention them because of course I'm proud of them.

I'm glad you have decided to send your manuscript along to
Abner Klang, who will make something come of it if anybody can.
United Parcel is cheap and fast. And now that you have for the
moment unburdened yourself of that work you are thinking of
writing my biography. Of course I am flattered, but I'd rather you
go on with more fiction. I don't at all feel like a desert flower
blushing unseen. I feel on the contrary sufficiently public, visible,
widely known among my friends and students and discriminating
readers. I am the world's happiest man, I am sure, needful of
nothing more than the abundance I have. My family is all in health.
How beat that? I own three sane cats and two insane dogs and
one swimming pool and one Monkey Ward Open Road Fitness
Cycle upon which I gave you a lift one day from the postal kiosk
to the dorm.

I should think you'd have understood me well enough by now

to know I wouldn't confuse you with the characters of your novel. How could I have found your characters "objectionable"? Your book is cleverly and gracefully written. Twenty critical people listened to it with absorption and genuine laughter.

Basically, I try hard not to think of the author but to think of the work. The question for me is not whether you are in your work (as I assume you deeply are) but whether there's more of value to your work than your simply being in it. Is there a plot? Is there a story? I know that students make fun of my demand that every work of fiction have a Beginning, a Middle, and an End. Beginning: the hero or heroine must have a problem. Middle: he or she must confront obstacles standing in the way of solutions to the problem. End: he or she must solve the problem in some satisfying way, so that the work produces catharsis, climax, pleasure, and relief.

You wrote for us who were strangers to you. No matter how much we may have liked you personally you could not have connected to us and made us laugh as you did unless there were more to the work than a bit of your private self revealed. Do I think you're a dirty-minded woman running around doing dirty-minded things like some of those dirty-minded people in your book? I have no idea. What I *do* know is that you seem to be a natural story-teller unable to resist a Beginning-Middle-and-End which kept us total strangers in our chairs except during those moments when we fell off them laughing. (I think possibly the funniest episode in your book was the one in which the mailman tries to conceal from the postal inspector the contraceptives in his hat.) Some of the students who make the most fun of my passion for beginnings and middles and ends write me letters years afterward telling me all about beginnings and middles and ends as if they just discovered them.

So I make no judgment of you, no guess at you. It's a class in writing. We are not psychoanalysts. I am not the judgmental university which threw you out of the dormitory—threw the baby out with the mother—nor am I engaged by the State to monitor your private life. Indeed, I tend to dislike the university and the State. I feel like the professional baseball player who said, "I love the sport of baseball, but I do not like the people who run the sport." I am not your parents. No sins in Sin City surprise me.

30/

If you were to tell me everything bad you have done for the past four years I would yawn. I would not call the police. You must not worry what secrets you reveal to me. I am your confidential teacher and Graduate Advisor. I often feel important when a student tells me I am the one teacher to whom she has felt free to tell everything, write everything.

I hope to see you back in class soon. I hope that whatever is keeping you away is nothing serious. I hope this letter reaches you in spite of its going to your parents' city address (the one shown in the student directory), for I remember from your manuscript our heroine's most tyrannical and unreasonable parents, who stopped her clocks, cutting her off from Time and Love which she so wistfully desired. But they dare not tamper with the mails, it's a Federal offense.

Yours very unsurprised,

FROM: *Lucien Youngdahl, physician, Mineral del Monte Indian Preserve, Mexico.*

February 9

Dear Dad,

Mother arrived safely. The last 50 miles were no problem by burro and bus. Things move swiftly enough in spite of their remoteness. My Company has just bought $50,000 worth of computers but still spends 12 cents per meal per worker.

If the zinc distresses your stomach by all means discontinue it. If one doctor "gets you down" go to another. I don't see why your complaint should embarrass you and obviously it doesn't embarrass you so much that you are inhibited from writing about it in all your latest letters and All Points bulletins and I expect you will write it in books and stories before too long. Your new Calling Card received and contents noted. I feel confident that you will soon produce another opus. It must be in your system now. From earliest childhood I remember you moaning and groaning to the effect that you would never write again, but I noticed you always wrote again. You tell about the poet whose son remembers him reading his books over and over again, but this does not seem so remarkable to me as I remember you sitting and reading your books over and over again and laughing. I couldn't understand how you could still laugh at something you had already laughed at so many times.

I regret that I forgot to mention your birthday. Happy birthday to you, happy birthday to you, happy birthday Dear Father, happy birthday to you. When I finish singing it my cheeks puff out like I'm blowing out a candle. How's that for conditioned reflex?

Mother is already at home with everybody here. She has been especially interested in some of the hand-made objects of the people and seems to know more about the origins and history of their things than they do. Certainly more than I do.

I appreciate your being so full of praise for the work I am

doing here and for the noble sacrifices I am making which you wish you were also able to make so that you too could be useful to society. I am sorry I came here, and as soon as it is possible for me to depart without leaving a trail of neglect I am going to cease being noble and return to civilization for several very tall glasses of water with lots of ice. I dream of ice. I think I might look for a job in an ice factory in southern California.

You seem to feel sorry for yourself because you ate dinner all alone with nobody but the animals for company. But at least you can pick up the phone and speak to someone in English. If I were you I would occupy my nights and days manufacturing ice cubes in the refrigerator. Secondly, we are all aware that when you complain how alone and neglected and isolated you are on such occasions you seldom or never mention that somebody very soon comes along to assist you through that bad period. You become compelled by pioneer frontier circumstances to accept dinner invitations in air-conditioned houses nestled among the millionaires of Paradise Valley and this takes the sting out of things. We also know that when mother goes away she takes the risk that when she next sees you you will be snatched away by some attractive woman, which has happened to many friends of the family in recent years.

I met mother in a heavy rain at a crossroads about ten miles from the Preserve. When I said to her, "What will Dad be up to while you're away?" she replied, "Up to is right. I'm so glad you put it that way. Up to some literary bitch plucked from classroom or espied at a Poetry Reading." I asked her whether your present medical affliction will dampen your enthusiasm for companionship. She replied with some skepticism whether you have an actual medical affliction. She believes it is a psychological affliction if it is an affliction at all. She is distressed that it may be her fault, of course, that she can no longer please you. It seems rather frank of me to be writing this way. I asked mother, "Is Dad at that dangerous age?" She replied, "He was at that dangerous age the day we met."

I honestly do not remember the incident where I fell asleep in the back of the car, having broken open a bank with the idea of running away. I am sure your memory is correct except that it was another child.

I have run on long enough. I have no good light at the end of the day. Mother is finding it more comfortable than I thought she would. If you can stand a few days of it you can stand more. She joins me in sending our love to you.

Your Number One,

FROM: Beth Youngdahl, c/o Lucien Youngdahl,
Mineral del Monte Indian Preserve, Mexico.
Enclosure: envelope of love powder.

February 9

Dear Lee,

You will be happy to hear that I arrived here not nearly as exhausted as I thought I would. It is not going to be all that uncomfortable, and I can see where I might even stay longer than I planned if that can be worked through the travel agency whose slave I believe I am. There was no need for such a long layover in Dallas. I could have taken other planes, but what I was waiting for was the travel agent's favorite airlines rather than the airlines leaving soonest. Crooks.

Lucien is not as bad off as he led us to believe he was. I never stop worrying. The discomfort is not so bad here. "Give it time," he says, "and the discomfort creeps up on you, while you are admiring the sensational sunrise and the silvery dew dripping and cascading down from the treetops you're suddenly stung by hornets. By noon the green forest is a desert." He is really in very good health, ruddy cheeked. We need not have worried about him so much. He is highly respected, which is good for him, his face lights up with that old look he always got when he was praised. His work is definite, no time for boredom or restlessness. People file in and out all day with everything ranging from splinters to serious maladies and long stories to go with them. Some things that would kill you in Arizona don't touch you here where people have built up immunities all their lives. One man has one hundred diseases at one hundred years old (estimated) as a result of the good fortune, says Lucien, of his never having heard about medicine until he was eighty. Then he started downhill. Lucien doesn't believe he can live past a hundred and ten.

Here was your Calling Card on Lucien's table. A familiar document lengthening. I think of all that I have been through. I hope that by now something has taken hold for you. You are a beast to live with when you are not into something. Bad enough when you are. It would be a great surprise to some of your admirers to see how difficult and beastly you are when you are writing night after night, you who are so charming on the dance floor after dinner when your wife is away.

Try not to over-feed the animals.

I gather nothing came of your visit to the super-specialist in Los Angeles. I wonder if you gave him a chance. I don't believe you gave the urologist a chance, either. Lucien sees you as the kind of patient who goes in with a chip on his shoulder. You go to those people to have your body looked at and then you don't let them look at it. This seems to me to be your admission that the whole matter is in your mind, something you should be seeing a counselor about, or talking to some trusted friend. You deny that anything could be going on in your mind without its telling you first. You prefer to brood. You know that I will go to a counselor with you willingly the minute you say. I repeat this in spite of the shouting and screaming generated in you by the sound of the word.

Lucien has been telling me how impotence is cured here by hypnotism, often with the help of a love powder ground from the beans of a tree I can't pronounce. The patient is relaxed by the hypnotist. During treatment the hypnotist gives him post-hypnotic suggestions directing him to carry on sexually, which he may do. They have about 95 percent success. I enclose an envelope of the love powder.

In difficult cases the family is concerned to discover whether the impotence is in the mind or body. The procedure is based on the fact (or belief) that all men all over the world have erections in sleep every ninety minutes. (This is a powerful thought.) The patient is observed by a brother or a male cousin in sleep to determine whether he has his sleep-erections on schedule. If the sleeper fails to have his ninety-minute erections the doctor knows the problem may be in the body, not the mind, although such cases are rare and account for the five percent. The others are assumed to be psychological and treatable by time, love, counseling, and love powder.

In one famous local case a man apparently pretended to be impotent to avoid marrying the bride his family had selected for him. The brothers of the bride, to save her honor, schemed to observe the reluctant groom in sleep, saw that he was having ninety-minute erections on time, and brought him before the Supreme Council on charges of breach of promise.

It is a serious matter to refuse to marry the bride chosen for you. However, the Supreme Council found in favor of the man, declaring that he was not responsible for actions performed in sleep. He was excused from the marriage with the proviso that he pray for forgiveness of those sins which had brought upon him the punishment of impotence.

Scandalously, very soon thereafter he was found to be courting another woman and he was once again brought by the family of his abandoned bride before the Supreme Council. By interrogating his new lover the Supreme Council learned that the accused was as sexually active as any man might desire. He was now in deep trouble for One) having breached his promise to his bride and Two) having lied about it to the Supreme Council, whereupon he nevertheless soon won his case and was acquitted by the Supreme Council by arguing persuasively as follows: that in pursuance of the proviso of the Supreme Council he had prayed to God for forgiveness of whatever sins had brought upon him the punishment of impotence; that God asked him what made him decide to pray his way out of things, and he replied to God that he was acting on the good advice of the respected members of the Supreme Council; that God praised the men of the Supreme Council for ordering him to pray, and as a bonus gave him back his potence. This report pleased the Supreme Council and made the members cheerful.

An odd feeling to see your All Points. Usually I see only Xeroxes you retain, but here was original copy punched through to the back by typewriter. Neither Lucien nor I can remember when he fell asleep in the back of the car as you describe. I know that you have told that story several times. Of course I do remember your announcing that you were now leaving us forever and slamming and smashing out of the house. We all waited for the sound of the motor. If you took the car you were serious. If you took your bike you needed only a brief cooling off. Does it not make you miserable now to think of the power you exerted over mere children? Once you took the car but returned because you required the bathroom and stayed forever.

Lucien's bathroom is a portable temporary addition to his house. Every few days some men come and take it away and leave him another. Did the young woman with the burning toilets send her manuscript to Abner and what did he say?

Here is my love,

February 9

Dear darling Schiff,

What a lovely surprise as I was in the library tracking down *Sex in the Seventh Decade (And After)* to find it with its jacket still on and your lovely face smiling at me in the silent stacks. I read it all weekend without interruption. I am not interruptible these days, my dear old friend, for reasons you very well summarize and explore in your chapter "Impotence: Causes and Remedies."

It was not always so. Once upon a time I was interruptible and distractable and for that reason took a longer time to read a book, and even as I read it my mind was on some lady or other whose telephone number sang through my head right along with the prose of the centuries.

Did I ever tell you I met Beth reading a book on a train from Kansas City to Salt Lake? I too was reading a book. If I went somewhere by train or bus I made it a point to try to sit beside an attractive woman, but I was always pledged to read a certain distance in the book I always carried before striking up a conversation with some clever opening. If I could catch a glimpse of the title of the book my prospective lady friend was reading I had a bit of a clue to her character. I'd give her my opinion, or I'd seek hers. On the Kansas City-Salt Lake train, once I had read my required quota, I introduced myself to Beth, she introduced herself to me, we will have been married forty years in June. She has gone off to visit Lucien in Mexico on the first leg of a tour of the children. I remain here teaching school and reading your book.

Why am I reading your book? I don't think you noticed when I was in New York and you were riding me around on those mad parkways and thruways how relaxed, how philosophical, how mellow I was, although in the past I had often complained of your driving and sometimes even insisted upon taking the wheel when driving conditions were unfavorable: for example, when you had had too much to drink (one beer), or when you were especially angry about some injustice in the world, as you so often commendably are. I was mellow because I was glum and indifferent to life, and the reason for that was that I had just discovered my impotence.

I think you subliminally knew that something was wrong, although it didn't too consciously register. You drove along with one hand affectionately at my crotch, and no response from me, nothing, no stirring. You must have sensed that something in me was dead or dormant because before long you removed your hand from my crotch and began most uncharacteristically to drive with *both hands actually on the wheel.*

I wonder if you thought, "How well he has learned to manage himself, none of his old wild impulsive plunging into the nearest AAA-approved motel or worse"—we've spent some delicious hours in some hideously unappetizing motels, haven't we? Yes, sir (you thought)—Yes, ma'am (you thought) Youngdahl has learned at last that there's a right time for everything and a right place for every right time.

Schiff, you know there's never been a right time for us. Every time was the right time and every hour was the right hour. Why then on that day should I suddenly have seemed to have become indifferent to you? I wonder that you didn't ask yourself that—what has happened to him who could always rationalize pleasure before business, who has been known to cancel a class to make love, who once slipped away from a colleague's funeral at a signal from *you,* my dear, because we both agreed we'd rather be at your place than that place?

And what can I do about my impotence? How do I recover? Write or wire. I have not only read your book and several others in the sexual hygiene genre but I have gone to three doctors. I had a horrible experience in Los Angeles (or in *greater* Los Angeles as my weird doctor kept calling it), where I went at the advice of my urologist here, to whom I had been sent by my G. P., a long-time trusted friend who in this case seems to me to have lost his mind. The doctor in greater Los Angeles looked at me—looked me square in my eyes, I should point out; and at no other part of me, though he wasn't in the least an eye doctor—

and shouted out without the faintest hesitation, "You need a penile implant." Believe me he was nothing if not an enthusiast. "It will be *gorgeous*," he exclaimed, "it will make a success of you." He mentioned the names of certain celebrities of greater Los Angeles (Hollywood) who had become successful only after penile implants by Dr. Emmer; for that was the doctor's name. He told me the story of a well-known lawyer of greater Los Angeles who had lost case after case before his penile implant but who is now besieged after every courtroom appearance (all victories, no more losses) by the women of the jury who have somehow learned of the ecstacy available from an attorney with a penile implant. He has a vulgar supply of witticisms: "A penile implant is no joke, but it will tickle the ladies."

I rushed from his office dazed, weak-kneed. He rushed right after me, out into the hall, saying, "Get used to the idea. Think of the long-term rewards. You will carry an erection with you into the grave—how many men can say as much?" At the elevator he seized me, preventing me from boarding. "I'm only acquainting you with the inevitable," he said. He offered me a riddle. I can't quite put it together. The point was that the first shall be *last*, I will last and last. I should have made notes on the spot, but I was too depressed to keep my wits about me.

Your book, on the other hand, has been tremendously encouraging to me. You insist that impotence is mainly in the mind. I hear your reasonable voice, your humor which never trivializes a subject about which, after all, the probable reader is anxious. As I read the book I could feel my mind striving for the readiness you describe, and as I write to you now I feel the real possibilities of genital stirrings. (Oh yes, I remember one more thing the doctor said in greater Los Angeles: "Science will give it back to you better than God made it.") At many moments I strongly felt your book was written just for me. I have had some of the experiences you cite as leading to a period of "felt or perceived" impotence. I have been "embattled or embroiled" at my place of work. Yes, and I have had some "hard or unusual" problems to face in my "work or profession," my writing, briefly put, which has been stalled for several months now and not the least hope in sight.

(I enclose herewith Calling Card Number 40, my annual gift to you.)

And we have all as a family known some recent anxiety over Lucien's depression following his divorce. I have had some anxieties from time to time about all the children, who are well but sometimes stubborn or headstrong, and now and again in bad need of money, which I supply without my former confidence that there's sure to be a windfall when the present book is done. Because there is no present book. There is one blank sheet of paper in the typewriter. I see myself passed along among my children from house to house, each child and child-in-law pretending to be delighted to see me moving in while counting the days until I start moving out.

I think the greatest thing about your book is its eloquent insistence upon demolishing myths and legends about the death of sex with the coming of age. Much as I thought I had observed about life I was nevertheless ready to believe, when this impotence came on, that this was what was supposed to happen, this was the schedule of life. Sex died. Men dried up. Women counted themselves out forever. The fun was done. The big Life Guard in the Sky was calling through his P. A. system, "Everybody over sixty out of the pool."

I too was about to surrender as Nature commanded, though now you tell me Nature hadn't commanded any such thing at all and I'm sorry to think I almost fell for it the way people fall for the things they are told Nature commanded—war is inevitable, the poor will always be with us. People don't care to be troubled with alternatives. My colleagues are always saying, "But that's how we've always done it." I live in a state of everlasting perpetual fury. The other day we fired someone from our Department because a very young very smart-ass professor (who himself just barely received his tenure a year ago) has a better instinct than I for parliamentary procedure. I lost the vote. I lose all the votes.

I marvel especially at your chapter "Getting Going Again," so wonderfully refreshing in rejecting all that's so awfully moralistic in our culture. That chapter and the one called "Frozen Thinking About Sex" (XI) overturn everything we ever even began to imagine in the State of Utah. I'd send your book to Beth if she didn't hate you. It confirms so many things we always secretly felt. I must also say that you certainly know a great deal about the male body, especially the genitals: I knew all those things were *there* but I never knew they had names.

I'll keep rehearsing in my mind your key sentence, your battle-cry and slogan and motto: "One time proves it." It's not a hundred or a thousand or ten thousand erections I'm after, but only one, to "prime the pump," whereupon, knowing it's primed, one knows there's nothing wrong, and off he goes again as good as new or even better.

The next day. I was interested to hear from you about your love affair with your new young man. It sounds to me as if you're either living out Chapter XII ("How Do, Partner") or you wrote XII day by day in the excitement of your new acquaintance. I am always jealous of men who take up with my lady friends. I believe every woman I know should be sitting with her hands folded beside the telephone, waiting for my return. "Every woman Penelope," that's my slogan—or it was until "One time proves it."

I am sure your man is a picture of perfect health. And so young! As I come and go across campus I spy all these young men with all their potentialities at rest in their cut-off jeans, and for the first time in my life I can begin to believe, through the crucible of experience, that old men hate young men for their virility and would kill them if they could, to assuage their own impotence. Until now all this was hearsay, but I can feel the truth of it by listening to my own uncensored, unrestrained instincts.

I too would take a lover if I were able. If things for me were physiologically top-notch right at the moment I'd be setting my sights upon a young woman here—a writer, of course (don't I always?)—who reminds me a great deal of you and has written a wonderful lively small masterpiece which reminds me a great deal of *A Klutz in Love*. I'm trying to get her to call it *Fire in the Toilet*. I have of course suggested that she send it off to Abner, which I think she may have done by now. I'm awfully eager to hear from him what he thinks its chances might be in the world out there. If by chance you're in touch with Abner I'd love it if you'd ask him if you can read it, too.

Well, you can imagine how it all began. She came into my class in the Fall and sat down and remained silent. I thought she might be one of those students who'd get a grade of *B* from me

/43

for Safe Driving, which makes my colleagues angry. But some young writers have just got to sit awhile without telling anybody what they're doing. She had already a little fame on campus for having been at the center of a controversy involving several young women—single mothers—who tried to keep their babies with them in dormitories. Once or twice she brought her baby to class. Through September and October she spoke in class twice in response to something another student had written, and I knew from what she said, brief as it was, that she had lived a long time with the problems of writing. Along in November she handed her manuscript to me with an assertion of ambiguous confidence sounding like a sentence from her manuscript, "Well, Dr. Youngdahl, here it is, I'm sure you might like it."

Yes I did, and the class did, and Beth did, and so will you because you too are a champion of the underdog and fond of hearty laughing. She herself may be, I suspect, one of those underdogs by conviction rather than heritage. Her family, I gather, owns a big prosperous ranch out in the County and gives little fortunes to little Right Wing political causes if only they are Right enough. Goldwater, for example, is not Right enough. She wears Western boots and a Western hat and now and again a T-shirt advertising an ecological issue. She comes and goes to class essentially alone, discouraging young men from making her acquaintance, either by intention or by her unwitting expression of intensity, which seems to say, "I do not wish to be spoken to right now."

Around about the time we were reading her manuscript in class she began to place herself in my presence as often as she could, sitting in on conversations in my office, leaping to serve me in small ways I really prefer to serve myself—answering my phone, running off on small errands for me, finding a book on the shelves. Putting one back.

Of course I enjoyed the sheer physicalness of her being there in the office. My skin tingled whenever we almost touched, my toes curled, my heart throbbed. You can understand, however, my not wanting to become physically involved with her until I'd seen her writing. I didn't want to make that boyish mistake I'd made in the old days of committing myself to someone whose writing wasn't really good, whom I'd need to keep encouraging for the sake of our relationship. That's a false life to lead, quite as flat to the taste as pretending to be in love with someone you're really not—the agony, the agony, the waste of time and breath, the long secret preparations for moments of ecstacy whose outcome is only to prove to oneself that one has been a liar. Touching her was thrilling. She waited to be touched, in doorways, on stairways. Walking across campus she constantly reaches for me, not exactly in affection but as if she fears I'm an old man about to fall down. She thinks I'm too weak to carry my books, and I want to tell her, "Listen, don't worry about me, some day you'll see how strong I am, I hope."

Every once in awhile she reveals a little more awareness of me than I suspect. The other day as I approached our building she was sitting by the bike rack waiting. I asked, "What are you doing?" She replied, studying me to see how I'd take it, "Looking for you looking for me."

She was right. I was looking for her. Here's a little incident that will tell you something about the physicalness of my feeling for her. It was exactly two months ago, right at the end of the semester, and my impotence had really put me into a state of depression. I had biked to school. Infrequently I do. I was tooling around campus on many errands, stripped down to shorts and jock, backpack on my back, swinging past the postal kiosk. There she was, waiting for the campus tram. She was scribbling away in her Spiral Notebook, repository of so much she sees and hears or so flagrantly and unashamedly invents. "Get on," I called, "I'll get you there faster than the tram."

"Oh, Dr. Youngdahl," she said, coming toward me a little, "I couldn't."

"Why not?"

"*You* couldn't," she said.

Couldn't what? I knew what I couldn't. Couldn't get an erection, hadn't had an erection in weeks. "Couldn't what?" I asked her. "Couldn't ride you on my bike? Get on my bike and we'll see," and she sat on my cross-bar and away we flew. And as we flew I went erect. She did not see it. Truly we flew. She knew my strength now. A man who could pedal a bike this fast this far with a backpack on his back and a good, sound, firm, solid, sturdy woman on his cross-bar was a man of some power and endurance indisputably. I deposited her at the dorm, and we parted.

Her closeness had aroused me as I had not been aroused for weeks and have not been aroused since—two months this very day. "One time proves it," you say. True, my spirits ascended, I knew there was nothing wrong with me. It wasn't surgery or medicine I needed, but a new state of mind. That much I knew, and I came up out of the depths of discouragement.

I know now that Mariolena (which is her name) can cure me. The other day she asked me if I'd be her Graduate Advisor. Yes, of course, I said. In my mind I said, "I advise you to become my mistress." I had not wanted her until I knew that she wrote well. But now that I knew she wrote well I was impotent.

My God, here it is the next day again. Subject: Mariolena Sunwall (continued). The problem confronting me now is to remain close to her until I am well. If I had been well when I read her manuscript we might have become lovers instantly. I hear you saying, "Go right to her. Tell her straight out what the problem is, and she'll help you." I may come to that. But I have been so distant from her for so many weeks, so merely advisory, so theoretical, that I'm afraid she might interpret any sudden warmth from me as following too close upon my praise of her manuscript— she'll think all my praise of her writing has been only toward the end of seducing her. So I can't venture that way until I'm sure she has enough conviction about her writing to survive any suspicions of me.

I can't go too fast toward her. I don't want the happy moment of perfect understanding to arrive while I'm still in the grip of impotence. It will only confirm her in the idea that a man at sixty is stone-cold sexually dead. And why should she not have such a foolish idea: after all, I too was a victim of that myth as recently as Friday, when I withdrew *Sex in the Seventh Decade (And After)* from the library.

Meanwhile she's educating herself about me, too. I see by her book-bag that she has taken good chunks of me from the library, just as I've taken you. Certainly my sexual life is implicit in all my writing; she can't possibly get the idea I've been indifferent to her sex. She reads me closely, I believe. She has mentioned writing my biography. She's ready to devote *one whole year* to it.

46/

But if I hesitate to go too fast toward her I also hesitate to go too slow. This is a community of thousands of distractions for her, among them ten- or fifteen- or twenty-thousand young men running around all day who, if not geniuses of literature, are capable at least of reliable erections. The competition is stiff.

Schiff, kisses to you and every other good thing you desire. Here I am. I am awake. I am ready. I'm not surrendering. I plan to continue. I chant to myself, "One time does it." I feel that I still have ahead of me a grand and adventurous life and I want to help it happen. I feel myself at last in command of almost everything, but then just exactly as I arrive at this supremely lucky time of my life—smash! Down go the wires! Down goes the apparatus. And with it down goes everything else. What can I do about it? How can I recover? Write or wire. I thank you again for *Sex in the Seventh Decade (And After)* and for any follow-up advice you wish to send along. I intend to recover and enjoy myself and win the prize for Comeback of the Year.

Yours as ever (not quite),

FROM: Ms. Mariolena Sunwall, student,
c/o Mr. and Mrs. Sanford Sunwall, Phoenix.

February 10

Dear Dr. Youngdahl:

I want to thank you so much for the reassuring comments in your letter of the 5th and for your renewed expressions of friendship and confidence in me, especially right now when if ever I needed someone I could "tell everything, write everything" to, this was it. For some time I have felt this to be true, but I was unaware whether you were feeling the same way. Your classroom and you as teacher have meant more to me than all the rest of the universe(ity) put together, and your agreeing to become my Graduate Advisor at a time when the wilderness seems to be taking over the university is a King Kong step forward.

This being true, you may wonder why you have not seen me in class the last time or two. (The reason you have not seen me there is that I have not been there.) It is nothing serious, only the same old conflict. As my money ran out I could no longer afford to live in Sin City. My gleeful parents said I could stay with them. By this they meant, as it turned out, speaking with their forked tongues as usual, not in the Spotless House in Phoenix, from which I might have access to urban advantages, but at the ranch, in exchange, of course, for the performance of certain chores and duties; where I would be obliged two or three times daily to repeat to them confessions of my having failed at urban life; and from which sandy place I was obliged to travel an arduous round trip to school in an unreliable car, with no place to leave the baby.

Do you know anyone who would care to own a practically new baby? I shall transfer title duly notarized without delay and will take an oath his odometer has not been tampered with. I think I wouldn't mind the drive so much if it weren't for him. I have thought of adding a short chapter to my book, featuring an infant age two who has spent more of his life in a Volkswagen bug than he has spent anywhere else. Dr. Youngdahl, in view of

48/

your inviting my total confidence on all subjects I can tell you for whatever humorous profit you may glean from the cramped situation that my baby was conceived in my car. After all, one must be conceived somewhere. Your eye's mind has instantly taken a picture of the moment. I know that. Our minds work very much alike. Chalk up one more triumph for Nazi industry.

I shall shortly drop out of school. The only reason I have not already done so is my fear of disappointing you, and secondly the other members of the class, because I know you take a curled up view of students who remain in class only long enough to receive critiques of their *own* work, and then disappear forever.

I accept with delight your idea for a title, *Fire in the Toilet*, and I have written to Mr. Klang on the subject, to whom I have sent the manuscript by United Parcel Service with my very last farthings. I have also addressed him on the subject of my name. I deplore "Mariolena" and must have some variation thereof from a wide selection such as "Marie Elena" or "Maria Lena" or "Marya Ilena," *etc.* It seems so awful to have an agent step in between oneself and one's work. To me the very word "agent" connotes a greasy ethnic man talking very fast out of one side of his mouth, lighting cigarettes one after the other and shuffling money under the table. To me, New York is an island littered with wastepaper surrounded by bodies of water overflowing with turds. Who is he to sell my book? Even if he does sell my book, how do I know the shekels he gleans will come to me? No, of course not, that's why he's doing all the shuffling under the table. I feel exploited by him. I mistrust him before United Parcel has even contacted him. What judgment will he make on my character when he reads in my manuscript accounts of the naked life led by Sun Devils and Snow Devils and Ski Devils and others—these lives which are the lives of characters I have invented or observed? Recognizing the prematurity of all this, nevertheless I cannot help but be saddened by the thought that if my novel makes me rich ten percent of my fortune will already have been consigned to a man I have never met born and raised on those littered streets on the turd-smelling banks. A stranger already into my baby for one tenth of my baby's inheritance! Where will it end?

Please pardon me for running on. My difficulties with my parents have perhaps overwrought me. I must live at the ranch.

I may not live in Phoenix, although our house stands there unoccupied. After the long drive from the ranch I must depend upon finding some sweet friend in Sin City kind enough to take my baby for the day.

You began, "I [you] was perfectly delighted to receive your [my] letter because you [I] mean a good deal to me [you]." No words could be finer to my eyes. If not for you I would be unable to say I am alive. On the strength of such encouragement as you thus give me I have determined to come to town and try with every extra bit of energy available to find rightful accommodations for myself and so live, if only in a corner of someone's small place, and be back in class just as soon as I possibly can. You may count on that. Once again, I thank you for everything.

Yours very respectfully,

Dear Mariolena,

Tell me how you decide to spell your name and I will spell it
exactly that way. Meanwhile I will spell it as I have been spelling
it and as it shows on your records.

I am delighted that you have fired off *Fire in the Toilet* to
Abner Klang. It seems to me that the preoccupations and consciousness of the principal young woman in your book exist, in
spite of all the free and confidential talk of recent years, as a
landmark in the liberation of the mind of a certain kind of young
American woman who may be more commonplace than we know.
If that be true she will emerge *en masse* as your book seizes the
world's imagination.

Toward that end your primary and almost sole ally may be
Abner Klang, and for that reason I might say a few explanatory
things about him. Abner is not for everybody. He may not be for
you. In the beginning I didn't think he was for me, either, and
early in our association I was on the verge of breaking with him
and delivering myself and my literary "properties" into the arms
of a streamlined agency, the soul of elegant décor, with lovely
prints hung upon the walls all painted plum. Everybody inside
those walls "loved" me and "loved" my work. My first book had
made a big splash and sold rather well when I was no older than
you. But that was what they were in love with, the sales and the
splash, not me at all, for when I came along with *new* work they
had no idea what to make of it. They had no figures on it, no
critical opinions to go by.

Abner's office may not have been much, but his interior was
magnificent. He gave me hope, encouragement, shelter, a hand
up, a handout, bucks, praise, cheer, and practically daily messages in one form or another crying across the wastes between

New York and Utah—*When are you going to finish your new novel? The world cannot be kept waiting much longer.*

In nearly forty years he has been my confessor, salesman, lawyer, negotiator, collection agent, broker, banker, promoter, advertiser, boaster, advance man, scout, cheerleader, and counselor. He has endured untold dozens or hundreds of lunches on my account (on *his* account), drunk with the thieves of publishing. He has been the bearer of all that missionary zeal in my behalf I could not work up even for God Himself: at the age when good Mormon boys went off in their neckties to effect the salvation of the misbegotten sweating peoples of Asia or Africa I drifted instead into Abner's office one day with the manuscript of *The Hard Puncher* in a beat-up package that had been back and forth between Utah and New York a dozen times at least (60,000 miles according to my Texas Instruments calculator); and it was Abner finally who took a chance on it after all those miles and all those rejections. I was made.

Maybe he will do nothing for you. That's the chance you take, but the place to start. He may be just the connection you need, wiring you to the world. He may not. I think you should try, while you are waiting for word back from him, to cure your mind of its tendency to associate the idea of Abner with the idea of a greasy ethnic man talking very fast and all that. I remember walking into his little office for the first time, fresh from the golden west, carrying in my unformed mind similar images of ethnic grease and money under the table. You are usually too good an observer to satisfy your style with ready-made images. Don't judge too fast. In that connection I might also suggest your inaccuracy in linking your Wolkswagen to Nazi industry. If the VW is a Nazi car what might you be who drive it? (Abner, incidentally, has revealed to me one prejudice over the years: he too dislikes Germans, so you'll get along swell.)

He is no sexual prude. He won't think the less of you for having written so dirty a book. In his learned comical style he will shrewdly differentiate your character from your writings, your person from the *personna* of your heroines. Many of the very best jokes in our jokebook came from him. He's a kind of national clearing-house for dirty stories which are also funny. He polishes them up and sends them into the world as it pleases the Lord to strengthen him to the task. He estimates (I believe him) that every good story he sends forth enjoys formal presentation in media, on stage, or in night-clubs within forty-eight hours. This makes him feel creative.

I'm sorry you are having so much trouble getting on with your schoolwork. Transportation problems. Baby-sitting problems. Can't you just bear down hard one last semester? I seldom hear of parents quite so singularly unsympathetic. Apparently they are unaware what a good student you have been, and of the great promise of your writing. If at any time you think my meeting and talking with your parents can be helpful to them in their understanding of you I shall be more than pleased to be of service to all of you.

Are they really as heartless as you make them out? I can even understand, for example, your mother's devotion to the idea of a "spotless" house, or your parents' insisting on your performing "certain chores and duties" when you're at home. How really awfully odious can those chores and duties be? I have sometimes been rather irritated when my own children come home and just fling themselves this way and that about the house and in the interest of spotlessness *clean out* our refrigerators in Olympic record-breaking time without offering to replace *anything* at all *ever*, even at their parents' expense. One of our sons once brought a few friends home one afternoon and they ate up a dinner party planned for that night. My wife, without a word, looped her pocketbook over her shoulder, glided off in the car, and returned home the following morning. Our guilty son telephoned the guests and told them she had fallen suddenly ill, which was not untrue.

This gives me a sudden great idea. Let me propose to you now, thinking of this house once filled with children, empty these days but for assorted animals, that while you are searching for quarters close to school you stay here. We have a guest house, comfortable and commodious, where many writers illustrious or struggling (at best the same thing) have remained for varying periods of time while recovering from chagrin, disappointment, failure, success, bad reviews, good reviews, physical afflictions including drug addiction and broken bones, such is the life of the writer in America. Poor Peter Bonfiso committed suicide in our guest house one evening, having moments earlier written his name and the date of his occupancy on the wall of the guest-house kitchen, as writers have done since we first suggested that space for that purpose. You will see this message Bonfiso left: "Three of my dearest friends in the world teach at this stone-cold university. None of them came to hear me read tonight." You too may come and write your name on the wall and make yourself as homely as you please until you can settle elsewhere. The house will be free until late March when a poet I never heard of arrives for public readings and other more or less uplifting cultural festivities.

I hope I will see you in class next week.

Yours very invitingly,

February 12

Dear Dr. Emmer:

Perhaps you will recall my having visited your office on February 4. I was directed to you by a urologist in Phoenix, to whom I had been directed for a second opinion by my physician. My complaint was impotence, so-called. Your recommendation was that you cure my condition with the surgical procedure known as "penile implant."

I hope I do not offend you when I tell you I have informally questioned people about "penile implant." I understand that two general methods are popular—or at least as popular as penile implants may be. Some people tell me that not every penile implant so magnificently succeeds as those you described to me in your office last week; that even reasonable success is by no means assured.

When I was at your office I quickly dismissed your suggestion that I submit myself to your surgery, but in this matter my mood seems to fluctuate. Since the onset of my impotence I had the feeling it would be but a temporary thing of the sort I have experienced occasionally in one way or another. I remember at one point of my life as a child being temporarily unable to make my legs run. Things come and go. I sometimes think this period of impotence will gradually—or even dramatically—pass, as other afflictions have passed, but the lingering of this matter has begun increasingly to worry me, depressing and distracting me in great degree.

I had quite dismissed from my mind all thought of a penile implant. Today, however, I received your bill marked "No Charge." You may be certain that that is the kind of bill I enjoy receiving. If the purpose of your billing me in that generous way is to call yourself favorably to mind you have clearly succeeded. My condition seems to resist every treatment or suggestion. No actions have helped me. I have been regularly taking zinc and I have had one injection of testosterone with another scheduled shortly. I have been reading books on the subject, and I have made every effort, by trying to understand psychological forces within myself, to proceed with confidence that I can best unblock myself by *believing* I can. "One time proves it," the books all say. Even so, not much has happened to encourage me. I enjoyed "one time" two months ago. Since then, however, nothing.

Now, to the point. When I visited your office you were eager to furnish me with a "patient-endorsement" list you routinely make available to interested persons, of whom I did not then—but now do—count myself as one. This, as I understand it, is a list of men upon whom you have operated for this condition; they endorse you. This morning, however, when I telephoned your office your nurse or secretary declined to send me such a list except in reply to my written request, which I furnish herewith. Please therefore send me your "patient-endorsement" list. Believe me, I thank you very much, and remain,

Yours very sincerely,

February 9

Dear Lee,

Point regarding commission novel. There's no point thinking about this further. Frank and Francine are not about to commission a novel from you. They know it won't work and so do you and so do I. Dismiss it from your mind. They said they'll think it over but experience tells me that the phrasing think it over means they already forgot it. In the end you give yourself your own assignments and you know it. You can't expect Publishing people to think up ideas for you. They haven't got the brains. You're a self starter and you always were. Nobody can help you but yourself. In the past you puked all over the place if I mentioned a Publisher's idea. Keep puking. Look at all the poor wretch writers that get an advance on an idea and never complete it. They put their heart and soul in a good Chapter One but they could never put Chapter Two after Chapter One and the book came out with one good chapter followed by twenty stinkbombs. What kind of a life is that?

Point regarding many aborted manuscripts. Whatever happened to the novel about the man that kills the horribly deformed child of a neighbor to keep the rest of the family from going down the drain? Problem: you have got to make the deformed child so horribly deformed we accept the murder. In addition, what about the boy who trains for years for the Olympics and blows it the night before running the streets? The story shows the power of sex in the young. It sounds right for Playboy. You were contemplating a novel about a man who needs to hate this woman to keep from falling in love with her. I don't understand what you're driving at but I guess you do. This happened to me in reverse. I fell in love with Dorothy first and hated her ever since. Five minutes ago she phones and asks, "How can we be overdrawn when there are checks still left in the checkbook?" This after forty-one years of marriage. A novel or a play about the breakdown of human relationships. This sounds possibly too big, you need to be a little more specific. You mentioned a novel following all the people in a movie company from one huge triumph through the years following, everyone watching it over and over again on film, the various people dying one by one. Whatever happened to the tale you were contemplating about a man who made love to a woman in every State of the Union? I was never clear if it was the same woman traveling or a different woman in every State. Then he tired of it and ended up campaigning against the admission of Hawaii and Alaska.

Soon you'll light a fire under yourself again. Something or somebody will inspire you. Take my word for it, even though it takes a little longer than it took in the past. Nobody is getting any younger. Don't be so anxious to think of yourself as drained of all fluids, all in a heap, all out of stamina, nothing but abortions underlined and stained with teardrops. I don't go for it. Relax. Don't be too choosy. Just start responding. You can't fail. Am I supposed to care what Graham Greene says?

Point regarding associating himself with downtrodden churches and lepers. The writers I know the older they get the better they get unless they lose their motivation. Several of my clients are older than you. You among them. Your only danger of losing your motivation is losing your love of money, which you often express in times like this when you decide you are all washed up you might as well elevate the world like Norman Mailer. You can't wait to become the Commanding General of the Salvation Army. I wish you would stop lusting to be poor. You can never be poor again. If you give away all your money you will only start piling it up again through your super agent. Give up the poverty ambition. Drown your guilts with your silver dollars in your pool. Be glamorous. You are not going to write *The Grapes of Wrath* all over again, it's been done, the grapes all turned to wine. Poor people don't buy books and rich people don't want to read about poor people. Take my advice. When did it ever fail?

Point regarding fifty new Calling Cards. Same received and contents read. They are just fine and make me proud and I have many uses for them. They advertise you as a hard working, successful, trustworthy writer that finishes what he begins and sells what he finishes. They probably are so impressive they earn you increased fees over the course of a year one hundred times in excess of the cost of printing. O.K., great. Keep printing. However, why do you go unnecessarily out of your way to insult Frank and Francine, the "business like house" which keeps your books a "top secret." I won't send them this year's card or I might tear it off at the bottom and tell them you printed short cards this year due to the recession. I just won't. They are every bit as anxious to sell your books as you are and maybe more so since they never work themselves up into fantasies of poverty. It is now definite without question they are heading for a divorce. They will remain business partners but no longer bed partners in case they ever were. Who knows what they were? Speaking of gossip—

Point regarding Virgilia Mac. K. McDevitt soon to be Mrs. Sky King. This is not gossip but the real facts. She is going to marry Sky King. You know who I mean. She has been going with him on and off for years and he has "proposed" quote unquote to her many times and she always turned him down proposal for proposal. I always told her she was crazy, a man with that much money you can forgive him almost anything, and now she sees the light at last and the bells will ring. I told her terrific, fabulous, but I hate losing a client. "You're not losing a client," she said, "you're gaining a *subsidized* client." Subsidized clients are not hungry, I said. She had the best of all answers: "Look at Lee. He's the proof that money does not end hunger. He rips off the university for seventy thou per annum and still turns out writing with speed." She takes a pledge of allegiance she will do the same. She is Sky King's connection to literature. There's nothing he won't do to keep her encouraged. She is to be envied. For example she has a new little paper edition of *Doctor's Out* out. I said to her what's a couple of thousand to you now? "True," she said, "it means nothing to me but everything to Sky King." He preserves her books in dust proof vaults one thousand miles underground. If he passes her books stacked on a rack he buys up every one. That's what I call a fan. All of my clients should have one Sky King.

I can't resist asking you how you feel about this. Some people say the reason she weaves in and out so many marriages and divorces is because she is waiting for you. I know that you and

Virgilia were always very close to put it bluntly. I don't think she is going to lead the old free life she led before. There's too much at stake now. Those husbands never meant too much, if you lost one you met another one at the next Publishing party, but Sky King is a bird of another stripe altogether. He doesn't come along every day. I wonder what is going to happen to the Bohemian life style of hers. Time will tell,

Point regarding Beth. I hope she has a good time on her tour of the children and returns to you refreshed in body and spirit as I am sure she will. Instead of looking on this as an opportunity for suicide look on it as the perfect opportunity to get some un-interrupted traction on new work. I remember in the past several occasions when Beth left you for a trip at this exact point in your work, finding you too gruesome to live with until you were over the hump into something new. Look forward to greeting her at the airport upon her return saying, "Beth, while you were gone I blasted my way into a new book I am so excited about I can't speak." It will be old times again. Pass my love and greetings to her. You are the only man that ever met me at the airport on a bicycle. I never got over it.

Point regarding going to Los Angeles for a second opinion. Whatever you have is nothing. It will pass. A man goes to a psychiatrist to discuss his screwed up life. After many sessions the psychiatrist says to the man, "I have listened to the story of your life for many days here from your own lips, and the only thing I can tell you is that you are insane."

The patient replies, "Doctor, I can respect what you are say-ing. I understand where you are coming from. You are not the first person to say such a thing about me and maybe not the last. However, since I have put a great deal of money in these treat-ments only to hear you say that I am insane I must have a second opinion."

"Very well," says the psychiatrist, "I will give you a second opinion—you're ugly, too."

(Credit Bob Dieppa.)

Point regarding novel manuscript by Mariolena Sunwall of Tempe, Arizona. I thank you for your recommend and I have also had a follow up letter from her with suggested title *Fire in the Toilet* and other data. As you know manuscripts by students are never any good but I read them anyway because you send them and in the long run they sometimes turn out to be profitable writers once they have written a book or two. There are not many natural writers like you turning out profitable books while they were still babies. God gave you the gift. I will read Ms. Sungold's manuscript the very first chance I get, always remembering that when a man has lunch with a woman and sounds so very excited about her writings I have got to be on the lookout to be sure he is not getting his literary taste mixed up with his wine. Mrs. Mannerly is shaking her head up and down saying "Amen to that." I must say to begin with that I cannot remember offhand any great novel with a hero for a locksmith. Maybe this will be the one.

Ever yours,

February 13

Dear Wally,

I have had several telephone conversations with your office. One of your assistants just phoned me to tell me that my blood tests have all turned out perfectly, so we know that my problem is not in my blood, which you said you knew anyhow. (Then why did we take $38 worth of blood tests?)

I had a second call from another of your assistants giving me the number and address of Haddock Hooper, noted quack. You mentioned him to me some weeks ago on my very first visit to you in this matter of my impotence. I have a negative image of him in my mind. In some ways I value him, as a social critic and activist, not as a medical person, as I certainly thought I made clear to you when you first mentioned his name to me. Now you come at me with his name again, which, on one hand, irritates me all over again, but on the other hand tempts me.

The deeper I fall into this state of impotence the more desperate I become, I suppose. I have a hard time putting it out of my mind for more than a few minutes at a time. I begin to understand so many people I have known in the past going from one thing to another in search of cures or relief for ailments for which there may exist no cures or relief and never have been—to spiritualists and Oriental mystics and astrologers and healers whose equipment consists of painted electric-light bulbs and Lourdes and witches and love powders concocted by the Indians of the deepest interior of Mexico.

I want to talk this over with you. I asked each of your assistants to put me on the line with you, but each time you were "with a patient" and would call me back. You never did. Maybe you never received my message.

Finally Penny called me back. Nothing has worked for me—not the zinc and not the hormones; and now you tell me there's

62/

nothing wrong with my blood. Penny said amazingly, "Well, how do you know it's not working?" I thought this was a kind of gossipy, unmedical prying. She means, of course, to say, "Since Beth is away how do you *know* it's not working?" This is some sort of affected innocence for which Penny has been famous for years: I am supposed to conclude that her world is so morally ordered that she has never heard of a man's having an erection while his wife's away. She tells me how busy you are, how drowned in patients.

But I too am a patient, am I not? I'd really like to do something about me first and you second. I went to the twelve-year-old urologist you recommended on the grounds of his being "relaxed." Yes, he was relaxed about medicine all right—all his tension was poured into real estate. He in turn, apparently understanding my impotence as minimally as you, sent me to a surgeon in Los Angeles who, as I walked into his office, attacked me with glistening knives, told me I must have "emergency surgery," and when I turned and bolted pursued me down the corridor to the elevator.

Several things you have done have really irked me. You told me you had read big studies showing the effects of zinc with relationship to impotence. You led me to believe your facts were from a learned journal. But when I mentioned it to Beth she said yes, she had read the same thing in *Popular Health* in the beauty parlor. Everything you said came straight out of that item.

Going to your office is an ordeal. I have mentioned to you several times (at first jokingly) that your little medical complex is the only place I regularly go to which has no bicycle stand. Thus I must either tie up my bike around the bottle tree in your planter or across the street at the Belly Whopper. I wouldn't *dare* cross that busy street until three o'clock in the morning, and the stench of the Belly Whopper is overwhelming. Your office smells more like a hamburger joint than a medical establishment. A hamburger juke joint. While I sit waiting for you to see me I must listen to the most awful radio music which is the hamburger sandwiched between commercials advertising new tires and financial credit. The last time I was sitting there holding my nose against the Belly Whopper the radio was *advertising* the Belly Whopper.

Now here is where my conversation with Penny shocked me most. Listen to this! I can hardly believe it. When I mentioned to her my small bicycle problem I added my observation on the irony of it all, for it was you who so strongly praised me some years ago for my faithful bicycle riding, who observed that the good effects of that exercise probably manifested themselves in my superb cardiovascular levels—telling me also in the same breath how you knew yourself also to be toned and stimulated in body and mind as a result of your daily devotion to your bicycle. Imagine my surprise, then, to hear Penny on the telephone laughingly assert that you do not ride a bicycle, that she cannot remember ever having seen you on a bicycle, that she wonders whether you can actually ride one, and that the very thought of your being seated upon a bicycle sends her spinning off into laughter.

Speaking of Penny, I become aware of certain possible consequences I should prefer to avoid. Over the years some of my colleagues in the Department have told me they hesitated to go to you for fear of Penny's divulging their medical histories to other members of the Department, so many of whom are your patients. I had no such fear. Now, however, I find myself taking a little different view of things. I am not especially concerned about my colleagues' knowing I suffer impotence, but I should certainly not want them to know that I have considered going to Haddock Hooper to be cured.

You recommended certain books to me. I found several of them at the library. Almost all the books on the subject of impotence seem to have been written by disciples of Haddock Hooper, dedicated to him by their authors, and filled with extravagant praise of him for his genius, his faith, his hospitality, his assistance, his charm, and the beauty of his soul.

My going to Haddock Hooper (I am not saying I will) will appear to those colleagues of mine who like me least to be a capitulation to all that quackery I have claimed to be against. Haddock Hooper appears to some of us to employ publicity as a substitute for substance. Now and again he appears on campus with his little roving band of Utopians, where he argues lost causes. I value him. I defend him. During the Sixties he did brave things to stop the war. He has been helpful to many people in individual cases of injustice.

But is he a physician? Does he call himself a physician? If

in my panic I abandon science and medicine for the healing grip of Haddock Hooper will my whole English Department know of it instantly through our beloved Penny? I'm just worried that in the spirit of friendly small talking she'll let everything out, just as she told me the truth of your not-biking.

I hope this letter finds you better than I. I hope that your children are well. Please send my greetings to them, and kisses to Penny.

Yours as always,

February 11

Dear Lee,

Point regarding novel manuscript by Mariolena Sunwall of Phoenix, Arizona. In a few minutes if the rain stops I am out of here on the way to Apthorp House with the novel entitled *Fire in the Toilet* under my arm to personally deliver it to Frank and Francine. Five minutes ago I said to Francine on the phone, "Francine, I am sitting here with a book of literary history on my desk." She said, "Bring it." I might not even wait for the rain.

I have a lot of reasonable doubts they are going to go for the title. They have come a long way over the years as regards language and generally lowering their morals, but it is hard to see them permitting the word "toilet" on one of their exquisitely designed jackets. They are squeamish. This is all the more laughable when you consider their own life style, they are known for fucking animal, mineral, and vegetable. It's a mad, mad world. I am speaking only titlewise.

As for the book itself they will be as floored by it as Dorothy and I were. Here is how the evening began last night. Dorothy said, "What shit are you reading tonight?" I said, "Something by a student Lee sent me, manuscripts by students are never any good, turn on the TV I'll be in in a minute." Two hours later she found me still on the bed exhausted with laughter. She said, "What? A fire in the toilet? There's no such thing," beginning from the beginning. After awhile she was reading parts out loud back to me that I already read and was still laughing from. We were down on the floor laughing with the rest of your class. I said, "Is it funny?" Dorothy said, "It must be funny, I'm laughing," and you know that Dorothy does not laugh easily.

When I came to the line "Earnestly they conversed together as they lied in bed" I collapsed outright. I think I would have collapsed even if you didn't mention it. I see millions of people collapsing along with you and I and Dorothy. In five minutes I am going to make history, savoring it in my mouth ahead of time saying, "Pal, you are making history now," snatching it up with my raincoat and umbrella singing in the rain like Bing Crosby while carrying it over to Apthorp House. This is it.

Since last night I am thinking about this locksmith. I'm thinking about the whole book. I can't remember the last time I was still thinking about a book the following afternoon. Better put in I think about his books and a few other favorite clients, but most books don't last overnight clients or not. I once didn't read one hundred books in a row. I'm thinking about the locksmith's whole family, not only the locksmith himself, and all their bathrobe ropes, and the Snow Devils and the Ski Devils and the Roller Devils and the Sperm Devils crashing through the night trying to catch up with our heroine, and our heroine's baby eating the dictionary, and the Egyptian's daughter groping in the bulrushes and the rushing bulls.

Off I go. Frank and Francine will love it. I was never so sure of anything in my life and you know you never heard me say I was sure ahead of time, but I'm saying it now, I'm off. I feel that I have brought a good one in, my gratitude to you as well, it goes without saying. Pray God I don't get smacked by a car in the rain. I am writing to her post haste.

Point regarding Mariolena Sungold being "shy, demure, and hidden." I know what you mean. Writers seldom look like their own work. You always look composed and dignified, a man that never raises his voice. Nobody knows what hell you go through between times to make the book come out looking so smooth people think they could have written it themselves. Let them try. Ha ha. It is no wonder Beth runs off to Mexico at such times. If Mariolena Sungold is shy, demure, and hidden I am wondering where she keeps it all. Her book is bursting with so much energy I get the picture of the author's eyes popping out of her head. When she is not writing she must be screaming. I cannot see her walking. How could she keep up with herself? She must run. When she walked off the two-story roof in Sin City I wasn't in the least little bit surprised to see her walk right back up again. It seemed right. Of course she did it exclusively to save her baby, but even so it would have been impossible if she was anybody else. And when she arrived home she discovered she forgot her adrenalin after all. It is a masterpiece. I am dying to meet her. It will be a disappointment meeting the writer. It always is. I'll get Frank and Francine to fly her in. I feel if I were on an airplane with her she'd be holding it up with her restlessness. How could she get past the weapons checking station as loaded with explosives as she is? There must be more to her than meets your eye. The rain let up.

Point regarding Mariolena Sunwall's manuscript getting to climaxes too fast. Going back to your letter of February 5 I see that you are correct on that score. I am sure Frank and Francine are going to love this book once the rain ever stops, while at the same time they are going to demand some rewriting where some events and actions go on too long and others don't go on long enough. Things need to be sped up and slowed down. In your letter of February 5 you say she may have hurried the ending, speeding things up too fast when she smelled success. I agree with you. Two of us can't be wrong. Mrs. Mannerly asks me why I worry about the rain when I have a raincoat and umbrella.

Young people get to climaxes too fast. Once there was a handsome and ambitious young man who saw a beautiful young woman on the street and made a promise to himself, "I will get myself into bed with her or die in the trying." He followed her and inquired who she was. She would not answer him but entered a fine automobile and he jotted down the license plate in his little notebook and through the License Bureau discovered that she was the daughter of a wealthy scion with an expanding estate in Purchase, N. Y., and many horses.

This handsome young man was poor. He had no contacts up there. There was no way in for him except up the lowest rungs of the ladder. Nevertheless, his erection for this young woman persisted, and he decided on a slow but careful plan which was sure to succeed.

He would begin as a stable boy on her father's estate. He would discover which was the beautiful lady's favorite horse and paint the horse's legs green. The lady would walk in one morning dressed in her fabulous tight pants and scream out, "Who painted my horse's legs green?" The young man would leap from the hayloft where he was hiding and say, "I did. What are you going to do about it?"? She would report him to her father. Her father would call the boy before him and fire him. The boy would plead sincerely for his job and engage in various business discussions with the father. Soon the father would see what a wonderful, smart, promising man the young man was and think, "He is a comer if ever I saw one," and he would send the young man back to his job in the stable. One more chance. Soon he would promote the young man from stable boy to assistant steward of the estate. Then to steward. In these jobs the young man would do so well he would soon be brought down to the city and work in the father's international offices on Wall Street.

Day by day the father would eye this young man, and after a due period of time he would make his decision and say, "Young man, I have eyed you for some time and in my opinion you are ready to become my partner in this business."

"Oh, Sir," said the young man, "I am not worthy of that."

"Certainly you are," said the father.

"However, Sir," the young man would say, "you know that the corporation rules prevent anybody from becoming a partner in this business unless he is a member of the family."

"Christ," said the father, "I forgot about that."

"Of course . . ." the young man would say followed by a long pause.

"*Of course,*" the father would say, and all efforts would immediately begin to organize the greatest marriage seen in Purchase, N. Y., in a long time between this handsome but obscure young man and the beauful young woman he saw on the street some time before. Soon they would be married and he would be rich and in bed with her nightly.

With all features and details of his plan firmly in mind the young man set about putting it into practice. He painted the horse's legs green. He climbed up in the hayloft and hid himself there. In to the stable soon came the beautiful young woman looking never lovelier. When she saw that her favorite horse's legs were painted green she cried out, "Who painted my horse's legs green?" The young man leaped from the hayloft where he was hiding and said, "I did. Let's screw."

(Credit Valerie Veatch.)

Ever yours,

/69

FROM: Barnabus Evan Emmer, M. D., Los Angeles. Enclosure: "Patient-endorsement list," naming twenty-one men at addresses in Arizona, California, Nevada, and Oregon.

February 14

Dear Dr. Youngdahl:

We are not surprised to learn that the condition for which you sought treatment from us on February 4 has not improved. Proposed remedies such as zinc, hormone additions or supplements and psychological regimens cannot be harmful.

We regret you sensed any hesitation when you spoke to our office on February 12 regarding our sending you our most recent and up to date Patient Endorsement List. We send you the aforementioned List herewith. The patients in declaring their agreement to endorse our medical procedures on inquiry have consented to our including their names on such a List to be distributed only to interested persons such as yourself. If we betrayed any hesitation in giving you such a List on the day of your visit to our office on February 4 the reason was because you mentioned your occupation as "Writer," which was revealed by "Calling Card Number 40," which you presented to us on February 4. A second copy accompanied your letter to us on February 12, received February 14. We have never sought publicity in any form, and for that reason we stress the importance of confidentiality. Our patients whose names appear on our List expect that the List will remain confidential.

You refer to two general methods of penile implant. We have two kinds of penile prostheses and can perform whichever procedure is suitable or desired. In one procedure a semi-rigid rod is inserted. In the second procedure an inflatable silicone rubber cylinder is inserted. Studies reveal that the "pleasure" of sexual intercourse has never been diminished. On the contrary, according to studies, it may be dramatically enhanced. Even those patients reporting only "moderate to fair" pleasure during sexual intercourse following surgical procedure for penile implant recognize the social and marital benefits also accruing as the result of their revived activities. Marital harmony was often restored. Studies reveal that marital "partners" and others report either "no difference" or "significant increase" in pleasurable difference in sexual relationships with patients following penile implant.

Where replies have been inconclusive the difficulty of interpretation has been attributed to difficulties surrounding subjective responses such as "pleasure."

We are pleased to hear of your satisfaction at receiving our statement in the amount of "No charge" and we are pleased to hear that your records accord with ours and consider said matter settled.

Sincerely yours,

February 14

Dear Beth and children,

Congratulations to mother, she is temporarily promoted from a mother to a Point. Letters arrived from her and from Lucien from Mexico this day. I had not been in touch with any member of this family since the day mother flew off a week ago Wednesday last and was feeling rather isolated. I was invited out to dinner tonight but I decline everything until after I start getting some work on paper. Now instead of getting work on paper I am writing a letter to you on paper that was blank all day from morning to night. I have no particular message except to send you all my love and to ask mother if she can tell me where the little Roll-a-dex is which rolls out crucial telephone numbers like the number of the boy who will feed the animals if by chance I should step out of the house for a day or two, which is unlikely. But may occur.

If I knew the boy's name I could look him up in the telephone directory. I could ask Information. But I don't remember his name, if indeed I ever knew it. I could tell Information, "He has long legs with knobby knees holding them together at the middle and wears a Pittsburgh Pirates baseball cap." Or if I knew his number I could pretend to know his name. It's as I remember it from geometry and algebra. I need to know certain things to arrive at an answer, but in the present case I possess too few known factors to calculate the unknown. I simply don't know enough about that boy to know more.

Anyhow, the occasion for my absence has passed. I was to have gone to Carefree for a day or two to visit with Haddock Hooper, whom Wally Drew recommends for the cure of everything that ails me, especially this small touch of "impotence," from which I have been suffering. Hooper is a quack. It made me awfully mad that Wally recommended him, and so persuasively that I was on the verge of going. Instead of going, I wrote a rather irritable letter to Wally. When it was done I questioned whether I ought to risk a lifetime's friendship to soothe my irritation, and I raced out and mailed it before my better nature could assert itself.

Instead of really trying to deal with my problem Wally sent me to the urologist I truly disliked (who sent me to a surgeon in Los Angeles about whom I have many doubts), and now he has been urging me to go to Haddock Hooper, a man of many admirable qualities whom you may remember as a constant crusader for virtue during the Sixties. The girls will remember our going in a mass with Haddock Hooper to Swim With the Sharks in the surf at San Francisco.

But I think Wally has lost his enthusiasm for his practice. Do you remember in the old days what a pleasant, lively, jumping place his office was? He really seemed to care about what he was doing. And Penny amuses herself talking on the phone only partly on business—it's gossip and slander; she has made the office a clearinghouse for medical news with a sexual emphasis: who is aborting these days and which little children are going into contraceptives and details of Wally's expert testimony at divorce hearings. That lovely little setting is wholly depressing now. The street has engulfed it with noise and the Belly Whopper has smothered it with frying onions: I was sitting in one of Wally's little examining rooms, the captive of his piped-in radio, which was delivering commercial announcements for the Belly Whopper even at the very instant I was inhaling the odor of the Belly Whopper through Wally's air-conditioning. There's captive audience for you, they had me coming and going—they had me hearing and smelling.

Mother writes excitingly, telling how well-respected Lucien is in the community where he is working, and Lucien writes that he misses ice above all. Mother arrived at Lucien's by burro and bus after an initial boost by jet airplane. She also sends me accounts of ways in which the people of Lucien's community deal with sexual impotence. One of their conclusions seems to be that a man who sins (I don't know how) receives "the punishment of impotence." I wonder if mother is speaking to me on the pretext of reporting to the world the nature of grand old tribal folk tales. What are my sins supposed to have been?

Earl, how is your novel coming? Thornton, how is your campaign coming? I know that some of you were planning to go help

Thornton in his campaign, and I am interested to know who went and how they helped. As you know, I root and pray for Thornton to win and love him none the less if he loses. I hope that everybody is well. I am teaching school and trying to write, but the writing does not happen. School happens because when I arrive there the room is filled with people and I have got to say something to them, I can't just stand in front of them mute. So I begin to talk and things begin to shape themselves. But writing is different, and I am stalled. Mother asks about "the young woman with the burning toilets" who has in fact sent the manuscript which she (mother) read to Abner, who is wild about it. Even Dorothy laughed. He has submitted it to Frank and Francine, from whom we now all await word. The young woman is named Mariolena Sunwall. Mother can never remember her name. Her manuscript is agile and funny and really ought to be welcomed in the world. I like to laugh.

Happy Valentine's Day.

Lucien in his letter does not remember the alleged incident of his falling asleep in the back of the car. I did not mean to fabricate. In the interest of an increment to family history, and in the belief that I was being accurate, I assigned a role to Lucien which may have been someone else's. Mother says she cannot remember the incident, either, but says she surely does "remember your [my] announcing that you were now leaving us forever and slamming and smashing out of the house. We all waited for the sound of the motor. If you took the car you were serious. If you took your bike you needed only a brief cooling off. Does it not make you miserable now to think of the power you exerted over mere children? Once you took the car but returned because you required the bathroom and stayed forever."

I remember that incident well enough. I did in fact depart the house by car and drove to Market and Ord, where I filled the tank with gasoline, my plan being to drive to Utah and live with my mother and other people who truly loved me, and farm, and write, and be a hermit. At the gas station I thought to use the men's room, but when I entered it I realized the men's rooms were going to be like this all the way to Utah. So I went home and used the bathroom and decided to remain the night and forever.

Forever and ever,

TO: *Twenty-one men named on the "Patient
Endorsement List" of Dr. Barnabus Evan
Emmer, February 14. Xerox. Enclosures with
each letter: 1) "Calling Card Number 40." 2)
Self-addressed postpaid envelope.*

February 17

Dear Mr.—————:

Dr. Barnabus Evan Emmer has given me your name as one
who has expressed a willingness to reply to questions on the
subject of your recent penile-implant operation.

Since I am a patient of Dr. Emmer weighing the "pros and
cons" of a penile implant I am anxious to gather for myself as
much information as possible regarding the effects of such a relatively new and unusual operation. I realize at the same time that
you had no such advantage of prior warning or endorsement. With
faith and courage you went forward with the procedure, for which
I commend you even as I send you this letter with its implicit
revelation of cowardice, skepticism, and scientific mistrust. Of
course if you speak to me you may be sure you do so in confidence.

You may wish to know something about the author of this
letter. Last month I observed my sixtieth birthday. I am a writer
(see "Calling Card Number 40" enclosed), professor of English
at Arizona State University, residing with my wife of thirty-nine
years, the former Beth Bingham, once of Bingham Canyon, Utah.
Our seven children, all grown and gone from home, reside in three
states of the Union, Mexico, and Canada.

I was born and raised in Ogden, Utah. In background I am
a Mormon, but at an early age I tended to disassociate myself
from my formal beginnings, even as I began to learn to be grateful
for the strength I inherited from my family and our larger community. I was at one time excommunicated from the church, and
I believe that I am still apart from it.

At age eighteen I entered seriously upon a career of boxing.
I was at one time heavyweight champion of Utah, afterward Mountain States Heavyweight Champion, and subsequently Golden
Gloves Heavyweight Champion. As a professional fighter, however, I began to falter, having become distracted, I now realize,

by questions of literature and alternative goals. "I was . . . becoming," as I have written elsewhere, "less and less the fighter, and more and more the social reformer. It had begun to appear to me less than purposeful to go about in life cracking the skulls of poor colored boys and poor Irish boys and poor coal-mining boys whose allies I should rightly have been." My career soon ended.

During World War Two I served as a National Parks fire warden in *lieu* of military service. After the war ended I became a student of English at Brigham Young University, and continued thereafter in graduate work at the University of California at Berkeley. My career as a writer advanced.

In recent months some sort of diminution within my physical system seems to have impeded if not (I hope) destroyed my power of erection. Recent medical tests have revealed nothing amiss— blood good, hormones O.K., blood pressure perfect. And yet I languish, I am spiritless. I am uninspired. I care for nothing much.

Out of this despair I am upon the point of entrusting so vast a portion of my fate to Dr. Emmer. I am anxious to solve the problem speedily, even by the radical action of surgery. On the other hand, I want to approach that hazard as effectively as may be possible, provided with every hint of safety, every warning of danger. I have prepared a questionnaire addressing itself to my primary concerns. If by answering this questionnaire you can shed light for me I shall be exceedingly grateful. But whether or not you enlighten me I shall appreciate your effort. For your convenience in replying to me I enclose herewith a stamped, self-addressed envelope.

As concisely as I can phrase them, their quantity as small as possible, my questions are these:

1. May I ask you how old you are?
2. How long was your period of recovery following surgery?
3. Was your penile implant by the method of insertion of a semi-rigid rod, or insertion of an inflatable silicone rubber cylinder?
4. Do you feel that the operation was worth having undertaken?
5. Does your penile implant work? If not, would the alternative method (see Question 3 above) have been preferable?

6. Has life generally been better for you as a consequence of this surgery?

7. Has your operation improved your marriage?

8. Has your operation improved your relationship(s), if any, with "partners" outside your marriage?

9. What advice have you for me which may be helpful to me in deciding whether to undergo such an operation?

I thank you very much.

Yours very fraternally,

February 14

Dear Lee,

Happy birthday Valentine's Day James Joyce's birthday, you were always a calendar-watcher. Your letter raises a real question nagging me for some years and all the more urgent now in view of my being about to marry Suekuykeen: What do you do with my letters to you? I *must* have them back unless you have destroyed them, which would be even better.

We are to be married March 2, commemorating a certain famous date in the history of his country, I'm not sure what, and don't care, don't care for his country very much, if the truth be known. We went there to sign our marriage contract. I have been in the most joyful and elevated spirits and am therefore pleased-not-angry to receive your annual Calling Card. Suekuykeen is solving all the problems of my life for me.

This is not the same thing as saying he is making me happy. Nobody makes me happy. You always made me happy. You *must* send my letters back to me. But you make promises *erectus*—you *imply* promises *erectus*—which you back out of when the excitement is over. It was always time to go home. It was always time to look at your watch. It was always time to look at your calendar. "Listen, Virgilia, I'll be back, you know I'll be back." Sure you'll be back. In a year or two you'll be back. Once it was three or four. Once you were in town and didn't call me, so even when you were back you weren't back. I told you I was angry. "Virgilia, we're never angry, we have never spoken a cross word to one another." After you left I was angry, never while you were there, always after, there you went, strapping on your watch, pulling up your calendar. I was always frantic then to find someone to make love to me to prove that somebody wanted me now that you had rejected me, and that began a whole new cycle of love with somebody I didn't even like especially, much less love, the

78/

neighborhood rat-catcher, anybody, so long as they had money. You are the only man I ever cared for in spite of your not being very rich. You had something. They had nothing. Only money. Suekuykeen has money. For God's sake burn this letter instantly.

That's a big part of what *Doctor's Out* was all about. You have so often praised that book and never seen yourself in it. A man has wanted for ten years to make a movie of it. Now he's ready and offers me big money for it and I turn him down. I have Suekuykeen. You were the doctor that was out. You miss that part. You read right over it. The new edition was nice, but it came like everything else came, not when I needed it but when I didn't need it any more. I needed it *then*.

That's funny, you and your little man out there—urologist trying to become real-estate tycoon. One knows the type. Suekuykeen had high hopes of becoming a dentist, but his family forced him into gold on a larger scale. Frankly, I thought you were coming down with impotence in Miami, though this may be hindsight. I do remember now that you mention it thinking then that something wasn't really right between us. You weren't good at all. No good. You were soft, you were flaccid, whatever it was you blamed it on drinking but you really hadn't been drinking at all. You kept falling out of me if you managed to get into me in the first place. I forget. I didn't make notes. You will remember that once upon a time I took notes of everything you said. It seemed so apt and wondrous wise, and I suppose it was, for now I'm wondrous wise, too. Look where it has got me. I'm the envy of the town. For God's sake destroy this letter.

We have an actual honest-to-God marriage contract witnessed in two languages, which he insisted upon to prevent himself from reneging on his promises. An old-country custom, he said, in view of men's tendencies to promise things beforehand and forget about them afterward. The old syndrome *erectus*. On the other hand he has also surrounded himself with lawyers who tell him how to extricate himself from promises he wishes he never made. I take comfort from the idea that his lawyers are my lawyers now (I think). I am walled against the world, defended six deep from eventualities. On the other hand, Abner alarms me by asking me how I hope to enforce in America a contract executed in the old country and delivered to his vaults there, whose family owns most of the country and everything that's in it.

So what did you do then? Did you go to the physician in Los Angeles recommended by the urologist in Arizona? Did you think of me when you were in Los Angeles? We'll never go there any more. Do you ever stop and think of someone and say, "I shall never go to bed with her again"? Are any of your mistresses dead? Thank God it's over. My friend Sid, who has been kind enough to give me all my letters back, to be destroyed, tells me of a new study of life expectancy that shows that many men suffer heart attacks while having an affair, the strain on the heart is enormous, they die during intercourse. This is what happened to Rockefeller. Sid says there's some sort of French term for dying during intercourse, we have no English for it.

Destroy this letter page by page as you read. If I had any medical advice for you on getting started again I'd give it to you, you may be sure. I'd go out there and prime your pump myself. But circumstances prevent. I adore the dialogue between you and the itty bitty little urologist on the subject of the woman on the bicycle. Was there a possibility of intimacy? "We'd have had to get off the bicycle." Don't lose it. It's the perfect impeccability of the grammar that makes me smile. Don't change a syllable. I change too many syllables myself,

So here's your story. Our hero is all washed up, through, the time has come when the mechanism breaks down (Stern) or you just can't bear the thought of one more effort (Updike). Nothing can revive him. A thousand girls on a thousand bicycles don't spin a single wheel for him. Our hero in despair speeds to his faithful old *Virgilia* in New York, living alone in the crumbling apartment she retains between marriages. It is rent-controlled. He first visited her here years before when it was smashing new. It reminds him of the days of his virility when they had no money but plenty of excitement. The tables have turned. She is about to marry a rich man and move out of that old apartment forever. It's not that Suekuykeen especially cares who my friends have been in the past, it's only that he doesn't want them around now. It's an old-country custom, I suppose, and I go along with all his old-country customs. Possibly they're in my contract. Whatever they are, I'm for them. I can't blow this one.

I love you always,

February 18

Dear Professor Youngdahl:

Yours of yesterday received. The world does not need more Mormons.

Sincerely,

February 18

Dear Dr. Youngdahl:

You often tell us that as writers we must not say "words cannot convey" or "words cannot express" or "I have no words to describe," or something is "beyond description," since we must make our words convey, express, and describe. That is our business. Nevertheless, I have no words to describe this day, which has been the most exciting and thrilling of my life.

This morning I received a special-delivery letter from Mr. Abner Klang, the literary agent to whom you recommended my sending my novel, as I did. He has read my novel with "overflowing enjoyment" and seems to believe the reading public will read it in the same way, "laughing all night." I had not so much felt the book was to be laughed at, but you and the class and now Mr. Klang and his wife, one Dorothy, all seem to be classifying the book as comedy, and I guess I am ready to go along. You have often mentioned instances of literary history wherein the writer thought she was writing one thing but the world thought she was writing another.

Mr. Klang is fond of the title, *Fire in the Toilet*, which you suggested, finding me very grateful when you did because, as you know, I was not having any luck finding a good title, and the class was not being helpful, either. He has taken my book to Apthorp House for their consideration. He feels that this may be "a historic moment in literature." Words like this have gone into making this day truly as I have described it in paragraph one above, "the most exciting and thrilling of my life." Yesterday I could not imagine myself being published by such a distinguished house as Apthorp House, and yet today I say to myself, "Why not? When Dr. Youngdahl was first published by Apthorp House he was no older than I." I thought of myself as being published (if ever I had that good luck) by some little group of people running off my pages on an old begrimed hand-operated press of the kind operated by students in garages in Sin City.

Mr. Klang's writing is amusing. I will send you a copy when I have a piece of change for the copier. I do not feel that he rewrites his letters or takes much care with them but dictates them madly to one Mrs. Mannerly, who "swallowed her cigarette" reading *Fire in the Toilet.* Time would be saved for me if I could write that way. I write fast but I laboriously rewrite. Yet I must rewrite. Mr. Klang feels that the editorial bigwigs at Apthorp House will order me to do some rewriting, which I am perfectly willing to do if their demands are reasonable. However, I will not at any point consent to censorship of my work on the grounds of "dirty" language or explicit sexual scenes. These things exist, as anyone knows who has lived for any appreciable period of time in Sin City.

In spite of his reckless method of writing Mr. Klang appears to me to be a thorough gentleman, as I suppose I should have expected, knowing of his long agentship for you. He calls you "one of my first friends." I love that man and look forward to meeting him if, as he foresees, Apthorp House, after reading my novel, "will want to fly you [me] in to gaze upon the creator of this universe known as Sin City."

So you think I am a shy person, according to Mr. Klang. I believe it is true—I am unnaturally shy and retired. I am a cross between Emily Dickinson and Flannery O'Connor and would stay in my house all the day if I had a house to stay in.

This raises the question of the timely arrival of your letter. I was dispossessed by my parents almost at the hour of your letter's mentioning the possibility that I might go and live in your "guest house . . . while you are [I am] searching for quarters close to school." This is the most fortuitous rescue imaginable. When my parents heard of the title of my book my mother exclaimed, "you are the Vulgarian we always thought you were."

I will stay in your guest house only under the strictest agreement that: One. I will vacate those premises not later than mid-March, as specified in your letter, and sooner if possible; and Two. That I will pay you a rental to be agreed upon. I would suggest a sum of $400 per month or fraction thereof. If in any way my being in your guest house proves to be an inconvenience to you I shall be under obligation to move out instantly if you will have the kindness to notify me of your desire that I do so.

I regret that I have been unable to return to class thus far, but as soon as I am relocated at a distance from my parents I shall do so. I shall also be making strenuous efforts to find a small menial job to support myself now that my father has declined to continue to assist me with my education, which, as he says, "taught you nothing but four years of dirty writing." This is a man, you understand, who drives off panting from the ranch periodically for points unknown with several of his buddies to attend exhibitions of pornographic movies at the "veterans' club" to which they belong, although none of them is a veteran of anything but alcoholic drinking and gaping eye-gawking. On the highway my father can never pass an Adult Book Shop without stopping. He has more than once left my child and me sitting in the flaming sun while he entered the shop to buy packages of hard-core pornographic movies, and magazines of filth. This is a disrespectful way for a woman to speak of her American father, I am sure.

If you would like me to withdraw from class I shall be happy to do so and accept a grade of "W". I recognize that I have not done the work apart from my one meager novel, and that my attendance has been but mediocre. It may be, however, that in view of your kind assistance in the housing matter I shall soon be re-located more swiftly than I had hoped, for which I am deeply grateful in advance, as I am deeply grateful to you for your having recommended me to Mr. Klang. Although I do not expect anything to come of it it has been a wonderful boost to my ego.

If I withdraw from school with a grade of "W" I can merely postpone my graduation to December, which would be no inconvenience but for the fact that my father has paid, as he puts it, "my last [deleted] tuition check to that [deleted] institution of higher [deleted].

Mr. Klang does not feel that we must make an immediate decision about the spelling of "Mariolena."

With good and abundant reason I remain yours very gratefully and, as in the past,

Yours very respectfully,

84/

February 19

Dear Virgilia,

You must know that I am all for your marriage, which I hope will be long and ever more prosperous and happy for you. I don't want to sound platitudinous. It's so easy to fall into trite phrases. For example, I keep wanting to say, "Beth and I send you . . ." but of course Beth doesn't send you anything. If she could send you something she would send you a bomb.

I however like you and love you and am fond of you and always think of you fondly in spite of the quarrels we have had over the years, the breaks and repairs, the partings forever and our coming together again.

What do I do with your letters? I re-read them. I bang pretty colored thumb tacks into their corners and hang them on the English Department bulletin board. I couldn't possibly destroy them. You would come to me before long asking me this or that about the letters, and I would remind you that you ordered me to destroy them, whereupon you would take off your shoe and beat me on the hat with it, or clobber me with your purse, claw at me, swear at me, as you have been known to do.

Please be at ease. Nobody is going to read your letters, tied in packages sealed in boxes locked in vaults of the First Western Bank of Arizona with orders that they not be opened without the most specific permission of me or my family until at least twenty-five years after my death. This means at least twenty-five years from this afternoon, by which time, really—tell the truth—will it matter very much to Mr. Suekuykeen to learn that you and I, when you were between husbands, resumed that old relationship begun when you thought me your wise old Professor of English and I was every bit of thirty?

What a little skinny thing you were when I first knew you. It was right after the summer, you will remember (and why shouldn't you remember? it was only sixty minus thirty equals thirty years ago, according to my little Texas Instruments calculator), and you were the color of a penny, tanned except where your whiteness traced the little swim suit you had lived in all summer: you had spent all summer, you told me afterward, burning your body for me in the Fall. I was stunned. I had no idea you or anybody except my mother thought about me in the summer. You were the first sexually aggressive woman I had ever met. I had been raised to believe that women detested the whole idea of relationships with men, although they sometimes consented to "do it" because that way they could have a baby, which women seemed to want as a kind of house-pet to fuss with while their husbands were off all day busy-busy at the office. I had been raised somehow to think women believed the sight of men's bodies was obnoxious; that a man who revealed any intimate part of himself must be arrested on the spot by the Chief of Police of Ogden. Indeed, did I not read all the time in the Ogden newspaper that this man or that was arrested for a vague but tantalizing offense known as "indecent exposure"? You never heard of a *woman* arrested for indecent exposure. Certainly not. I prowled the streets for hours searching for women indecently exposed but never found one. I never knew that the girls in school talked about *us*, although I knew we talked about *them* and compared their bodies one to another and argued what was desirable, if not indeed what was real, for we knew very little. (Of course my sisters talked about *them*, but everybody knew my sisters had dirty minds: one by one, as each of my sisters married, my mother told her, "Remember, nice girls don't move.")

So you can see that because of my Utah delay I got a late start on world-weariness, for which I am grateful in general, and to my family and our Mormon setting in particular. Delayed beginnings extend pleasures at the farther end, where I am now. I am rendered incapable for the moment only. I am determined to have many good times yet. I have not broken down. I am ready and awake. I'm delighted you were amused by the tale of my young lady on the bicycle. I suppose you might have guessed she's a student, taking notes, as you did once upon a time, on each syllable of priceless wisdom as it dribbles from my lips. She is herself rather a writer. Abner is extremely enthusiastic about a novel she has just sent to him, which I think you will enjoy: do make him Xerox one for you.

Finally, one request. I want to go to your wedding. I can find an excuse to go to New York. Will you send me an invitation? You say that Mr. Suekuykeen doesn't want your old friends around. In the big crowd would I be noticed?

Yours with affection always,

FROM: A. *Whalen Drew, M. D., Scottsdale,*
Arizona.

February 19

Dear Lee,

It is understandable that you are becoming a little "desperate,"
to use the word you use. I was a little upset by your letter at first.
We go too far back for arguments. I don't think we ever had one,
did we?

I don't believe you need to worry about Penny telling any of
your medical history to people in the English Department. She is
professional in her considerations and so am I. Your "secret" is
safe with us, although I hardly even think to call it a "secret" since
many other men in the English Department and elsewhere
throughout the University and elsewhere suffer the same small
problem.

It usually just goes away. Notwithstanding we made the $38
blood test only because that was all that was left to do before I
could bring myself to say to you, "I don't know what to do now."

Since nothing shows up I felt that your problem may be "psychological," and that was the reason I had my assistant give you
Haddock Hooper's number. I was only "thinking ahead" as well
as I could, although I suspect that my thinking has slowed down
along with the rest of me. There's nothing I would rather do than
retire, but we cannot afford it now or in the foreseeable future. It
looks to us like we must work until we drop. Of course you are
under no obligation to visit Haddock Hooper, but even if you did
you could be sure that nobody in the English Department would
hear about your doing so from our office. Everything remains in
complete confidence. Nobody has access to our files except Penny
and I and one girl of our office staff under complete supervision.

You mention "gossipy, unmedical prying," to use the words
you use. We do nothing of that sort. I can tell you in all honesty
Penny has no curiosity about your relationships with Beth or
others. The tables are turned in this respect. You once made me

a character in your book. That was a form of gossip, but I recognized it as part of your business. Gossip is not part of my business, however. You employed me amusingly, so I am told, although I never wanted to read the book even when people showed it to me. You are a somewhat unusual person and I have always been proud to inform people we come from the same town, but I tried to read your books and I must confess I was stumped. Penny is the book reader. She bought every book and brought it home and I would earnestly try to read them without success. I got a few pages into it and succumbed to a headache. Of course we read the duck book with the children and we have given many copies away as presents, but I don't suppose that counts. After every book Penny wonders which things are true and which are not, and she goes through them matching up the people with real life. I could never set down events that were not true, and the fact that anyone can do so amazes me and earns my fascination and admiration. I was trained not to.

Your "impotence" may be the result of a general tiredness. I am tired. We wish we could retire. I do not know if I am "impotent" but I am too tired to find out. Maybe your general tiredness is the result of having practiced your trade to the end. You can do no more now. You always seem to be filled with energy. I don't remember ever telling you about my "daily devotion" to a bicycle, and I am sure I never did because it is not true. Some years ago I was prepared to install a bike rack in front of our building, but I changed my mind for some reason. Maybe I said to myself what I often say, "I have put enough of my life into this piece of real estate. I won't put one more dime into it." I don't have control over everything. I have no control over the magazines coming to my office. I could not have told you things out of *Popular Health* because I never read it. I only fall over it in the waiting room. We have tried to work without the radio music you complain about, but if we turn the music off or even down people complain that it is much too quiet, they really need something to cover up the silence, the walls are so thin the sounds go right through to the embarrassment of patients who do not want to know what is going on in the next room. We did not realize the walls were so thin when we bought the building. Penny and I have often bitterly realized that when we bought the building the real estate people covered up the thinness of the walls by walking very quietly on the other side.

I don't hear the music if it's on or off. I don't smell the hamburger fumes from the Belly Whopper any more. I guess you have got to come to our office on days when the wind is right. We never really wanted to settle the office here, but we thought it was best, all things considered, and it barely was. It kept up with inflation. We went broke buying it, we remained broke paying for it, and we'd go broke if we sold it and tried to move. At sixty a doctor doesn't move. We never earned as much money as people think we did. My retirement plans looked sensational twenty-five years ago when I charged ten dollars for an office visit but they look like pancakes now.

You can understand why I am tired. Maybe I also should consider going to Haddock Hooper, "noted quack," to use your words. I mentioned him only because I ran out of things to tell you from the medical point of view. I have heard of people he has helped. He apparently has some sort of unique philosophy on life and a new outlook along the lines of Hindu faith healers and so forth, mixed with health fads and diets and mental healing, which may be the new thing. He specializes in sexual dysfunctions, breaking bad habits, curbing vices, quitting smoking, alcoholism, and others. I don't recommend him or not recommend him, I only mention him. He is not even a physician. In spite of his reputation I don't think he is terribly expensive, either. He charges as you can pay.

I hope this letter clarifies the points you raised. In the meantime please send my love to Beth as she travels on her tour of your children. Thank God our children are well, we have nothing more to ask.

Your friend,

February 20

Dear Abner,

I do deeply appreciate your friendly and supportive letters of the 9th and the 11th, not the least of them being your useful equestrian story about the horse with green legs, which I delivered yesterday to my writing class, prefacing it with the idea that the tale has a moral to it. It's true, they hurry their stories; they ruin everything by climaxing too fast; they've had wonderful endings in mind for so long they can't wait to get to them; they plunge like thirsting maniacs through the desert. They must learn to enrich the interior of their fiction with all sorts of details and characterization along the way, stopping and pausing and enjoying the sights and sounds and tastes of things, not merely leap down from the hayloft in a frenzy, *etc.*

Students say, "Yeah, I see what you mean," and on the whole they do, but seeing's not doing; it's a long time between perception and practice. The whole matter arose, of course, in connection with counsel we want to give Mariolena Sunwall about rewriting her novel, but she was absent from class yesterday and has been for several weeks. I have the feeling you are in closer touch with her than I.

There's no doubt you and Frank and Francine are correct about the inadvisability of their commissioning a novel from me. You are right. Your lecture on self-reliance did me good. As always, you have helped me get up off the floor, off on a better track, depending upon whether this is a boxing story (let's hope not) or a story about steam engines. In short, I am at work on a new book at last, which serves, I think, my interests in growth, love, education, personal striving, Tolstoyan reform, and all those yearnings within people I think I admire (of whom, I modestly suppose, I am one), who wish both to achieve something publicly good and privately decent.

/91

This work I am thinking of focuses itself around the idea of impotence. Here is the narrative line: a certain likeable man suddenly finds himself, in a certain year of his life, incapacitated in that way. He is our Hero. Let's call him that for now. Later I'll change his name to something less obvious. Distressed by his impotence, he seeks its causes through inquiries among various people of his acquaintance, among his family (his son, for example, may be a physician, his daughter a psychiatrist, *etc.*). If he turns out to be a bookish man he'll read books on the subject. He comes and goes to doctors. In his relationship with his wife she plays a new role, to help him she overthrows their conventional backgrounds and becomes a whirling dervish in their newly acrobatic bedroom where, prior to the time of the action of the book, they had always been essentially well-behaved. All this potentiality has yet to be worked out, but of course it will build as I engage in long detailed examination of everything, long past the mistake now of the over-eager young fellow sailing down from the hayloft.

Will Hero discover the cause of his problem? Will he cure it? Will he have strengthened relationships along the way? What will all this tell us about humankind? Will we laugh—that's the main thing, we must laugh. I think of certain highly comic possibilities: for example, he discovers a wonderful and thrilling readiness in a woman he has admired for years at a distance. But now, just at the point of her readiness . . . this. Or he discovers a young woman, the merest beginner at love, who takes unaccountatable possession of his soul, offers herself in readiness when . . . this.

Anyhow, these are the lines I've been following for the past few days, with some feelings reminding me of old feelings of success, the smell of a few little blank pages covering themselves with the letters of the alphabet and all the useful tools such as periods to end sentences with. Question marks to end questions with? Exclamation points to exclaim over!

I gather from your letter of the 9th that it isn't the money Frank and Francine balk at so much as the idea of a commissioned novel. Let's therefore ask them for the same $20,000, except that we will apply it now not to a novel they have thought up but to this novel which is coming right out of my head. Frankly, my idea is better than one they'd think up anyhow. I really do feel myself breaking through on this. My standstill is over. I who thought I was dry forever should have known better. My mind teems with many details for this new book—as I write this letter to you I keep interrupting myself to make notes.

All right, there we are, one more crisis behind us. So I feel and hope I feel the same tomorrow and the next day and the next. Many a crisis popped up ahead after I thought it had been put behind.

Abner old friend, old pal, of course I am delighted that you and Dorothy and (I hear) Mrs. Mannerly were able to enjoy Mariolena Sunwall's book so much. You must pat Dorothy one thousand times on the top of her head for laughing in bed. Could be a title for something, *Laughing in Bed*, so many people tell me they read This or That of mine laughing in bed, it always pleases me. I don't mind people's enjoying my books in the bathroom, either. Some writers seem to object to that. I really don't know why. *Laughing on the Toilet. Fire in the Bed.* But the main point is that you and I know that if you and Dorothy and Beth and I have all liked it so much Frank and Francine are going to like it, too.

Sure, some rewriting, Francine and Frank are going to want that, they wouldn't feel whole if they took a book just as it came. Our Mariolena will do what the book needs. She is truly a writer. You know, these students of mine are all so much better and smarter as people and critics than they are as writers. So when a real live writer like Mariolena comes along I rejoice, and in the midst of my rejoicing I apologize to you for all the rest I send to you, who seem to waste your time. Isn't the one in fifty worth it then?—one Virgilia, one Schiff, one Mariolena? Answer: Yes.

Francine's and Frank's divorce probably comes as no surprise to anyone. One only asks why now? Why at all? Why bother? What can they now do bad in the eyes of proper society or distressing to each other that they haven't been doing for a quarter of a century? So down they go, out of matrimony, but remaining in business. It's so meaningless I feel I ought to send them a greeting card.

No, I don't at all mind telling you how I feel about Virgilia's marriage. I look forward to attending her wedding. Fly in, fly out, not miss a class. Every time she marries I maintain the discretest confidence. I view each marriage as a new job she has taken, and I want her to have her best shot at it. I had a letter from her earlier this week sounding a trifle desperate, ending "I can't blow this one," and for that reason I'd keep to myself my opinion of the matter except to speak as freely and as confidentially with you as always. Not for immediate publication.

Yes, we "were always very close to put it bluntly." Well, not always. Only for the past thirty years with unlimited time-outs for her to go courting and marrying and divorcing. Each time she called time-out I thought the game was over, but if this was a game, which it was not, it had no rules, and she wrote it all up here and there and walloped me and slandered me and hated me and abused me and then seemed to invite me back into the game again, and I like the loving little puppy dog I am raced to the dressing room and got all dressed in my uniform again and resumed.

She wrote me up not only in *Doctor's Out* (which she thinks I never noticed) but also in the story "The One Who Always Came Around Between Times." One of the first things she did as my student was to write a story about me so wide of the mark neither the class nor I recognized me. This taught her a good lesson, and the next story she wrote about me she shot me straight through my heart.

In her academic robe thirty-one years ago come summer right there in the middle of the basketball arena she said to me, "Don't you want to sleep with me?" Sure. "Lend me five dollars," she said. Sure. "The five dollars has nothing to do with it," she said. I hadn't supposed it did. "I cost a lot more than five dollars," she said. Under the academic robe she was naked. She wore it to bed. A lot of students do that to satirize the ceremony.

But she scolded me for making a five-dollar whore of her, and she has been scolding me and loving me for thirty years, and borrowing from me and hating me and sending my books to me with all her interlinear conjecture on my loathsome character, and insisting that she is not a whore, which I never said she was. Her *father* said she was.

If you read her carefully book to book you see her gradually separating the idea of money from the idea of sleeping-with. She has made her obsession with money pay money. I don't suppose Suekuykeen will read her well enough to find out the things she

94/

doesn't want him to know. He's no scholar. (But he can *hire* scholars, can't he?) I think it's a truly hopeful sign that she's not pretending she's marrying Suekuykeen for the pure love of the man: she admits that he is in possession of fluid money, and I gain the idea that she intends to see that some of it settles on herself. When she married poor MacGregor she went around telling everybody she was marrying him in *spite* of his money. When nobody believed her she became furious and said she never gave money a thought: then along came *Cash Sale* where people were hiding money on their bodies, chewing it up and swallowing it, the surgeons were planting it inside friendly bodies, and Virgilia gave interviews saying this wasn't money she was talking about, it was a theological dialogue based on a Sixteenth Century occurrence. It might have been. I'm an Eighteenth Century man myself.

Summary and Conclusion: Please keep me posted regarding Apthorp House's response to Mariolena's book.

Confront Frank and Francine with my idea for a novel as I have outlined it to you herein, and secure $20,000 advance.

Your Western Scout,

FROM: Mr. Arishima *"Don"* Kuraji, Prescott, Arizona.

February 19

Dear Honored Professor:

My answers are as follows.

1. 61.
2. 30 days.
3. Rod.
4. Yes.
5. Yes.
6. Yes.
7. Yes.
8.
9. Undergo.

Respectfully,

FROM: Ms. Virgilia Macgregor Kuhmerker
McDevitt, writer, New York City.

February 22

Dear Lee,

Your letter infuriates me. I want to have my letters back or destroyed. You should have destroyed them by now.

In your earlier letter you spoke of an "occasional meeting."

March 2 I will be married. On that subject let me address you in the Johnsonian construction you called to my attention when you were my wise old Professor of English at thirty and I was your impressionable sunburned student—"You are not to believe . . . you are not to imagine . . . You are not to think . . . and so forth" . . . You are not to attend my wedding. You are not to telephone me or send me night letters or Telegraph or funny postcards or timely books or flowers or gifts or greeting-cards. You are not to imagine that we are any longer connected to one another by those ties which have bound us in the past.

Gratefully and appreciatively,

February 24

Dear Abner,

I hardly expected to write you so soon again. I was just simply awfully delighted to receive your call and to be able to put you so promptly in touch with our Ms. Sunwall. If I am delighted you can guess how delighted she is, though she played it rather cool. When I gave her your message she said, "Oh, by the way, what's his number, I'll probably give him a call, I wonder what it's about."

I'm sure she's right, though, not to count her chickens before they've. I have so many students who dream reality in without much basis. If they meet a traveling third assistant editor at a summer workshop they conclude that they have established the unbreakable connection not only with posterity but even with New York publishing. Still, I suppose one must do it. One knows very little about the working of things. Do you remember my first advance on my first book, it was $250 and you had to fight for it, as I recall? Frank and Francine deducted from that regal sum several petty charges including $8.00 for "hotel." The Algonquin. I had thought they were to pay it. They had not thought so. You then deducted your commission not from the net but from the gross. I was flabbergasted. Still, it came finally to nearly $210— plenty of inspiration for me, you may be sure.

This news will send Mariolena hurtling years into the future now with the firmest image of herself as a writer, even if nothing immediate comes of Apthorp House's enthusiasm, which, as you know, happens. Since she has been in straits I had some days ago offered her our guest house. She arrived over the weekend to take it over, so to speak, with her baby and her books and her Spiral Binder and her worldly possessions in her Volkswagen bug. You remember our guest house, I'm sure. Your signature is on the wall. Hers is now there, too (and her baby announced in parentheses), in the rather large hand of a woman confidently poised on the threshold of literary distinction, you may be sure. Yet she is as independent as she can be. She insists upon paying me rent as soon as she has some money.

She came to class today, She gave me permission to announce that she has received this encouraging word from Apthorp House. The class applauded. It's not every day that students from Gila Bend and Buckeye and Yuma receive word from Apthorp House. Mariolena acknowledged the occasion by removing her cowboy hat and shaking out her hair and declining to attend a party in her honor, which one of her classmates had immediately proposed. Instantly famous, instantly a recluse, no party for her, Arizona's own Garbo.

Class continued. I thought that was as it ought to have been, with the focus on the work, not the market. I don't mean to underestimate the significance of your world as the objective of hers. Can you imagine the meaning of the phrase "Apthorp House" to aspiring writers from these little distant places? You, Abner, and your neighbor Apthorp House, represent the seat of all sophistication. For these children Frank and Francine's silly little trademark-drawing of a house (it always looked rather like an outhouse to me) looms as large in their heads as the Statue of Liberty. They have been reading Apthorp House books and authors through their solitary childhoods—and now! what! the Apthorps themselves have read the book of their classmate Mariolena! How can I tell them or anybody that two more fucked-up citizens than Frank and Francine nowhere exist? These world leaders of art and commerce, two of the maddest hats the universe has ever seen, are the judges whose good opinion my students seek. I want to keep it in perspective. I take the stance of teacher: of career they hear enough.

One thing our classmates promptly asked is whether our new star Mariolena will receive at this point any money for her book—not that they wish to pry, you understand, but they do wish they knew (if there's money to be got) exactly how much and when she will receive it and how much her agent receives as his "cut." Some of their questions are answered, and certain inaccuracies generated, in an article in the student newspaper which I enclose herewith. Her financial position is basically rock-bottom. Why should it be otherwise at her age at her point of career? We were

there, were we not? Her parents have quite divested her of everything on the grounds that she has disgraced them in several ways.
She was expelled from the dormitory—or at least her *baby* was
expelled—a year or so ago. At about the same time she was expelled from her home: *i. e.*, her family threw her out because the
University had thrown her out, so goes her tale. She lived and
wrote and kept house and raised her child in her orange Volkswagen plastered with idealistic ecological stickers of the sort I
should plaster to my own vehicles but somehow don't. I have
become too sedate. I am really a thousand times more radical than
my bare bumper suggests.

Mariolena makes me feel somewhat guilty, as my own children sometimes do, about my outward moderation in social and
political matters. She can't believe I've never smoked marijuana.
She urges me to take it up as a way to get my literary creativity
really going again. The few pages a day I've been doing don't
impress her as much. And yet, when I told her how bad I think
it is to take any sort of smoke into one's lungs for whatever reason,
she instantly agreed, sold all the marijuana then in her possession, and is on the lookout for a good clever anti-marijuana bumper
sticker.

This faith in me is flattering. She spends day and night reading
my books, and although she sometimes misses some of the di-
mension of it she always seems to laugh in the right places. She
is precocious. She is also the ancient peasant of faith, gazing upon
me so attentively when I speak that I truly do wish I were saying
more. I can't help myself. I do the best I can. If it all sounds like
old stuff to me nevertheless she marvels at my wit, my wisdom,
my merest halloo to the postman, sterling things I say to the burly
man delivering bottled water, to telephone solicitors calling me
up to invite me to have my roof shingled, to dance at the fireman's
ball, each little endearment I speak to these my three cats and
two dogs. My every goo-goo sounds profound to Mariolena. She
wants to transcribe my "lectures" on writing—so she calls my
remarks springing unplanned from the top of my head—for she
plans now a book of my lectures on writing as a supplement
(Volume II) to my biography, *Sunwall's Life of Youngdahl.*

I am the first literary man she has ever met. All her family's
associates are bookless, avaricious, mercantile, criminal ele-

ments, she tells me, cattle thieves, lying landlords, drunken pornographers. I have never met them.

Apparently she has undertaken revisions of her book. But I had had the impression, both from you and from her, that Frank and Francine are delirious about the book "as is" and don't want a word changed; except that, as you predicted, and as I too should have expected, they don't like the idea of the world "toilet" in the title. No problem, I'm sure. You know, here's an idea for a title: *Lying in Bed.* Because we were all amused early in the book when the young lady says, "Earnestly they conversed together as they lied in bed." It sent me sprawling and, as I recall, left its happy effect even upon you.

Of course I am anxious to know how things work out as they go forward, but please understand that you are under no obligation to tell me anything. She is yours now and not mine, and nobody may come between the writer and her agent, it's the sacred relationship.

Even this moment your client is jumping up and down on my diving board with her baby in her arms. It's truly remarkable. I never really dared to do it, though Beth could. Beth could spring high into the air with the baby in her arms, and the babies always loved it, even if their father didn't. Beth could jump up and down on a diving board for a quarter of an hour without stopping.

Mariolena isn't really the indifferent mother she seems to have wanted us all to believe. She often tells her baby she intends to sell him first chance she gets, and she pretends to be indifferent to his falling into the pool and drowning, but she doesn't sell, he doesn't fall. After she leaps up and down on the diving board a few hundred times she sits down cross-legged on the board and scribbles away in her Spiral Binder on her revisions. Apparently she intends to rewrite whether Frank and Francine call for it or not. Some of the class criticism of her book has taken hold, she sees that she has swooped down precipitously on certain climactic events, she wants to slow things down and deepen certain characters. Her classmates have conveyed to her the parable of the horse with green legs.

I thank you for your encouragement all along. I now do indeed look forward to the real possibility of greeting Beth at the airport with the news that I have broken through into new big work. To

/101

prove it I'll show her my $20,000 advance. Yes? She is back in the United States now. At the moment she is either visiting with Thornton & family in Dallas or moved on to Kentucky. Thornton is running for public office, as you may know. Earl is teaching in Bowling Green (Kentucky) and writing a novel which I think is very good. Bernique is in Owensboro (also Kentucky), where she has just more or less celebrated her thirty-fifth birthday. Somehow it was rather a trial for her. Her excellent husband rented a billboard to announce the event but kindly did not mention her new age. I can send you a photograph of it if you like.

Clipping enclosed.

Jubilantly yours,

The halls of the Language & Literature Building were buzzing Monday with news of the New York acceptance of a novel by Mariolena Sunwall, Liberal Arts senior, majoring in English. Ms. Sunwall's novel, which she has been writing for the past one year, has not yet been entitled. Title discussions are under way between Ms. Sunwall and her New York publishers, Apthorp House.

Ms. Sunwall is the daughter of Mr. and Mrs. Sanford Sunwall, of Osage Verde Ranch, Tonopah, where Ms. Sunwall was born and raised prior to entering ASU.

Ms. Sunwall declined to divulge the sums of money she has received for her novel, but "it is more money than my mind ever imagined," she revealed. According to Ms. Sunwall she established contact with Abner Klang of New York, an agent of established reputation. Reached in New York, Klang revealed he has "high hopes" for ASU's Ms. Sunwall's career as a novelist and described her as "an example to youth." He declined to reveal the sums paid to her by Apthorp House but differed with Ms. Sunwall on whether or not the sums were greater than the mind can imagine. "I can imagine it," said Mr. Klang by telephone.

Ms. Sunwall first became famous on the ASU campus last year when she and several undergraduate women engaged University officials in a dispute over dormitory rights for single mothers.

Ms. Sunwall's major work in English has focused on creative writing under Dr. Lee Youngdahl, also a noted novelist and writer of fiction. "I believe in him," Ms. Sunwall said. "If he says it I do it. What did this University do to deserve him?" Professor Youngdahl described Ms. Sunwall's book as "tonic."

February 23

Dear Dad,

Loved your letter. What a writer you are! Loved your Calling Card #40, too, and think I might get up a Calling Card myself just as soon as I have a few more items in print to put on it.

I met mother in Dallas and we helped out Thornton in his campaign as well as we could, and we all wonder how it will come out. Too close to call—that seems to be the concensus there. We are all exhausted. Mother begs to explain that she is too exhausted to write to you at the moment, but soon will, adding only at this point that the Roll-a-dex directory telling the number of the boy who feeds the animals "ought to be right in plain sight on the telephone table," and, second point, do not over-feed the animals and "do not allow the boy to over-feed the animals once you find the Roll-a-dex."

I thank you for your inquiry about the progress of my novel in your Valentine's Day All Points. Right now my problem seems to be different from yours. You seem to be stuck in your writing, whereas I, far from being stuck, seem to be spilling it out by the ton. When I began I doubted that I could write two hundred pages, but following your suggestions I let my stream of consciousness carry me away until now I have five hundred and fifty pages of memories in search of some shaping. Mother's being here, and running around with Thornton's campaign, stimulated many memories. Every time Thornton spoke he reminded me of something that happened between us as kids. Once he and I forged a check for five dollars. I don't believe you ever found out—oh, you must have. Thornton and I worked hours and hours practicing forging your signature, lurked several more hours to get our hands on a blank check, and took it to the Friendly Market where Ben gave us a five-dollar bill. I remember very clearly thinking at that moment that life was going to be awfully easy from then on. All we had to do when we needed a bit of cash was to forge a check and get the money and never worry about earning a living. I wondered why nobody had ever thought about that before. I was at that time (still am) uncertain what I was going to do for a living, and this solved the problem.

Have you any word on the student's novel of "burning toilets" mentioned in your All Points? Mother seems to have found it amusing. Mother seems to be rather optimistic and upbeat about Lucien's progress in his job down there. She's more worried about you. She wishes you were into a book. You're a beast when you're not writing—"bad enough when he is"—that's her verdict on your character. If anything, I've got *too* many stories fighting for places in my novel, so many memories I can't keep up with them all. A friend of mine found it useful in keeping track of her past to buy a computer, and she had really gone far and deep into her life when one day she pushed the wrong button and wiped it all out. Now she's back to paper. Every little thing sets me off—a bit of a tune, a phrase somebody speaks, mother lifting her eyebrow the least bit skeptically. A computer couldn't handle me. In your All Points you said you went to Los Angeles and the doctor "called for" his knives. Off I went. I was back in the old house and we were all singing—

> Old King Cole was a merry old soul
> And a merry old soul was he.
> He called for his pipe and he called for his bowl
> And he called for his fiddlers three.

Called for, called for, called for his fiddlers three. That threw me. What the hell was that all about? Called for them at their door, of course, that's where you called for kids, you knocked on their door and out came the three fiddlers. Somehow when I was five years old in my fantasy when we sang that song I called for the fiddlers three at the Rucklers' house and that was that for then and always and now and forever, I'll always see that same unvarying scene.

I am sorry to hear about your physical affliction and wish I had something helpful to say on the subject, but that particular problem has never been mine. Some day I suppose. Mother is distressed about it and feels guilty for having gone on this trip of hers. She apparently does not fully believe you when you speak of two possible cures. You say Time or Nothing will cure you, but she is still afraid of Somebody Else. Well, say I, let's throw out Time, leaving us with Nothing or Somebody Else. If there has got to be a cure wouldn't it be better that it be Somebody Else rather than Nothing?

Mother declines to accept those alternatives. "I am not a damn computer," she says. "I can think up my own alternatives." Why don't you go for marriage counseling? Mother laughs. Nevertheless, a lot of people I know go for it and say that it helps. A close friend of mine had the experience of coming with his wife to a parting of the ways. They had been very good pals for many years. Then they married, only to find that they had enjoyed each other much more as pals than as newly married people. It was necessary to continue the older pattern, which meant that when the spirit (the flesh) moved them they went out for some "fresh meat," as they called it. I realize how offensive such a phrase must be to you, and they themselves were covered by guilt until their marriage counselor urged them to go right on being pals when they couldn't stand being husband and wife, and they have been trying that method. Soon they will be married five years so there must be some wisdom to it.

I believe with mother that once you get rolling with a new work the problem will care for itself. It won't be Nothing and it won't be Somebody Else and it won't even be Time, really, except insofar as Time is a function of your Getting Back to Work. Anyhow, she says, there's no use talking about your going to a marriage counselor, she "can't picture" your going to such a person after all these years. But even talking about something is "picturing" something. If you can mention it it exists, and you can begin to "believe it in" (Robert Frost).

I couldn't picture a lot of things about you until they happened, or until my own experience made me aware that it was *logical* such a thing happened to you, though I had no direct proof of it. All my thoughts lead back to memories. I couldn't picture you swearing, although Thornton told me you could swear like a plumber when you cared to. Then one day I heard you break loose: you cracked your head on a kitchen cabinet door—one of those doors that catch shut by a magnet except when somebody (in this case you, dear father) slams the door too hard and the magnet fails and the door swings open and the poor joker (once again you) who thinks it is closed finds out the truth the hard way.

And that's about the local news.

Getting back to Calling Cards: please tell me whatever gave you the idea of getting up Calling Cards in the first place, how you went about it, problems and pitfalls.

Love and more love,

P. S. It was I, not Lucien, who fell asleep in the back of the car.

February 24

Dear Mr. Youngdahl—

I could not believe my eyes. Author of the *Hard Puncher.* I thought you were dead. Or maybe it was me that was dead and went to heaven. Author of the *Hard Puncher* writing a letter directly to me. The greatest book ever written including the bible. Over the years I gave away dozens of copies to people for birthdays and Christmas and good will contacts on the road.

If you're on your way out the door for your penile implant, stop! I didn't go through with mine either altho I know that some people go through with theirs and are fully satisfied. I hope I'm stopping you just in time the way somebody stopped me just in time. I'll describe it. If I can be of service to the author of The *Hard Puncher* I have not lived in vain. "Question 9. What advice do I have for anybody wanting to decide whether to undergo such an operation?" My advice is give it a second thought.

I never boxed altho I did everything else, wrestled and weight lifted and high dive and ran the dash as well as played on every team game going. I was one of your all around athletes and proud of it. I was one of your macho men, as they call them, and proud of it. I was one who was never a quitter in any sport at any time, and never a quitter in non-sports, either, could outlast anybody in any tavern, bar, or saloon and hold the record for broad jumps (jumped more broads), the latter because I had and still have such perfect muscular control over every part of my body. I have been a non-stop business man for thirty-four years and sold a million dollars in every kind of conceivable surplus back in the days when a million dollars was considered a real achievement. Nowadays I do a million dollars in the first quarter.

One day about two years ago I noticed that my cock was just not about to stir for anybody, and I knew from sports that such things happened. I know from sports that I can talk freely with you, the Hard Puncher himself wasn't too queasy about such things, was he? Altho it gives me a start seeing myself writing down such things in this way. I write a lot of letters in sports controversies to the newspapers and various writers. An arm can go temporarily dead. Once my timing went completely off for a period of weeks. I needed glasses. Another time I couldn't leave the ground. Couldn't go in the air for anything. There was nothing anybody could do about it. People say that the worst thing you can do is press. "Take your mind off it, don't think about it, and it will come back." Ballplayers play through batting slumps. You can't keep a good man down for long. This went on for a couple of weeks.

I belong to the Bay Side Athletic Club, not the best, not the worst, "everything money can buy, but you can't buy your way in." My observation is you *can* buy your way in. I spend most of my time there. I would rather go there than home, rather go there than work, altho I'm a good family man and a good company man, but I spend as much time there as possible. I was there one day at the time of my cock crisis feeling rather sorry for myself and brought up the question to a long time friend of mine named Tiffin, who for many years held the California record for several high school swim events. "Let me give you the name of a good cock doctor." He gave me the name of Dr. Emmer, who in turn gave you my name as one you could write to for an endorsement of his product. I signed his consent to that.

Now I don't really know about his product. I never had it done but I was so close to having it done he had my name on his list and either he or his girl forgot to take it off. That's O. K. Listen, if his small mistake brings me a letter from the author of *The Hard Puncher* who am I to complain.

A few days before I was scheduled for surgery I went to the club to clean out my locker, knowing I would not be back for several weeks, maybe longer, when along came a long time friend of mine named Dave Kendall, who has had a locker next to mine for years. We are not good friends. Not enemies. Just visual friends. When I see him there he is. When I don't see him he's nowhere. Nowadays, however, I think of him favorably because if I had not seen him and struck up a simple conversation with him, his locker being right next to mine, my life might be greatly different today.

I said, "Hello, Dave, I haven't seen you in some time," which opened up the flood gates. "Well, the reason you haven't seen me in some time is because I have just had surgery and am only now getting back in some sort of shape." He swam. It was all he ever worked out at. He swam for two hours without stopping. "All right," I replied, "what did you have surgery for?"

"This," he said. He dropped his pants. I was clobbered. I had never seen a cock hard before, not for years and years. Why would I? You know, when you're a kid in school you horse around in a locker room and a kid might get a hard on (I never did, but I saw others), but many years passed thereafter and I just never had occasion to see one. I bet I began to back away from Dave Kendall, we were alone down there down that alleyway between the lockers and he said, "Don't be afraid of me, Charlie, you asked about my operation and that's my evidence." It was Dr. Emmer's specialty, the penile implant, recommended to Dave Kendall by Tiffin, they were fellow swimmers, the same Tiffin who had recommended him to me.

Holy God, was that going to be me in a few days? I didn't need a permanent uninterrupted lifetime hard on for God's sake. I became weak all over. There was something going on here that I hadn't given sufficient thought to. I went heavy, like the time I could not get into the air, I was frozen to the spot. "Why don't you put some pants on," I said. SUPPOSE SOMEBODY WALKED AROUND THE CORNER OF THAT LOCKER ALLEYWAY AND SPIED ME STANDING THERE IN INTIMATE CONVERSATION WITH A NAKED MAN WITH A HARD ON AS BIG AS THE RITZ. WHAT KIND OF A QUEER FAGGOT WERE PEOPLE GOING TO THINK I WAS? Of course I could talk my way out of it.

"It's just something I've got to live with," he said, pulling his pants back up, thank God. He told me the details of his life. He was married many years, but during the last ten years his wife was very ill. They had no relations during that period and his cock dwindled and died. After her death he was extremely lonely and still being a young man began to take up with various women of his acquaintance, and everything went well until they discovered that he had no interest in jumping them. One after another he lost them as friends. They wouldn't go out with him, no matter what fine food and entertainment he offered, the bottom line was the old desire for romance which they wanted with reasonable

110/

frequency. But Kendall's cock was dead and if this kept up for long he would be out of his mind besides. Then Tiffin told him about the implant, and he has never been so popular. It's a story with a happy ending.

Well, that was all very well from my point of view, I'd have given anything for a cock as big and hard as Dave's except I wanted to have some control over it. I could do almost anything in this life, but I cannot bring myself to walk around in a locker room with a hard on, maybe in a ladies locker room, but I have never been invited in. Dave Kendall's way just wasn't my way. I couldn't do it. Maybe I could work around it some way. But how? One of the things you like about a club is the comradeship of the men, you work out and then you stand around in the steam and the shower bare ass naked (pardon my language) but if some member ever had a hard on staring you in the face you're going to start drifting away, and I saw that as a danger of the penile implant, I could hear people all over town talking about it, all of a sudden Charlie Martinak is coming out of the closet as a queer faggot. Any closets I've been in I've come out of. That's not one of them.

I never went down for the surgery by Dr. Emmer, although obviously he or his girl never took my name off their list. Can you imagine a job where a man operates on so many cocks he can't remember whose he did and whose he didn't? I'd rather sell surplus.

Now to get to your letter. The most amazing part is coming. I put my gear back in my locker and I left the club. I made up my mind I would just resign myself to a no-sex existence. If we fought a no-win war I could live a no-sex existence. It was the same thing. I told Mrs. Martinak I was not going to have the operation done. "O. K. whatever you want to do about it it'll have to be, won't it, beggars can't be choosers." I gave up. My broad jumping days were over forever. I was a very young man, fifty-six. I began to live a regular life trying to put it out of my mind as much as possible, running my business with extra energy, working out at the club longer and longer, expanding my territory. Here's where the amazing day came.

Following every sport going, I mixed business trips with sporting events. I went to my customers and took in sporting events at the same time. Los Angeles. Las Vegas. Phoenix. Denver. Salt Lake. Everywhere. Formerly business trips meant I might

/111

jump a broad or two. In fact, that was half the purpose of them. I spent a lot of hard earned money in those days broad jumping on short business trips. My accountant shook his head. "How come you took that trip when you didn't make any money on it?" No answer. "It's costing the firm money." "I am the firm." But now that I was no longer interested in broad jumping a business trip combining business with a sporting event was easy on costs, and there were times when I began to feel how lucky I was now that my cock was dead and buried forever. I was just getting used to it. I wasn't thinking about it any more. I was flying all over my territory more thoroughly than ever before, seeing more sports, making more money. On this particular day I was on a flight I took many times, Republic 550 7:55 A. M. to Palm Springs-Indio. Fasten your seat belts.

Sure. Why not? But just at that very moment, as I was fastening my seat belt, I said to myself, "What's this?" and what it was it was something MUCH MORE THAN THE BUCKLE OF MY SEAT BELT, it was my cock forming the biggest and most mammoth and impressive hard on you or anybody else might have seen in a long time. My jaw dropped open. It didn't seem to belong to me. It was from another world. I was out of my mind with frenzy. I was back from the dead. There was a lady in the seat next to me and I grabbed her arm and said, "Look at this."

Now whose jaw dropped open? Hers. She yelled out, "Let me out of here," beginning to unbuckle her seat belt. The stewardess said, "Sit back down, lady, the captain has got the fasten seat belt sign on." The lady said, "I don't care what the captain got on, look at this man and what he got on and you expect me to sit here beside him all the way. Nothing like this ever happened to me before on Republic Air."

And I bet nothing like that ever since.

"What's the trouble here?"

"This lady is crazy," I said.

Saved. In my opinion I came back from the dead because I stopped thinking about it. When I surrendered victory came. When I accepted the no-win war I won. Lee Youngdahl, author of *The Hard Puncher*, whatever you do I plead with you, don't do it. Relax and it will return. "Question 9. What advice have I got for you which may be helpful?"

112/

My advice. Don't.

Your long time admirer,

P. S. I have to tell you about a kindness I did I'm proud of. As the airplane touched down in Palm Springs-Indio and we all began to stand up and collect our overhead possessions and so forth I said to the lady beside me, "Keep the faith. Believe in yourself. You saw what you saw. I was in a slump and suddenly recovered." She said, "I'll say." She even smiled a little.

FROM: Alvin Oatkus, Esquire, for Klaridge,
Claus, Nugent, Peart, Limbeck & Weddle,
Las Vegas.

CERTIFIED LETTER

February 25

Dear Professor Youngdahl:

Acknowledging receipt of your letter form communication February 17, postmarked February 17, Tempe, Arizona, addressing Mr. Skipper Rothgery, and accompanying advertisement entitled "Calling Card Number 40," purporting to be a list of your literary writings, seeking information from the above named Rothgery regarding his supposed "penile implant," as, for example, "May I ask you how old you are?" in a group of nine questions of that nature and category, Rothgery neither affirms nor denies the occurrence of any surgical procedure or other procedure of the kind or nature intimated in your said letter form communication.

Rothgery declines at this point in time to reply to the questions you have submitted to him.

Rothgery affirms that the letter form communication referenced above was sent to him absent his solicitation, nor did he invite or solicit all or any part thereof of the nine questions of the nature and category referenced above.

Be informed herewith and by this codicil, sent to you postal certified, that you may not broadcast or publish news or information connecting or associating Rothgery to the alleged surgical procedure commonly called "penile implant" without Rothgery's express permission to do so in writing. Violation of this demand may be viewed as defiance of Rothgery's wishes and rights in every respect, and a violation of his every private right to which he is entitled by the laws of the State of Nevada, the Constitution of the United States, and all other codes or regulations where applicable.

Very cordially,

114/

FROM: Beth Youngdahl, c/o Earl Youngdahl,
Bowling Green, Kentucky.

February 25

Dear Lee,

Please put some sort of sign on the fence asking United Parcel
or others "Do not throw objects over the fence." I have sent several
boxes of interesting objects of art and use from Lucien's. His
friends crated them well but wonder why I am afraid that someone
will throw them over a fence. I say our truckmen are in a hurry.
They wonder why.

The little packet of love powder I sent you separately. It is
guaranteed to make you loving in your old age if not sooner.
Sooner has almost passed. On the plane out of Texas I was talking
with a physician who attributes your "impotence" to tension and
anxiety. You are afraid of "performance failure," she says. When
your writing gets started your everything will get started, she says.

Leaving Lucien's was more difficult than arriving, made so
by the rains. We were two days on the mule-drawn bus and bus-
drawn mules to the train to the plane. The last thing Lucien said
to me was to tell you that if the zinc bothers your stomach just
discontinue it. He talked frankly and gravely with me about your
"impotence," commiserating with you all the way until at last I
spoke up. "What about *me*?" Years ago the ladies magazines discovered that I too had rights, but it was a jolt for Lucien to hear
it directly from his own virgin mother. The truth dawned on him.
"I never thought of you . . ." His eyes had a new view of his
mother. She was not yet that old. He has been talking over your
situation with the wise men of the tribe. Wise men are only counselors who never received certificates. Of course you feel that your
experience has endowed you beyond certificates. Still you might
go speak to someone with a certificate. I touch this point gingerly.

Riding through town seeing Thornton's face on billboards. It
was a shock. Two days by mule and bus we saw no billboards.
The mules tow the bus through stretches of mud and then go

/115

back into their trailer and the bus does the towing until we arrive at the next mud. Awfully clever. I have many photographs of expanses of mud.

I have heard that the man to see for "impotence" is Haddock Hooper. You will remember him from the occasion when you went swimming in the ocean daring sharks to bite you. I was opposed to that venture. It was idealistic but risky to life and limb. A father of seven really had no right to do it.

Thornton's politics are much more direct but I'm not sure that he has a right to do it, either. He knows what he's into. Bernique was there when I arrived and Earl arrived soon after. Thornton tried to appear to be happy to have me. He'd sit with me with his legs crossed as if he were totally at leisure, but his appointments were uppermost in his mind. Telephone ringing once per minute. "Yes," he said, "and some of them ringing the other side, too. Whoever loses his telephone will stop ringing." They will be crushed if he loses, but it will be a kind of relief, too, and he vows he will go back to his firm with the resolution that he will never run again. I was introduced from platforms. It was as if he took his mother with him everywhere he went. I received many cheers for being his mother.

Why are you so hard on Wally and Penny? Don't turn on old friends who have proved themselves. Beware women who love you when your wife is out of town. They should be awarded the experience of seeing you in your natural state when you are into your writing and sweating and your beard is growing and you have refused to bathe or shave until you have turned a particular corner in your writing. At such times your breath may be very bad and you sit in your own smells like the late professor in his library spot. Does your little bitch with her bastard hang around your office all day or has she given up? They never give up. I see by the news the man with the unusual name (S--------n) will be spending $100,000 for his wedding with your long time New York fuck. You got her for $5 as told in her book. You deny it was you. Sometimes you see yourself where you care to. For example, I did not intend to connect the punishment for "impotence" to sins of yours, if any. I was only telling the tale Lucien told me, which the people of his community told him. It may all have lost in the translation.

116/

The Roll-a-dex should be on the telephone table. I can't imagine where it is if it's not. He is a reliable boy and feeds the animals without over-feeding them. His name is Todd. Ask children in the neighborhood where a boy named Todd lives. We call him so often you'd think we'd remember his number. I notice how fast things slip away with distance. Things at home don't seem to matter as much. At home I can't wait until the newspaper comes. If the boy skips us I die and hate him. Now it doesn't matter if I never see the paper again. The paper boy might know where Todd lives.

On to Earl's. Bernique has gone to Owensboro. With each child I must readjust my thinking. I say, "What did I know when I was thirty-eight? Thirty-six? Thirty-three?" I must calculate the year and remember where we were that year. Then I can begin to relate to the child. Thornton still a child though the billboard colors up his cheeks and presents him as a Leader Of Men. What did I think my mother knew when I was thirty? Earl's friends are much different from Thornton's. Much less turned to the outer world. They talk more about the body and inner things. Nothing could be more inner than anal itching. One of his studious friends brought up the subject and they talked about it half the evening. Was it from too much coffee? From perspiration? They just chattered about it as if it were car parts.

Students drop by to discuss their writings with him. Only yesterday he was showing his writings to you, waiting tensely for your opinion. Now his students wait tensely for his. I want to say, "Don't be tense, it's only Earl, he won't hurt you." He feels that's his duty, not to hurt them. He said, "I realize now it was dad's encouragement that helped. I guess he meant me to remember the encouragement above the criticism." He can't understand why you have run out of ideas. He has a thousand stories and says he'll never run out. So he thinks. I said nothing.

With love,

February 26

Dear Lee,

I am delighted and flattered that you sit around all weekend admiring my photograph on the jacket of *Sex In the Seventh Decade* (*And After*), but it's simply crazy for you to worry about your so-called impotence when Haddock Hooper is right there and you can go to him. I can't believe you haven't. Or have you? Under other cover I am sending you a copy of *Any Cure is the Right Cure*, which is the foremost book on curing yourself of impotence or anything else you imagine you have. If you want to know why the smile is on my face on the jacket photograph it's because I make it a habit to read Haddock's book whenever I feel myself sinking.

Haddock is not only a genius, he's an *intelligent* genius. He is the most open and accepting and welcoming man that ever lived. He wanted me to go west with him when he started up out there, but I was already ensconced here and couldn't leave. He is the wisest and kindest man I ever met and may be the wisest and kindest man that ever lived. Some people don't like him. He arouses animosities. He made many enemies in the east and is now making them out west, but he will conquer them all with his sweetness and his love and his vision. He conquered me. My own practice is adapted from many things he taught me, not only in the classroom but by example. You taught me writing and he taught me practice and they were both so much the same method I never understood why you resisted him. It wasn't he resisting you. He resists nobody.

Haddock will get at whatever is blocking you and free you in no time at all or less. He is always available. You may have noticed that *Sex in the Seventh etc.* was dedicated to him.

For God sake probably the last thing anybody in the world needs is a penile implant. Exactly why do you feel the need for a

118/

lifetime erection twenty-four hours a day? Isn't that overdoing it? I didn't notice that anything was wrong with your crotch anyhow, subliminally or otherwise, when you were here. If I assumed anything at all I assumed you had your mind on other business. I drove with my hand in your crotch by habit. It was not a test, it was friendship. Who needs two hands to steer a car? I didn't notice anything wrong or right, responsive or not responsive, and I did not detect any new maturity in you. You have all the maturity you need.

I easily discern many reasons for this "impotence" of yours and they are all related to your super-maturity. In all the university you were the only serious teacher I ever had. You connected the idea of teaching to the future of the world. You worry. You are too responsible. You battle the elements at the workplace and in your art. You are scrupulous about how you treat the very enemies who are trying to do you in. You worry about other people's fate. Do you still tell them in class that as they are sitting there dreaming and sipping their sodas in cans somebody somewhere is being tortured to death? It pepped up the class. You have been having difficulty getting going in your writing, which is of course a source of anxiety and helplessness: it contributes to a feeling *akin* to impotence.

But it is not the same as impotence. Rationally you know that you are only passing through a period of dryness in your writing. That is writing. Impotence is sexual. You feel impotent because you lose all the votes in your neurotic Department. The university throws your young friend out of her dormitory with her baby. She fights back but of course she loses. But even she, low as she may be on the power scale, is unattainable for you. You do not know whether to move toward her slowly or with speed. You are afraid she will discover your "impotence." Your last blessed erection was invisible to her as she sat on your bike looking forward. You are worried about your cash flow. You have anxieties about your children, who have dispersed, leaving your home unguarded, imperiling themselves in the alien world. You imagine yourself in your old age carried in a helpless state ("impotent") from house to house, from child to child: they smile at you but they do not want you.

For the moment all indicators seem to be pointing in a discouraging direction, as if you are losing power, losing control, losing command, and so it is natural for anyone to feel that this is not simply a momentary conjunction of events but the gloomy outcome of every theme of your life.

I on the other hand can see off at a distance from you that you have been through all these phases before. It is you who are basically in control. It is the outer world which has not yet matured. *Go to Haddock Hooper.* You will thank yourself all the days of your life. I believe he is only a short drive from Phoenix. I will write him a letter and tell him you are coming. No, I have just telephoned him, forgetting the time zones, waking him up. He growled at me and then expressed his love for me, nothing human is contradictory. He says, "I remember him well, tell him to come, no appointment necessary." When you see him, kiss him for me. Don't be embarrassed to kiss him. He kisses everyone who goes to him, male or female, acquainted or not, kisses and hugs and long history-making embraces, for when Haddock embraces he seldom lets go, the other person must let go, so that now and again if neither person lets go they stand there embracing for the longest time. Upon meeting Allen Ginsberg, Haddock and Ginsberg embraced for two hours. Joan Baez and Dick Gregory ninety minutes. Norman Mailer, Jane Fonda, Brando, Jerry Brown, poor Elvis Presley for varying periods of time. I do not mean he embraces only celebrities and achievers, but all sorts of people all over the world.

For Haddock, nobody is more important than anybody else. If he is with a patient when you arrive he will interrupt their session and welcome you, and you go in and kiss him and hug him and kiss and hug his patient, too, regardless of whether you ever met either of them. (Of course it is also your sacred right not to kiss.) You sit right down and join them in their session. *Their* session becomes *your* session, everyone is counselor and counseled, everyone learns from everyone else every minute. There's no telling lies.

When you and Haddock meet it will be a case of two of my favorite people in all the world meeting. He knows your books. He said so on the phone. He will read you thoroughly and tell you things you never knew about yourself—things you discharged from your mind into your books. But those things are only the fruit of the tree. The roots remain. (I wonder what he means, though, when he says he knows your books. You've got me worried. You were always so impatient when somebody rushed up to you and said, "I read all your books," when all they had ever read was *The Hard Puncher.* Or seen the movie. Only recently could I begin to appreciate your impatience. People rush up to me—I see them coming across the crowded room, they have the unmistakeable wild look on their face, "Listen, Dr. Schiff, here I am, I am the original klutz herself. How did you know the story of my life? You must be my premature reincarnation.")

I'd have answered your letter sooner but I wanted to read that book with the engaging title, *Fire in the Toilet,* which Abner sent me at my request. How could I resist a "lively small masterpiece" reminding you so much of *A Klutz in Love?* This girl is heavenly. I want to embrace her and her baby and her keychain and her locksmith and all her Devils. I am a fan of Sin City and join my name to the petition making its official seal the beer can crushed in the mighty hairy hand of the young man clutching the bicycle wrench. The high point for me was hearing God say at last, after all that long night of waiting for Him, "Do not duplicate." Abner had me on the phone half an hour regaling me with scenes I might have missed, but I missed nothing.

Abner would like me to write another *Klutz,* of course, but of course I cannot, as I am no longer a klutz: writing *Klutz* de-klutzified me. Instead, I am writing proposals for grants for studies which might become books which will not sell like klutzes sell. How can I help it if I too have matured? I cannot suppress my own growth, for that would be to deny my whole idea of life and growth. Abner says, "Stay like a klutz, live in a box forever." I cannot bind myself as Chinese women bound their feet to keep them small. Not quite women's liberation, wouldn't you say? Almost the first thing that ever terrified me in a book was my reading about Chinese women binding their feet. I declared I would fight to the death against the Chinafication of America.

Go to Haddock Hooper. Please keep me informed. Tell me how it all comes out. The next time you come to New York your crotch will be its old crotchety self again. Don't forget, the seventh decade may be the best of all. Then I got to thinking that according to my logic the eighth should be even better yet. I'm working on it. The older you grow the clearer you realize that everything you learned about love and loving was folklore. Now you test everything for truth. I have begun to find that many men in their eighth decade (ages 70–80) look back upon their *seventh* decade (ages 60–70) as a period of trial and innocence. At age 60–70 you are warming up for a passionate love life yet to come. At age 70–80 you will be ready to begin. When we women will be waiting. Alliterating.

This at least is really the way my interviews are beginning to shape up. After a dozen more interviews I'll be able to write my grant proposal. I'll make it a book *The Eighth Decade May Be Better Yet*, although Abner says I should call it *Son of A Klutz in Love* no matter what it's about.

If I thought your wife was still in Mexico I'd come out and visit you and put you back in shape. Or you could come here and be put back in shape. May she be held in violation of *habeas corpus* in a Mexican jail.

Always your student,

February 27

Dear Lee,

Point regarding newspaper clipping from Arizona student paper. Clipping received.

Point Regarding novel about incompetence. Here I was just virtually writing you a letter about a number of things when your letter of the 20th arrived infuriating me. Anybody but you I would have torn it up.

To get right to the point just let me tell you dismiss from your mind all ideas about a novel about incompetence. Who needs it? Half the world is incompetent already and the other half is their dependents. We need to be cheered up, not bawled out. I always admired your idealistic way of going about things. However, whenever you are between novels a screw goes loose. You start in talking about a better world, a better society, a world without grief, growth and love and being ethical etc. etc. etc. three or four times and they always lead to some third-rate idea like incompetence.

I hate this sort of thing. You are still in a slump, although I know you are going to climb out of it. On second thought I'm tearing it up anyhow. That page anyhow. There's no such thing as medical aid for incompetence. I think this is one time you strained your mind from over-reaching.

Just to be on the safe side I mentioned your idea to Frank and Francine. He didn't go for it. She sniffed. I repeated your plan of having a Publisher think up an idea and you'll fill in the novel. "Oh yeah," said Frank, "and then when the novel's a smellorino Lee will say no wonder, even a genius like me couldn't write a novel on such a lousy idea as that." They'll go for any idea in the world as long is it's yours and not theirs and as long as it's not incompetence.

Let's have a novel about that beautiful, ravishing girl on the diving board, that's what the world wants. Leave out the baby.

/123

Make her a virgin. The baby gives her away. Let her fall in the cold water and the hero saves her. They smoke marijuana together. Try it, it might float you out of your doldrums. Take smoke in your lungs. A little moderation never hurt. Anything is worth the price of getting started again. Here's a working title, *The Girl on the Diving Board*. I realize as a title it's for the birds but I never pretended I was a novelist.

I mentioned your suggested figure to Frank and Francine, $20,000. They have no problem with that. Write up a little five or six page outline denoting your general direction for *The Girl on the Diving Board* and your check is in the mail. I can see her from here flying up and down in the air over the diving board. She is "the ancient peasant of faith," quotes around it. Even when you're in a slump you're a genius with phrases. For God sake, however, don't get too poetic. I can see her now and her criminal family, cattle thieves, making use of your western background, lying landlords, drunken photographers, put it all together, I'm sure you're on the edge of a breakthrough. Don't ever forget we're all cheering for you. Who wouldn't cheer for their bread and butter?

What have you heard about their divorce? Nobody in New York talked about anything else for a week. If I hear one more word about it I'll plug up my ears. I sat in the courtroom half of one of the days, I was so ashamed of myself I sat in the back. Francine was asked when she slept with him last. She replied, "Some time during Eisenhower." He accused her of weird investments. She claimed they were shelters. "Yeah," said Frank, "she sheltered many young men." When he went to the Frankfurt Book Festival one year he brought home a beautiful Italian authoress, lavishing her with the most expensive gifts and luxuries. "Therefore," said the Judge, "you were angry at him because he slept with that Italian woman." No, said Francine, she was angry because throughout all the time Frank and the authoress spent together he forgot to get her to sign U. S. rights. It cost them a million lira.

Francine accused Frank of publishing too many of his friends. Frank blurted out, "How can she say I have friends?" Once in a fit of anger she printed up stationery changing the name of Apthorp House to Apthorp Hotel for Women. Nobody noticed. It looked very genuine. It was all fairly good natured. They came and went to court together, sharing the same cab back and forth from the office, enemies in court, partners in business. Nobody knows what really went on. So much for the facts. Mrs. Mannerly went back on the following day and wrote down all the settlement figures. It was stupendous. He is getting Fifty-Eighth Street, she is getting Martha's Vineyard, and they are giving away Key West as a home for disabled fishermen.

Point Regarding Mariolena Sunwall's novel manuscript entitled Fire in the Toilet or Lying in Bed. Mariolena called me as soon as you got word to her, which I appreciate. I like the sound of her voice. I am excited at the thought of meeting her. I am always excited at the thought of meeting a sterling author and always disappointed in them. They are never as good as their books unless they are lousy writers, at which time they are often very entertaining in the flesh but you forget them as soon as you say goodby. All of us here live in hope that one of these days we will discover a writer whose personal character matches up with their writing. We are huddling over our calendars finding a date for her coming. She will be asking you to excuse her from class. It's news to me you needed to be excused in college.

I hope she behaves decently when she gets here. I could never understand why writers try and bite the hand that feeds them. You used to be like that yourself. She launches an attack on Frank and Francine. "Hey, Mariolena," I replied, "listen to a little reason. I love your book and Dorothy loves your book and Professor Youngdahl and Beth love your book but Frank and Francine Apthorp are the ones that count. Fifty million people can love a book but you are nowhere without a Publisher." Well, but they are censoring her. They censored James Joyce and John Milton and others and now they are censoring her.

How?

Well, they are taking the toilet out of her title.

How else?

"Well, how are you spelling my name?" she asked me. I replied we are spelling her name any way she requests us to spell it, the name Mariolena is a different question from toilet. She then spoke as follows in case you heard it otherwise. "I'm trying to think what Dr. Youngdahl will say about this. Let me check with him."

"No," I said, "don't check with him. I mean to say, check

with him to your heart's content, but I know what he will say to you if he hasn't already. Mariolena, my dear, in the final analysis the people who are paying you hard money and Publishing your book are not your fellow students in your class in Arizona and not even your wonderful, kind, honest professor Youngdahl. You are now out in the big world to the east of Sin City and you have got to look around you and decide who the people are who are holding up the other end of your lifeline to the future, to wealth and fortune, to the midnight talk shows, to the national book club prizes and the Pulitzers and the Nobels and all the dollars and bucknicks which accompany the literary life." She listened courteously. I felt she was receiving what I was saying in the spirit of an open mind, and I thought it was the time to go the whole way with her. I want you to hear it from me and not somebody else. "Mariolena," I said, "no matter how you spell your name you pronounce it the same way and no matter how hard you look down the line at your lifeline there are two people at the other end. One is your Publisher and the other is your agent. Ask Professor Youngdahl on this one. He will agree your agent is the most important relationship in the world as long as you live. Children will desert you when you're old and gray, husbands will commit suicide, lovers will fuck you and wave to you at the window climbing into their Porsches and Triumphs and flying away in a cloud of dust, but your agent goes on and on, so you must not bawl me out for spelling your name wrong. You aren't even sure yet how to spell it yourself so why should I."

She took all this quietly under advisement. Then she said, "If you have finished running down Professor Youngdahl on the long distance telephone I am hanging up. Please United Parcel my manuscript back to me without delay."

"If you hang up on me," I said, "I will not call you back."

"If you called me back I wouldn't pick it up."

"Don't you prefer to think it over?" I asked. She said no, not on the long distance phone. I said, "Don't worry about the long distance. I used to be a rich man." She broke into speech and didn't stop. She began telling me her ideas for her new book. A biography of her baby. Did I hear her right? I said, "I understand the lovely child is only two years old." "You heard me correctly," she said.

She has a sound in her voice giving me the impression she believes she has lived forever and knows everything everybody in the world ever knew. She avoids anything half way. She has all her answers ready even before I have got them out of my mouth. This makes her hard to work with. Therefore you and I have got to take this matter up together. Don't blame me if I scold you, but I have got to speak to you with as much honesty at my command, as follows—

Point Regarding Mariolena Sunwall Prevented from Becoming a Cow Shit Eating Chicken. When you predicted that Frank and Francine would love her book I was a little skeptical, but now that they have proved you right you go up still one more notch in my estimation. Better put in he was always at the top of the notch, how could he go higher? Francine said, "Abner, you were right, it is literary history, I love it, you have got us over a barrel, go easy, she is only a little girl starting out in the west so we must limit her advance to $10,000." I could have got more, but I won some contract points instead. I have already got a paperback lined up. Could be six figures. In the meantime the money alone is enough to give her encouragement to last awhile and clear up a few debts besides. On the telephone she enumerated all her debts including $400 to you. You're your usual princely self helping out a damsel in distress. I'll get her money from Frank and Francine while they're hot and speed it along. I can't understand parents like hers allowing her to live in dire straits. They have a genius in the house and won't feed it.

However, you also are to blame. There is no point in the world in bringing a young writer along this far to the point of a Publishing contract and then ruining her by filling up her mind with all kinds of doubts and reservations about herself, and guilts that she is selling out her simon pure amateur western Christian virginity to the fleshpots of New York.

Nothing was ever truer than you put it in your letter of the 24th, you had the impression from everybody that Francine and Frank want her book as is, not a word changed. Yet you say she has undertaken revisions all the while leaping up and down on the diving board hundreds of times in her Spiral Binder. "Apparently she intends to rewrite whether Frank and Francine call for it or not." And you simply stand there and watch her and make

/127

no effort to stop her. You could at least say to her, "If you don't stop this minute ruining your future I am throwing you off my property."

On the telephone she told me she is intending to clean up the book in various ways, developing the characters, deepening the plot. Never mind *deepening,* you might as well *bury* it, if she keeps deepening and developing and messing and fussing we're all dead, Francine and Frank want it "as is." Capitalize it and underline it, AS IS, *as is.*

Now who are the great critics and editors whose advice she is following in this matter and what is their track record? It is not only you (that's fine enough) but also the students in her class in Arizona. These are the very students you mentioned to me their excitement when they heard that Apthorp House was taking the book, who until yesterday were fresh out of Buckeye and Yumer according to your letter but who today are advising Mariolena Sunwall how to write a novel for Apthorp House. She is listening to them. She is spewing out their criticisms to me over the telephone. She cannot even yet decide how to spell her name.

And the professor who is supposed to be clamping down and exerting control over these young maniacs is simply standing by and watching in approval without applying restraints. What chance have we got? You have woven her mind into a tangle. You are making her think too much about every little decision—should it be a comma or a semicolon, should the character really do this or that, is this where the character is truly coming from? None of these are the right questions. The only question is not what do her friends in the class want but "What did Frank and Francine buy?" They bought the book AS IS *as is* and they can throw it in the garbage can AS IS *as is,* too, such is their power, as you well know.

Do not sophisticate her too much. You are ruining her. Do you remember in the past from time to time you would tell me about certain chickens on the farm which become unsaleable in the market because they escape from the chicken coop and eat cow shit? Nobody wants to buy a chicken full of cow shit. Maybe for a pet, but not for eating. This is a brilliant symbol. Mariolena is sending me new material, revisions of her book. It will be worse than the earlier material. You are allowing the natural chicken to escape among the cows and ruin herself for the market.

Pardon me for going on so frankly now that I am started, but I feel that this is what you already did to poor Halina Schiff. Everybody in the United States with half a brain loved *A Klutz in Love* and gave away ten copies to everybody else, cheering the whole world up, translated in every language including German. If the Germans can laugh it must be funny. People still introduce me as the agent for *A Klutz in Love* who formerly introduced me as the agent for *The Hard Puncher*, and I hope they will soon be introducing me as the agent for *A Fire in the Toilet* or *Lying in Bed*.

But then you sophisticated Schiff. You ruined her. You drive your friends out of business. They become squinty eyed living in the library. They become obsessed collecting more college degrees. They got so many letters after their name there's no room to address their envelope. Starting off as promising properties they end up beggars. Poor Schiff is sweating her ass off writing on sex in the 70's and 80's. Who in the goddam hell is going to *read* it, Lee? I stand at my window and I see the people in their 70's and 80's and they are not reading books looking for hints on their sexual future life. No way. Sex in the 20's and 25's, *now there's a market area*, millions of kids the result of the baby boom with money to spend and never a thought about saving a penny, looking for instructions, frantic to read about other people living it up, having a good time, joining the Sperm Devils in Arizona, laughing and skiing and rollicking. Why not A Klutz Goes to College and A Klutz Goes to Hollywood and any number of others I can think of?

No, instead of tapping into the living market poor Schiff is tapping into the 70's and 80's, which is the equivalent of tapping into nowhere. She might as well tap into the graveyard. Excite the tombstones. A great deal of this is your fault.

Isn't what I'm saying making sense to you? If you don't mind me speaking in a very personal way you could apply some of these thoughts to your own present situation and profit from it. I could be wrong. First time ever. You are too worried about writing some sort of a book that's better than any book you did before. For you,

/129

just another routine masterpiece is never good enough. Nobody is demanding you do better every time out. You are driving yourself crazy setting new goals.

If you want to teach Mariolena Sunwall something teach her to relax. I can hear the tension in her three thousand miles away. By relaxing she can make it happen, not by demanding too much of yourself. Her book is perfect enough. Save some perfection for the next time out. But no, it's got to be so perfect even Professor Youngdahl will admire it. That's you. Nobody will be able to read such a perfect book except you and the librarian. When thousands of copies return from the stores Frank and Francine will say, "The end. It wouldn't have sold even if we put toilet on the jacket. This is one protégé from Lee Youngdahl too many." If she revises it too much she will bleed the life out of it and it will sell to the paper pulpers. Pardon me for telling you but you over revised like this on *The Man Who Loved Women Who Write* which I recently saw in a trick shop on Sixth Avenue. I opened it up and a jack in the box popped out.

Point Regarding Social Notes. I am glad to hear that Beth is back in the USA. I always get sick in Mexico. I don't know why I go. I only go because the medicine is so good. In the USA it's illegal. I appreciate the confidential rundown on your long friendship with Virgilia, describing her in cap and gown. I am sorry she is angry at you at the moment, but I am sure that once she has settled down in matrimony with Sky King she will be secure enough to invite you back in her inner circle. It is going to be a very big wedding to which everybody in the world is invited except you. Literary New York will be there. People I have not seen in years. I'll do business. It may be the biggest thing since Truman Capote's party fifteen years ago. Time flies. I look forward to it.

Ever yours,

*FROM: Haddock Hooper, D. D., Learning
Together West, Shoestring Ranch, Carefree,
Arizona.*

Enclosure: descriptive pamphlets

February 27

Dear Lee,

Our mutual friend, Dr. Halina Schiff, has urged me to be in
touch with you.

I want to invite you out to see us, and for us to see you,
whom I have not seen as often over the years as I'd have liked.
I remember lunching with you on your campus some years ago
at the height of a commotion or crisis related to the war, and I
have heard that you have written excellent works on topics of
interest to me, as described by our good mutual friend, Halina
Schiff. She reminded me on the phone just yesterday that it was
you who created the slogan "Nobody Wins a Race," which inspired
us through the Swim With the Sharks campaign. I am eagerly
looking forward to meeting you again.

I pray that you will accept my invitation. I hear from Dr. Schiff
that you have been having a bit of trouble with something you
call "impotence." We have never called it that here. If we come
here feeling that way we get over it as soon as possible, with as
little delay as possible, since we do not feel it is in the interest of
our human community to live that way. Our system is to release
feelings of frustration and unproductivity, replacing them with
feelings of pleasure and sympathetic strength.

Since receiving Dr. Schiff's call I have been meditating on
your "problem," as people call it. Tonight at our Round Table we
agreed that a "problem" is basically an opportunity. For every
"problem" good friends create a solution, replacing a negative
condition with a positive. In the process we learn more about
ourselves and about anybody else who might have encountered

/131

the same "problem." Every "problem" gives us the opportunity to see the world in just a slightly different way than we have been seeing it before, telling us what it means to be in "somebody else's shoes." Many people will agree with me when I opine that the whole "problem" of the world is our inability to see other people's points of view, our blindness in failing to recognize other people's realities. We often think that only "our kind of people" feel pain. My eye often falls on a bark painting presented to us by one of our fine Native American neighbors. The painting speaks this legend: "No person on earth feels less than you."

Many of these positive ideas about life are pondered in my book, *Any Cure is the Right Cure*, a copy of which is being sent to you. When I reflect upon the period when I was writing this book I remember with special warmth my closeness at that time to Dr. Schiff, who was my editorial assistant. She and I first became acquainted when she was a student at Learning Together East. From her I often heard your name. Hoping to be a writer, she had studied with you before her residence at Learning Together East. It was during her residence that *A Klutz in Love* appeared and for a moment seemed to repair the world with laughter. In her generosity, following the great worldly success of her book, Dr. Schiff assigned some of her royalty payments to the Learning Together East-Learning Together West Foundation. To this very day sums come to us to be put to good purpose.

Maybe you will also be interested in another connection of our lives. More than twenty years ago I encountered your work during a honeymoon trip to New York, when my new wife and I saw *Boswell's Manhattan Journal* at a Broadway theater. I remember the play especially vividly because of an incident which occurred. Two Scotch military men entered the theater and were pelted with fruit by some English people in the audience. The actor playing Boswell interrupted his performance and delivered a telling speech against the narrowmindedness of the English people. Several policemen quelled the disturbance and the play resumed. Your play outran my marriage.

You are welcome here at any time, but the sooner the better. "No appointment necessary." Somebody is always here. If I am momentarily out, enter and visit with whomever is here. Sometimes by the time I return people have come to good terms with whatever was on their mind to bring them here, and have gone home without seeing me. For everyone here is teacher. As we say, "There is no front of the room," and of course there is no head place at our Round Table. If nobody is here, enter and make yourself at home. Our dogs never bite.

Bring your spouse or a friend, or both. We welcome all people of all ages, backgrounds, occupations, races, religions, connections, or sexual preferences. You may remain an hour or a week. Dress is informal. Charges are optional—from each person according to their evaluation of our mutual counsel. Very few people who have shared with us deny that many of their "problems" drift into the night, becoming lost among the stars after a meditative walk along our well-remembered "Moonlight Trail of Rocks."

I am eagerly looking forward to seeing you again. Arrive as soon as you can and remain as long as the busy world can spare you. Please bring linen and a pillow (we supply blankets). If you plan to swim, our swimming pool is heated to eighty-eight degrees year-round. We also enjoy, of course, Hot Tubs, and programs in Massage, Counseling, Yoga, and Hypnotism serving every requirement. We are proud of our austere, sound-proof Meditation Spaces. I am hoping that I will see you here soon, and I can guarantee you (within the limits of our respect for a Nature whose scheme we may not yet fully comprehend) that the "problem" you bring here with you you will leave behind when you depart.

Yours in wellness,

P. S. Descriptive literature enclosed.

TO: *Beth Youngdahl, c/o Earl Youngdahl, writer,*
Assistant Professor of English, Western
Kentucky University, Bowling Green.

February 28

Dear Beth,

I am pleased to see you have arrived safely in Kentucky.
Halfway between Bowling Green and Owensboro will be the halfway point of your travels. Stop and plant an historic marker. I am
sure you helped to provide Thornton with a good mother image
for his constituency. No doubt you look every bit the mother,
though you complained five thousand times over the years that
you wished you weren't. I remember your standing over a hot
stove one day. You held a nursing baby in one arm. With your
other hand you were stirring a pot of beef barbecue for thirty-five
Indian Guides. "Lee," you said, "are you sure we planned this
thing right?"

It wasn't planned at all, I suppose. It was spontaneous and
unrehearsed. I savor the sweet portrait you write of Earl's meeting
with students dropping by to discuss their writings with him. You
observe that he is my direct descendant, that he divides himself
between tenderness and sternness. I wonder a little bit then why
you feel compelled to attack my student Mariolena Sunwall, "little
bitch with bastard"—that's the title of your portrait of her—whose
name you can never remember; she who hangs around my office
all day, so you say. Is she as student any less real than Earl's
students? Am I as teacher less real than Earl? Nor do I think her
child ought to be designated "bastard." One of our grandchildren,
too, arrived quite without her father's knowing even to this day
of her existence, yet we accept her as one of ours.

As a matter of fact Ms. Sunwall, "the young woman with the
burning toilets," according to your earlier letter, has received enormous encouragement from Frank and Francine, who adore the
manuscript you read, and who are flying her into New York one
day soon in her jeans and a pair of borrowed shoes.

I've got a bit of a foot in the door on my own writing, punching

134/

away at an idea Frank and Francine will honor with an advance of $20,000 as soon as I can get up a little outline for them. Abner tells the latest gossip of them. Did you know they have been divorced, but are still doing business at the same old pushcart, forever and ever, they promise. Alas! in their settlement they gave away the house in Key West where you and I, you will recall, spent happy days with them and hordes of other people. I was always impressed by their doubts about the identities of their guests. I remember a little dialogue. *ME*: Who are those nice people in the room next to Beth and me? *FRANK*: Damn if I know. Friends of Francine's friends maybe.

You must not hurry home. You are missing nothing. I wish you wouldn't keep transporting your paranoid suspicions of me across international boundaries and American state lines. What will father be up to while mother is away, Lucien inquires. Up to is right, mother replies. Up to some literary bitch. The old bitch image again. Literary bitch. Hanging-around-the-office-with-bastard bitch. For awhile I've thought there's a paradox in your carrying with you everywhere this dreary conviction of your wicked philandering husband side by side with your keen concern for his (my) recovery from my impotence. I think you want me to be rescued—but first punished: thus the parable from Lucien's group in which "impotence" is so clearly identified with "sin." You deny the connection. You say the connection was in the legend itself, as it came down through the ages to Lucien, who doesn't speak the language terribly well to begin with.

But I say it's you who made the connection, consciously or not: God was punishing the man for the sins of his profligacy. Now that's just plain old back-home Utah stuff if you think about it for a minute. You have decided I am guilty and you have administered my punishment all in one blow. Genital punishment for genital sins. All little boys in Utah understand that primitive code and believe in it until or unless they escape, God punishes appropriately all sins of the flesh—swear and your mouth will be washed out with soap, window-peep and go blind, masturbate and your hands will fall off. I thought we were long gone from Utah.

Everybody is at me to go to these witch doctors called counselors. How would you have known that Haddock Hooper, world-saver and pious fake, is "the man to see" for impotence if you

/135

hadn't heard it from Penny Drew, Gossip Queen of Paradise Valley and the Western World, who got it from her husband, unless he got it from her, along the medical/dental/gossip grapevine. I see where you tried to sandwich a paragraph in there between your mentioning Hooper and your mentioning Wally and Penny, as if you'd buffer the connection, or as if my mind, failing like my lower organs, couldn't carry anything longer ago in my head than one paragraph. You arrive at Lucien's and all of a sudden he's directing me to a psychological counselor. You arrive at Earl's and all of a sudden he too is directing me to a counselor. "Mention it to your father . . ." I can just see it. Nudging with the elbow, little hints behind your hand, an old family scene, passing the buck to the old buck.

Just for the hell of it I phoned Penny yesterday and pretended I knew she's been talking to you, and she revealed it easily enough. Penny the hillside spy with her birdwatching binoculars. She is the most insufferably depressing person I know. Poor Wally, he wrote me a sad letter. I suppose I should be more sympathetic. He is tired of doctoring, but trapped in weariness and noise and the odors of the Belly Whopper and real estate and rising costs.

I put this paper into the machine with the idea of writing an All Points, but I wanted to say some things privately to you. Maybe I shouldn't have said them. Nevertheless I send it. Why waste paper? I have put a big emphatic sign on the fence directing the United Parcel man to be gentle with your packages from Mexico. I have sprinkled the love powder you sent me into the pool and into my coffee but I have not yet been restored to anything, especially an erection. When my last erection occurred you were there, although in your fantasies you dwell upon creations of your imagination, bitches here and bitches there and my long-time New York fuck, as you so daintily entitle the poor (soon to be rich) woman upon the basis of evidence gleaned from her fiction. You as one who has observed at first hand the stink, sweat, and tears of the writer of fiction in his solitude must surely have learned to distinguish by now between fiction and actuality.

The Roll-a-dex is not visible anywhere, neither on the telephone table nor anywhere else in the house nor, as far as I can see, anywhere else in the world. I feel I must now take to the streets crying them up and down for a boy named Todd, in the event I go anywhere longer than it takes me to go to school and back. I have no plans.

Everything is well. Enjoy your visiting, travel slowly, kiss everybody for me as you go.

With love,

March 1

Dear Dr. Youngdahl:

I want to thank you so much for your glorious hospitality to me during this trying period. Now I will be out of your hair for a little while. I have left everything in a jumble, but of course I will pick it all up when I return. I have also left a few last-minute things in the guest-house dryer—no problem, I am sure.

Off I go into the beckoning, hazardous future. Off I go on my first airplane flight. I congratulate myself. I seem to be flying both upward and forward all on the same day.

Please consider this letter my formal request for leave of absence from class in order to confer with my agent and publisher in New York. Since the book which is to be the subject of our New York conferences was written during my period as a student in your class this year one might argue that my trip to New York is certainly a legitimate absence. I look forward to further comments Mr. Klang and Frank and Francine Apthorp of Apthorp House will be making on my manuscript, just as I looked forward to comments made by you and by members of our most stimulating class. I dread a possible disagreement with my New York conferees. I have been hopeful of making certain changes in my manuscript, along the lines suggested by you and by our class, although Mr. Klang insists that he wants the book exactly as he presented it to the Apthorps. His is not literary reasoning but business reasoning. "Yes," he says in his clever lickety-split way, "if you don't reason in a business way the Apthorps will give you the business."

We will also be discussing title choices and the spelling of "Mariolena." I shall be fighting bitterly for your candidate and mine, *Fire in the Toilet,* and for one of the following choices of spellings of my name: "Maria Elena . . . Marya Elena . . . Marie Alina . . . Maria Ilena . . . or Marialena."

138/

If on the other hand you prefer, in view of my absence, that I withdraw from your class I shall be willing to do so, accepting a grade of "W". I feel that I have done the work when I was there. I have read my classmates' manuscripts and offered criticism as aggressively and as constructively as possible, as you have directed us to do. Thus I feel that I have done my work well but not completely. My failure of attendance has been unintentional. As you know, my parents have made life for me rather a raging inferno. Exiled from the ranch, forbidden the town house, I required time to re-locate myself in Sin City and might have successfully done so had I not suffered serious financial setbacks. But for you—had you not so generously, so graciously, and so self-sacrificially permitted me to install myself in this wondrous guest house with its echoes and ghosts of literary visitors I should still be "floundering through the streets" like the maiden of my tome. I have signed my name to the wall. I shall return in victory from New York.

Or it may be that you in your judgment will decide that in spite of my absence from class I can nevertheless be thought of as a student who is proceeding satisfactorily. It is not as if I have been merely indolent. *Au contraire*, I have been deeply absorbed not only by *Fire in the Toilet* and its revisions, which I fly now eastward to defend, but with my new biography of my baby, to be entitled *Life Seen by the Eye of an Orange Bug*. I think this idea is unique. It amazes me that I cannot call to mind many biographies of babies. Mr. Klang also thinks very highly of the idea and will discuss it with me when I am there. True, in an earlier letter to you I thought I could merely postpone my graduation to December. That would mean your giving me a "W." I should dearly prefer graduation in May, and I therefore hope you can pass me, even with a low grade in view of my absences.

You know that it has been my ambition to pay you a rental fee of $400 per month for your permitting me to use your little guest house, but since I have now found myself with little enough in the way of a working exchequer I must add the rental sum to the sum of cash I have borrowed from you. And to that sum we must also add the bottle of money I have borrowed (took the money, left the bottle) from the table in the front hall. This comes altogether to a total of $515. I have also taken with me yesterday's

New York *Times* to read on the airplane if, in my excitement, I am able to read at all, so that I will understand what New York is all about when I land there. Since I am informed that the weather in New York at this season of the year may be egregious I have borrowed from your closet a "genuine French fur" coat, if the label does not lie. It looks like mink to me.

If while I am gone you wish to reach me I will be a guest at the historic Algonquin Hotel, about which I have read so much in the lore of literature over the years. Nor can I omit to mention the loving and humorous accounts of that place as told by the young, romantic narrator of *The Utah Manner*. Places which only print has placed before me will in a few hours "achieve," as the poet says, "the materiality of touch."

I will be depositing my VW and my baby with acquaintances in Sin City. I am not quite sure of their names but they have a decidedly reliable air to them. I have asked them not to reveal my baby's whereabouts to my parents, who would cause him to be taken into custody by the so-called "humane" authorities if they could. At heart they are kidnapers.

For your confidentiality in these family matters I shall be grateful to one to whom I am already grateful beyond words. You have often cautioned us not to speak of anything as being "beyond words," for words are the writer's craft, and she whose craft lies "beyond" her concedes defeat before she has begun. I do not concede defeat. In spite of your caution I tell you that I am grateful beyond words . . . beyond words . . . beyond words for everything you have done for me. I wish only that in some way I could repay you. Nothing of mine would I withhold. Alas! that at the moment I have nothing. But here I am at the doorstep of a career, and I might have something yet.

Last September, if anyone had asked me, I would have been forced to guess that my literary beginnings were years over the horizon. But you have brought me along swiftly beyond any expectations I may have had six months ago.

Please, please, while I am gone, welcome Spring, your lovely house bathed in the odors of blooming garden, your numerous friends, your admiring students and colleagues, and your achieving family so busily creative here and there in the growing nation.

You are the best man I have ever met. I know you will say,

140/

"But, Mariolena, you have not met many men." I think you would say it more cleverly somehow. You deserve every good thing that can possibly come to you.

I will keep you informed.

Your very respectful student,

P. S. As I was departing this morning the animals clamored to be fed, but I did not feed them. They are already fed more than enough.

March 1

Dear Mariolena,

I was astonished when I arose this morning to find that you had gone, and with you my wife's coat and the bottle of money (or at least the money therein) we have kept on the hall table for several years untouched by human hands until by yours today. I thought I was to have driven you to the airport.

You say you owe me $515. Into that sum you put "rent." I have repeatedly told you we do not charge rent for the use of our guest house. You may call the sum $115 if you like—sounds about right.

I must say, too—I suppose it's a small matter—that I'm a bit puzzled by your speaking of today's flight as your "first airplane flight" since on a number of occasions during the past months you have mentioned airplane trips to far places, sometimes reluctantly to faraway social occasions which proved to have been planned, as you suspected, by lustful men. On other occasions you went flying at the bidding of your parents who were forcing you to visit disgusting relations. Don't I recall your telling me, too, of trips you have made to ski—or at least to sites where people ski—yes, here it is in your letter of just a month ago today, "flying up again for a long weekend skiing in Colorado," where you actually worked at your writing, choked on smoke, fought off male beasts, and simply didn't have a very good time at all. I am sure you can explain these discrepancies.

Above all, I am troubled by your having taken my wife's coat, egregious as New York weather may be said to be. I assume that you will guard it with your very life and deliver it into my arms instantly you return to these parts. If my wife knew I have become a coat-lender I would be in serious trouble.

I regret this letter. It seems to have an angry tone. When I am angry I write. It seems to be the natural way to work it off.

You must not construe this as my intending in any way to spoil your good time in New York, or to wish you any the less the great good excitement your letter anticipates. Perhaps it is the excitement itself which accounts for the failure of some of your facts or even some bizarre lapse of your memory, although I confess I have never heard before of anyone being so unclear upon a question so unambiguous as whether she had flown in an airplane.

Please do not neglect to carry my greetings to Abner and Frank and Francine and to other friends of mine to whom you will surely be introduced.

Yours puzzled,

March 1

Dear Abner,

Impotent, not incompetent.

From the sound of your letter you were so excited in antici-pation of your welcoming Mariolena whom, by the time you re-ceive this, you will have met, that your eyes crossed when you tried to read my letter. I should think a man of your age, at large in one of the world's super-cities, in daily contact with learned and sophisticated women, would have managed to focus his at-tention upon his business correspondence even in spite of the pending arrival of a beautiful girl hick straight off her father's sandy ranch in the middle of nowhere.

You scolded me, I'm scolding you. If you'll only read it right—"impotence"—you will now be able to follow my "outline denot-ing . . . general direction," for which you ask, of a novel we might entitle *The Woman on the Diving Board* or *The Woman With the Spiral Binder*, at least as working titles until we find better ones. Please notice that my "general direction" is toward a novel com-bining both your idea and mine: impotence, mine; the woman on the diving board (yours), perhaps that "beautiful, ravishing" per-son you mention, perhaps not; we'll see as we go.

Let me break it down into some basic stages of my premise. If you like it, please have Mrs. Mannerly type it up for transmission to Frank and Francine.

Premise. Stage One. Better still, Roman numerals. *Stage I.* A man of some means and some leisure befriends an attractive woman who, for various reasons, soon finds herself emotionally dependent upon him. He seems to her to be wise, gentle, witty, and considerate of her: she has not been accustomed to fine deal-ing, and she appreciates him a great deal. Let us say that he is a sixty-year-old professional man—physician, lawyer, maybe a fin-

144/

ancier: I have saved a lot of notes and odds and ends about financiers and would enjoy creating one.

Stage II. Our novel may begin with the man's rescuing the woman from some situation of danger and embarrassment. He assists her to avoid financial disaster. And because he is gentle and prepossessing she is prepared even to love him as passionately as one might wish. The man, however, is impotent. He cannot make physical love. He possesses desire, yes, but not the ability. In the hope of the return of his powers he has submitted himself to several medical options or procedures, but for the moment he remains impotent. *Stage III.* The woman—our heroine—knows nothing of his impotence. She knows only that in spite of her readiness, in spite of her having transmitted signals of the kind always successful in the past (not that she has had *millions* of affairs, you understand: she is a woman of taste) he has not responded to her sexual invitation. *Stage IV.* As a matter of fact, from our heroine's point of view, our hero's impotence does not necessarily disconcert her. Recovering from a difficult past, she is pleased to be able to enjoy a gradual process free of commitment. She is once more free to devote her energy to her art, perhaps painting, and now at last in the safety of his relatively undemanding presence she is able to concentrate upon her work as she has not been in the past. He is supportive, her mentor, her lifeline, her patron. He is her affectionate companion, her nonsexual lover. For the moment he is everything she requires. Never was life so good to her, time so spacious, prospects so likely and bright.

Stage V. The advent of a happy turn of events brings with it suggestions of ominous developments as well. Our hero, who has appeared to our heroine to be almost saintly, has been also her artistic inspiration: for here is a man who is truly a good man, truly selfless. He has transcended, after all, mere body. So she believes. With a single gesture, in supporting her he has both preserved a human being and advanced the idea of art. She whose art has been so much a reaction in bitterness to the brutality of men she has known, seems to be upon the point of the restoration of her faith in all men, of whom our hero exists as the symbol of benignity. But we know—as she soon must learn—that our hero has sought recovery from his impotence. At last his recovery

/145

seems to approach. His sexuality returns. How will this affect her happiness? And to what extent will our hero, having discovered his potentiality for disinterested good action, sink to a lower estimate of himself even as he achieves the return of that pleasure he so earnestly sought?

Stage VI. Trouble lies ahead for a number of reasons as soon as I can think of them. His never having approached her sexually has given her the impression he is sexually indifferent to her. She has learned to live with that. How will she adjust to the change in his life? She is severely depressed by the disillusionment of her seeming to discover now that saintliness was nothing but impotence. Perhaps no saint is possible.

Stage VII. He fears that his new nature will shock her. Remember what happened to Adam and Eve when they discovered their nakedness. He is disappointed to see the dissolution of his saintly self with the return of his sexual power. He sees how he endangers her: he who had so praised and honored her interior artistic life had scarcely had another choice. First choice was body. His sweetness was but the absence of lust.

This strikes me as an excellent plot, with endless ramifications and permutations clearly potential on this broad, basic plot. I know that Frank and Francine will respond to it. You might remind them how much in its outer form it resembles *Dreams*: and you might remind them—having reminded them of *that*—that they published *Dreams* with spiritless reluctance, enjoying thereafter the satisfaction of knowing how successful a book they had given the world in spite of themselves.

But, Sir, let's talk money for a moment. You mention an advance for me on this book of $20,000. For my first book from Frank and Francine I received an advance of $250. Granted inflation and other economic changes these forty years, nevertheless I cannot help but gasp in wonder that Mariolena, for *her* first book, at the age I was when you carried my first book to Apthorp House, is to receive $10,000. That being so (which is right and proper—I wouldn't want her to have a penny less), I should receive, at my age—sixty, 2.7272727 times the age of Mariolena, according to my Texas Instruments calculator—not merely twice her advance but 2.7272727 times her advance, or $27,272. An odd figure, to be sure, but fair.

146/

I don't mean to make a big thing of money. I really don't have any *use* for money in the state I'm in—an idea which affects my thinking about my impotent financier: what was money always for if not to entertain women with, to take them places, to buy clothes to wear to please them with and make them say, "I love your clothes, take them off," for haircuts and underarm deodorants and automobile gasoline and tickets to all sorts of desirable occasions such as moving pictures, and food and drink in nice restaurants?

I am of course always interested in the gossip of Apthorp House, and I shall now be eager to hear from you how your client Mariolena fares inside those doors. Frank will be mad for her—if he's not too busy. Scold me all you like, but I don't think I have entangled your client's mind, corrupted her innocence, or poisoned her against commerce. In certain students hyper-energy turns to wisdom. She has things she insists upon saying to the crazy stinking world which is oppressing her. Mariolena moves me. Many students move me. I was there myself in those unencumbered days before I needed $27,272 to prime my pump. Recently I came upon Mariolena on the campus mall standing under a sign announcing "Half the world is hungry." She was furious. She had just this minute found out about it. She put down her books so that she could clench her fists. She was shocked, debating heatedly with other students what might be done, not tomorrow, not next year, but right now, today.

How can I stop her from revising her book? All that critical energy that produced her wild book also produces her reaction against it. She sees in March that what she wrote in December won't do any more. I think that what you and Frank and Francine have got to do is to encourage her to think forward to the next work—the biography of her baby; and if her biography of her baby is a dumb idea she'll know it herself soon enough. But point her forward. Go with Nature, which insists upon growth. You mustn't expect her future books to be *Fire in the Toilet* again and again, or Schiff to go on writing *Klutz* again and again or Virgilia to go on with *Doctor's Out* again and again.

Now what will I do all evening? I have shopped for groceries and pumped air into my bicycle tires and laundered my clothes and showered myself. In the old days, alone in the night, if I had

/147

been a good boy and written my daily measure of book, I might have stepped out to call upon a lady somewhere not too far away, sans souci, nothing on my mind but pleasure, nothing to oppress me but marital guilts crushing me to the earth. Impotence cures guilt. I can't be bad if I want to. And I do so want to.

Of course I'm sorry to be missing Virgilia's wedding. I'm sure it's going to be the grandest and most memorable opulent more or less literary occasion of the decade. Please do breathe my name affectionately to the bride somewhere beyond the hearing of Mr. Suekuykeen. She has forbidden me to write, wire, send her gifts; or, I suppose, even to think happy thoughts for her, but I shall be doing so nevertheless.

Yours,

March 2

Dear darling Schiff,

I thank you so much for your lovely letter with all its encouragement, backed by nothing less substantial than your offer
to transport yourself across State lines and see to me yourself.
Prime my pump. "One time proves it." You can see how well I'm
mastering the jargon of corrective sexual hygiene.

But I am no better than I was. No worse, either, I suppose,
but just where I was except days and days older and still not
enjoying the remotest hint of the resurrection of—I was about to
say *desire.* No, the desire is there but the equipment won't work.
A mechanic with his head deep down in the engine of my automobile once said to me, "It's a car, it's got to work." The job was
to figure out how.

I had a nice little letter this morning right on top of yours
from your old friend and teacher and fellow-learner East and West
and all around the town Haddock Hooper, inviting me to his ranch
or school or whatever it is in the desert, where he will so pow-
erfully doctor me I might be cured even before I see him. His
patients cure other patients. All doctors should have such magical
waiting-rooms. But he isn't even a doctor, is he? No matter, all
I need do is step inside his door. Even his dogs are gentle and
mild. My imaginary impotence will go away, no more zinc, no
more hormones, no more gloomy thoughts of penile implant.

I wish it could be, but I doubt it. My physician—from whom
I wouldn't have expected it—has sent me a copy of *Any Cure is
the Right Cure,* and another copy is on the way from you, and
one from Haddock Hooper himself for the postman to throw over
the fence into the pool soon to be overflowing with copies of same.
I'm not at all sure I would enjoy being kissed at his door by
Haddock Hooper. The only men who have kissed me these last

thirty years or more are my sons, and they not often, I suppose. I hold back somewhat. I wish I didn't, but I do.

I'm amazed that you haven't outgrown Haddock Hooper. He has dreadfully simplified everything. If only we all love one another and keep our voices down we will survive and flourish and endure. I wish I could have your faith. Of course you know him better than I. To you he has been "the most open and accepting and welcoming man that ever lived," *etc.*, and he wanted you to go west with him. I can't blame him. I'd want you to go west with me, too. But I wouldn't want *him* to go west with me. You see what I mean—that your intellect has merged with your emotions, and my Haddock may not be your Haddock.

No doubt I'm too old-fashioned to accept undocumented revelation. My old-fashioned self immediately rebelled at his addressing me by my first name. When a doctor's not really a doctor he first-names you to put you at ease. He claims more meetings with me than I actually recall. I did love The Swim With the Sharks he promoted when he and I and my daughters and many other nice idealistic people went to California and swam in the ocean with sharks to prove that two species said to be enemies might live together harmoniously: *i. e.*, no nuclear bombs. I created a slogan for the group: "Nobody wins the race." Haddock was convinced I was a genius—one four-word sentence earned me immortality and election to Haddock's private Parthenon. Later I found out that Haddock might be more of a realist than I suspected: he had actually done a certain amount of ichthyological research in advance, so that we knew just which sharks to encounter at which season with respect to their having eaten or not having eaten their lunch.

You seem to conclude that I am nothing but a bundle of self-fulfilling prophesies: I feel myself impotent and therefore I am determined to prove that I am. One kiss from Haddock Hooper will cure me. It's all in my mind, you say. But that's not true, really. Really not true. Really untrue. Really a damned lie. And a damnable mystery, too. I want to. I want to be swept up into all that restless distress I used to know, lost in the depths of reveries of somebody else's body, but I want to be able to be effective, too, and do something about it.

You predict happy days ahead for me, not less than two decades of life after impotence. Meanwhile, if I am not dead, I appear to be. According to one of those authors taken from the library shelf with *Sex In the Seventh Decade* (*And After*) I suffer "fantasy failure." This failure, he says, has affected many people in both their sexual and occupational or artistic life. That's me; sexual life gone; writing coming back a little. Our author distinguishes between "cerebral" and "tactile" love. As we grow older, he says, we become less cerebral and more tactile. To illustrate: in the old days I developed erections on many occasions simply by lying (standing, sitting) thinking about somebody. Nowadays, however, according to the author, mere old imagination won't do it any more. I've got to touch somebody. I tried it. It didn't work. My cerebral blew out and my tactile followed, the whole system a wreck. Here is what happened:

Mariolena Sunwall came and stayed in my guest house for a week, parked most of the time on my diving board writing two books at once. She carries with her everywhere she goes bright orange Spiral Binders, writing one book with the Binder right side up and then flipping it over and writing the other from back to front. It makes sense. I spent years writing on both sides of the page until Beth said to me one day, "Lee, we're poor no more." In the Spiral Binder right side up Mariolena is revising *Fire in the Toilet* and in the Spiral Binder upside down she is writing a biography of her baby, a boy of two who speaks remarkable thoughts which only his mother can hear. He was conceived in an orange Volkswagen approximately the color of the Spiral Binder, but who his father is I do not know. Not me, that's for sure.

So I sat here for some days gazing out my window at the swimming pool with the diving board with the young lady on it, thinking how, in the old days, my blood pressure would have been spiking high scores. It used to be that a lovely guest in the guest house kept me awake. I plotted silent visits downstairs and around the pool and through my guest's door. It never much happened, but it always kept me awake planning. Or I'd have strolled out there onto the pool deck and said, "Mariolena, my writing is done, how's yours?" and we'd have spouted and cavorted in the pool together, you may be sure. I don't *throb* now. There's something truly wrong, not with me but with my body.

A couple of times I did come down from my lookout and

strolled to the diving board, but not an awful lot happened. She was absorbed in her writing. Now and again I touched her—the top of the head, the back of the neck. She interpreted these touchings, I think, as affectionate grandfatherly communication, as well she might have, for my body felt nothing, either. If I don't throb she won't throb back. Nothing. There she sat writing and there I sat not writing. How many kinds of genteel misery can a man endure?

I don't know how conscious she was of my being there. I was that old man who now and then came out of the house in his antique swimming trunks and grunted greetings and swam awhile and climbed out and went back in his house.

There occurred one moment of excitement which seemed to me (but may have been my imagination) charged with desperation, frustration, when, just as I was leaving the deck, she flung aside her Spiral Binder and plunged into the pool and swam furiously, blindly, smashing at the water. I felt that she was very angry at me for my indifference toward her, but she may have been merely angry at her Spiral Binder, caring deeply how she writes. But I don't know . . .

I was just beginning to be the faintest bit worried at not hearing from you. I'm glad you waited until you could read *Fire in the Toilet.* Yes, God as locksmith, it's priceless. Who could think up such a thing? "Do not duplicate." I swear I really worry about my keyring these days. By now you have perhaps met her. She's in New York getting together with Abner and Frank and Francine.

I saw a few seconds of Virgilia's wedding on the TV news this evening. Were you there? I couldn't catch a glimpse of anybody except her and Suekuykeen. Virgilia specifically and firmly disinvited me, though I don't know if I could have gone anyway with Beth away and animals to feed and my hungry typewriter confronting me. I stayed home and taught school and kept company with my warm, loving bicycle. I won't kiss Haddock Hooper for you even if I see him. Ask me another. I'd kiss you for you.

Kisses kisses and more kisses,

FROM: *Mr. Del Vandenberg, Cannon Beach, Oregon.*

February 27

Dear Mr. Youngdahl,

The question is hormonal and the champion hormone is testosterone derived from the Greek language meaning "to arouse to activity." That's what I heard.

Like you I began by thinking the magic cure was the knife, and Dr. Emmer was enthusiastic about doing it, as you probably observed for yourself while there. He showed me testimonial letters he had received from men who were now living life enjoying penises of strength and durability to match anything they had known in their heydays. According to them Dr. Emmer did it. In the long run I accomplished it otherwise than by surgery and will tell you how. My guess is that he failed to remove my name from his list of "jobs done," since he had planned to do me but was never needed. I'm sorry you were forced to the trouble of writing me a letter although it is a pleasure to answer on a subject turning out so right.

Being logical about it I thought I should try the hormones first as someone else advised. I took shots of testosterone regularly in my butt for five months without results. Such shots should be administered only by a prescribed physician.

You know what testosterone is. In the early days I could not spell it, but I learned to spell it after receiving several letters like yours from men betwixt and between not knowing whether they should have Dr. Emmer do the job or maybe ride out the storm in some other way or not.

I am no youngster. I am eighty years old. I was not at all sure there was going to be anybody to appreciate my penile implant even if I had it done, which was another word I learned to spell for the first time. You're never too old to learn. My wife has been dead for several years. In fact, more than several. "Time goes fast when you're having fun." That's what they say.

/153

At seventy-eight after first noticing my failing powers Dr. Emmer said, "Let's do it. Let's go into this together," but at the time I thought I should try the hormones first as another party advised and did so. Nothing happened. I took shots of testosterone regularly for five months without results. Although the word is from the Greek language meaning "to arouse to activity" it wasn't doing anything for me in the way of "arousing to activity," and I lined myself up with Dr. Emmer after all and prepared my mind for it and notified my lawyer and began to close out certain affairs just in case.

Now it just happened to happen that right about the time I was in the bank closing out certain affairs of mine my estate officer there was a lovely young woman for many years a widow. She and I began keeping company as time allowed. It was during this period that the testosterone began to work, I was "aroused to activity," so was she, and I became active again as I had not been since my seventy-eighth year. For this reason I was inspired to discontinue the idea of having Dr. Emmer do the job down in Los Angeles, although I was grateful to him for offering. I notified him in ample time, of course.

I hope this letter answers the questions you have asked me to your satisfaction. I did not go right down the list as you advised. I was never a person that could do it that way.

Yours very cordially,

FROM: Beth Youngdahl, c/o Earl Youngdahl,
Assistant Professor of English, Western
Kentucky University, Bowling Green.

February 27

Dear Lee,

Now I understand that your bitch in her bikini and her bastard occupy my swimming pool all day. I had better not see her there. You did not inform me you had cured your impotence.

To Owensboro.

Beth

/155

March 3

Dear Beth and children,

When I am lying limp and useless and empty of desire in my coffin mother will be checking to see if I'm having an affair with the mortician's wife. Saturday I received mother's excellent long letter from Earl's recapitulating her tour thus far, to which I instantly and lovingly replied, but today her bitter little note accusing me of crimes I have not committed, I assure you, to wit: "Now I understand that your bitch in her bikini and her bastard occupy my swimming pool all day. I had better not see her there. You did not inform me you had cured your impotence." If the truth were known she'd be contrite. But how can the truth be known when mother depends only on *understanding* something? Hearing what from whom? As if we didn't know. Penny Drew the town crier, purveyor, voyeur, galloping through every middlesex, village, and farm examining everybody's pool to see who's in it.

How I wish you (Beth) hadn't spoiled your lovely letter with this sour note. But I had with so much pleasure intended to write an All Points this evening that I am going to do it without distraction. (Quite apart from anything else, I might mention that I thought mother was going to Montreal before Kentucky; *then* California. When I go on a trip I write out beforehand for mother the route of my travel and where I'm going to be and with whom every day at which hotels. Mother is like one of these missiles our insane President is hoping to hide in the earth and ride around on underground railroads to confuse the Russians.)

Who is this "bitch in her bikini and her bastard [who] occupy my [sic! our] swimming pool all day"? We may wish to collect a few details in order to set this story down in some sort of accurate form.

The woman in question is a writer of some talent, one Mariolena Sunwall, single mother of a two-year-old son. She has been a student of mine. Several months ago she completed a novel which made me laugh very hard in the most sympathetic manner. Your mother also read it, smiling as she went, erupting now or again into loud laughter, exclaiming at one point, "Wow, this kid can really write," to which, with her penchant for punning, she soon added, "She can juggle a lot of balls at once."

I prevailed upon Mariolena to send her completed novel to Abner Klang, who in turn trotted down the street with it to Apthorp House. Frank and Francine instantly committed themselves to its publication, probably under the title *Lying in Bed*, which I suggested after rolling on my tongue eight or ten times Mariolena's striking sentence, "Earnestly they conversed together as they lied in bed." Apthorp House will pay her an advance against royalties of $10,000—a considerable sum to a young woman just starting out in the literary way. Day before yesterday the young author pursued her manuscript to New York, where Abner and Frank and Francine will wine her and dine her.

In the continued interest of accuracy I might observe that by the time mother's brief but forceful indictment arrived here the bitch and her bastard had cleared out of our guest house, where I had sheltered them overnight. Her own family, although wealthy (they own 63,000 acres of ranch near Tonopah; or 36,000; whatever), withhold from her every form of assistance, and complicate her life with various forms of vengeance upon her. Some of their actions against her are so complicated and spiteful as to invite description, but that belongs to another account. I might, however, employ this moment relevantly to observe for mother's benefit that when one of our daughters became the mother of an illegitimate child our family one and all rejoiced in that child and welcomed her forever and ever, quite as if the situation weren't in the least bit the infant's own fault. We did not call her a single dirty name.

Nor do I believe, either, that the attire worn by Mariolena at our pool may properly be called a bikini. It looked to me like shorts and halter, as Penny Drew herself, with her keen medical scientific vision, might have detected had she cared more for accuracy than for inflammatory gossip. And what was Miss Sunwall doing by the pool? She was revising the manuscript of her novel, sitting cross-legged hour after hour on the diving board. Glenna used to sit that way over her homework.

Even more to the point, what was I doing poolside (was I even poolside? was I upstairs in my aerie?)? What were *they* doing? Were they cavorting and splashing and making love underwater? On the diving board? On the deck? Where was the baby all this time? If only Penny Drew had advanced to the pool, down from her hillside, she might have been able to tell a more complete story than she told.

Mariolena has been my student this year only. We enjoyed her novel from beginning to end in class. It is a somewhat imperfect book. But it is often capable, skillful, whose author's genius lies much in her instinct for turning accident to purpose. She explores what-might-be with an inventive vocabulary. Her story follows a young woman's career on a large university campus from the bottom of a long dormitory-waiting list to the very top— a pinnacle she achieves by sleeping with a University Housing Official. This Official is one of her triumphant creations, a terrible comic indictment of human behavior as we see it in many university bureaucrats. He assumes no blame for the consequences of his action: when the young woman becomes pregnant he expels her from the dormitory on the grounds of the child's being fatherless. But *he* is the father—if she as student is to be punished shouldn't he as bureaucrat be punished? Oh no (his reasoning), in becoming father to the baby he was acting as private citizen, not as official. Well then, maybe she too was private citizen, not student. No, the Official insists that he can occupy two places in the social scheme, but the girl cannot. He is privileged. Why is he privileged? Why, he is privileged because he is an Official and has officially designated himself privileged.

Our heroine, after a period of public protest, moves from University housing to Sin City, where she becomes entangled with a locksmith. Like the Official, he is a rather faithless fellow, supplying keys to her dwelling to young "scholars" of the University who may wish to call upon her without the formality of knocking at the door. In the course of moving from place to place to avoid the treacherous locksmith our heroine offers a close history of a variety of men of all ages and types and colors and nationalities and physical and mental peculiarities, all dominated by the ambition to open her door with their keys. It is a comprehensive catalogue of one young woman's experience or imagination of love and confusion, preserved with humor from despair. At the end, the locksmith is promoted to God— "a significant promotion," we hear.

I haven't always been sure how much control she exerts over her humor. Sometimes when we were all laughing she seemed puzzled that we found it funny. At other times she smiled alone. She hears every syllable of her own, however, and with her darting eyes seems to be ceaselessly searching the room, as if vigorous action of her eyes assists her hearing. Then comes a moment when she seems to fear she has seen too much, and she withdraws behind the brim of her Wire Brim western hat. Years ago I wouldn't have dared to read her work aloud in class. The "moral majority" would have come down on me. I found that the succession of young men in the book became tedious, somewhat linear, but when I tried in class to skip a bit here and there my students cried, "No! No! More! More!" I could see, however, that Mariolena, too, saw how too many young men became too many, too much dirty stuff became more simply dirty than amusing, and she has wanted to make some changes. She grows right before my eyes. But the Apthorps don't want any changes at all, and I assume that's what they're talking about in New York.

Although mother permitted the novel to entertain her she took an immediate, instinctive dislike to the author. This was true textual criticism—the power to love the book even as one hates the author. True, mother had never gone so far as to *meet* the author until one day not long ago the class gave a little party in the banquet room of a tavern, to which mother and I were invited. We entered. Mother stood a moment until her eyes adjusted to the new light, and when they did she pointed a finger at Mariolena off in the distance and said, "That's she."

"Who?"

"Mary Mary Sunspots, who calls you up for literary conversation at various hours of the night and day."

"I recall only one or two such calls," I said.

"She's got a massive crush on you," said Mother.

"How can you tell?"

"I can feel the vibrations back and forth."

That, then, was mother's hard unassailable evidence, vibrations felt in a tavern.

I do not intend at this time to assert or deny anything in general. Mother has not, in any case, accused me of anything in general, citing only one particular case—one bitch, one bastard, one swimming pool. And you will ultimately judge me generally by my actions, measuring me at last not against claims or denials but against your knowledge of humankind and its moral achievement. You will decide which things matter greatly and which do not.

I will, however, testify flatly now, *in this particular case*, in the matter of Mariolena Sunwall—speaking as much as possible in the mood of an affidavit, swearing to you upon my honor as your father and your husband, pledging to you that I tell you the truth, the whole truth, and nothing but the truth—that I am blameless in spite of whatever vibrations your mother Beth Youngdahl may feel or have felt. This is not to say that I do not cherish Mariolena Sunwall as my talented and promising student, and offer her assistance now and then (*i. e.*, a room, a space) in moments of material need. In the same way I have assisted students in the past, male or female.

This All Points replies not only to mother's charges but also to Earl's letter of the 23rd except that I have yet to reply to his question about the Calling Card, to wit:

I remember exactly the moment the idea of my Calling Card entered my mind. Your mother and I were at BYU. I had had some stories published by that time, but the thing that was exciting my life as nothing had before was the imminence of the publication of *The Hard Puncher*. I was the author of a book soon to be published in New York. I was where Mariolena is now, just on the verge of things, just about to emerge from total anonymity into—what? Slightly less anonymity.

I was exhilarated. I was even superior (within the limits of my democratic convictions, which were active and unrelenting). But nobody shared my exhilaration except mother and Abner Klang and the Apthorps.

But they were in New York. What about the people of Utah, especially my classmates? Why couldn't they in some way both share my exhilaration and recognize my democratic superiority? I was exactly in that dilemma of the man who is wise but poor, of whom Johnson spoke to Boswell on Monday, June 3, 1782: "Consider a man whose fortune is very narrow . . . what good can he do? or what evil can he prevent? That he cannot help the needy is evident; he has nothing to spare. But, perhaps, his advice or admonition may be useful. His poverty will destroy his influence: *many more can find that he is poor, than that he is wise*; and few will reverence the understanding that is of so little advantage to its owner." (Italics mine.)

My achievement was invisible, like the poor man's wisdom. Well, there was a classmate of ours named Sam Sloat who worked in a print shop and who perceived my tendency to mention, if I gracefully could, my forthcoming book. Therefore he printed up some cards and handed me a thick little packet, saying, "Now you don't have to worry whether everybody at a party knows who you are. You just go around handing these out." My Calling Card was this:

> *Lee Youngdahl*
> *Author: The Hard Puncher* (novel)

Every year I made some more, adding accomplishments of the interim, if any, and carrying my cards about with me, as I do to this day, even as some men carry fresh cigars. I wouldn't go abroad without my Calling Cards in fresh supply any more than I'd go abroad without my pencils, my eyeglasses, my driver's license, my trousers zipped. I send about fifty each year to Abner Klang, who says they pay off by identifying me to ignorant editors, producers, *etc.*, as one who is prolific and reliable. Once I found a Calling Card marking somebody's abandoned place in a library copy of *Dreams*. This depressed me for a couple of hours but I recovered.

I send my greetings and my love to everyone everywhere and to your spouses if applicable, and to your children.

Forever and ever,

March 2

Dear Dr. Youngdahl:

I say to myself over and over, "I am in New York," and it
must be true, and why not, for look at how many other people
are here, too, people *do* get to New York, even the humblest sorts
of people I see in their pitiful states walking the streets outside
my hotel. So what's so hot about it? I'm sure I have yet to find
out.

Abner met me at the "JFK" airport. He told me once you met
him at an airport on your bicycle. This was a memorable impression for him, since he mentioned it not only when he met me but
twice afterward when he saw somebody riding a bicycle. He checked
me into this interesting hotel, saying, "How about if I give you
an hour to change for dinner?" I had nothing to change into, but
we went to dinner at The Two Fishes. Tonight the wedding.

This morning I went promptly to his office to arrange my
schedule and my life. All the while he dictated mail to Mrs. Mannerly in a way I had never seen before. I was not certain which
things he was dictating and which things he was saying aside.
She is very fond of you and told me she has written you four
thousand letters—one hundred letters a year for forty years. Her
hair was knotted up in a most unusual way and I asked her what
style it might be. "Mine is the style of the future," she said. Abner
unleashed a volume of obscenity. *My God, is he addressing that
to her?* No, he was just thinking out loud. She knows when he
is dictating and when he is thinking, and when he stops dictating
she sits frozen waiting for more. Yet I had the feeling that certain
phrases or expressions he addressed to me crept into the letter
she was typing. For example, he asked me how many "kids" are
in a class at Arizona State, and it appeared to me that she just
crackled right along, inserting his question and my answer. Somebody out there will have some information *gratis*. While he dictates

162/

he also signs other letters and documents and even reads manuscripts, books, and scripts, saying, "Regarding your manuscript which I have received this date and which I have read with deep interest . . ." although he only that minute picked up the package itself and may have still been struggling to rip and wrestle the wrapper off. Nevertheless he was offering an opinion of it.

He turns everything down. It appears to me that the literary future for younger people may be very discouraging. "Always was," says Mrs. Mannerly. Hundreds of people seem to want Abner to be their agent, and for that reason I realize how fortunate I am to have broken through almost effortlessly, thanks to your unnerving support. You have no way of knowing how much you mean to me.

Abner talked forcibly on the telephone with Frank Apthorp, with whom I am to meet and have lunch tomorrow. Abner assures me that if all goes well I will leave New York with a check for $10,000 in my possession. I take this to mean I must capitulate to everything at lunch. I see the meaning of temptation now. I wish I had a friend to hold my hand. A Letter of Agreement will be thrust before me with the coffee cup.

When Abner picked me up for dinner he said it was marvelous what a change of clothes would do. I don't know if he was deceived or gallant. I bathe, I put on *clean* clothes, but they aren't really a change. They are my classroom uniform. We went to The Two Fishes restaurant where he spent more than two hundred dollars for our party, consisting of Dorothy Klang and Halina Schiff. "Schiffy" struck me as an amusing Jewish person. Dorothy said that she, too, was Jewish. They started to look at each other, smiling as if they thought me innocent. Abner twirled his eyes around the restaurant and said, "It's possible that everybody in this restaurant is Jewish, including the two Fishes themselves." The owners are brothers named Fish.

I said, "I am not Jewish."

Abner said, "We thought you were." They all smiled. "Schiffy" took hold of my hand. I needed that. She stopped my trembling. Afterward she and I had a long talk here, eating fruit until one o'clock in the morning. To my surprise, she encouraged me to join Abner and the Apthorps in accepting my book as is, without any significant rewriting, and accepting *Lying in Bed* as the title, rather than *Fire in the Toilet*, which the Apthorps find obnoxious. Of course both titles were your recommendations. Your name arose several times. I told them of our first lunch together, when the wine spilled, and your sophisticated way of managing that incident. Dorothy said of you, "Yes, he will have appeared to have been uniquely sophisticated." I thought that that itself was uniquely sophisticated. In geography Dorothy is weaker: she said she has been in only two States of our Union, New York and California, and yet she constantly mentions doing one thing or another in Connecticut. I was almost confused myself. "Isn't Connecticut a State?" "No," she said, "it's just where people live who work in Manhattan." I believe she believes it.

Abner left me on this note of warning or wisdom: "Remember that the Apthorps have yet to sign your check. All literary arguments reduce to that." I can go home without my check. I have my airplane ticket. But then I thought how very handy and helpful the check will be to baby and me. "Schiffy" said, "Don't insist on 'toilet' in the title. It isn't all that revolutionary anyhow. The best way to rewrite this book is go home and write the next. I am waiting breathless to read the biography of your baby." All along she had thought the biography of the baby was a fine idea. Dorothy said, "I wouldn't read a biography of a baby. I only read biographies of celebrities."

"Once my book is a best-seller," I said, "my baby will be a celebrity, too."

"But your book can't be a best-seller," Abner said, "if you don't let them publish it. Once it is a best-seller you will be in a strong position for future work with Frank and Francine, but not one minute before." When he says "one minute" he taps his wrist as if he is wearing a watch. When Abner replies to a letter he goes over and holds it up to the window as if the light shining through the letter will reveal to him meanings between the lines. I said, "In Arizona such letters would be much more meaningful because the sun is so much brighter." He knew what I meant but he did not smile. He told two superlatively bawdy jokes at table but he did not smile at them, either. Mrs. Mannerly said, "He often laughs but he does not smile." At table when "Schiffy" and I smiled he and Dorothy did not. He said, "Two smilers at one table are enough." I *love* "Schiffy." She will guide me over any confusion

I may encounter here. I told her I read *A Klutz in Love* at least four times. Said she, "I read it more than that."

Imagine sitting at a table in New York at an unbelievable restaurant with three people who have read one's book and keep mentioning highlights at which they laughed. "We broke the bed laughing," said Dorothy Klang. I wonder if I shall ever again be at such a moment of my life.

I finally met a Christian. As you undoubtedly know from your many visits here, the Algonquin does not issue room keys but little electrified cards you slide into your jamb to open up. A young man with his card in his hand came up to me and said, "I believe our cards went into the wrong mailbox by mistake. Give me your card and I'll give you mine." I replied that I thought him handsome, attractive, no doubt brilliant, ingenius, and musical but I was in town for a short time only on important business and dared not accommodate him; that if he were ever in Phoenix, Arizona . . . It's a lucky thing I didn't set my book in the Algonquin, for if we have no keys we have no locksmiths. I would have found a way.

I no sooner admitted myself with my electric card to this room than Frank Apthorp called to welcome me to the city and to tell me he will be spending a sleepless night anticipating meeting the author of—"Well, "said he, "that's what we'll lunch about." He was excessively courteous.

I will keep you informed.

Your respectful and devoted student,

/165

March 3

Dear Professor Youngdahl:

In response to your inquiry regarding my surgery procedure at the hand of Dr. Emmer, I am pleased to be able to give you the information as I see it. Since it is a confidential subject I hope it will remain in your private file, as I am sure it will. I have confidence in you because I am a graduate of Arizona State University and a contributive alumni. So we are Sun Devils together. I am pleased to know that you are among our faculty.

The surgery was a moderate success. Success for whom? I rate it adequately satisfying for myself, but it may not be in the way you think. It has been satisfactory for my wife, let us say, but that is not why I had it. It doesn't bring me big pleasure to know that I am bringing pleasure to another, for I have never been an appreciator of that philosophy. If I cannot feel the pleasure myself I am disappointed.

"Does your penile implant work?" Do you mean to ask if it works for her or for me? It works extremely well from her point of view, but for me it is only boring. "Has your operation improved your marriage?" Yes, certainly. I wouldn't have any marriage without it. My wife is thirty-five years younger than I am and might be even younger. It is possible she told me a slight untruth. This young woman hovered about, and after the death of my wife she moved in and swept me off my feet. I can see now that she led me into it, but at the time I thought I was getting the better of the bargain. From the beginning it was apparent that her idea of the marriage had been financial. I was the support of her romances. She kept company with former "associates" of hers.

When I went to Dr. Emmer he painted a new picture in glowing terms, and I have been left moderately disappointed, as I have told him. I am surprised that in view of my disappointment he has given out my name to others. You are the second man I have heard from. If Dr. Emmer had put my wife's name on the list instead of mine you would be reading a letter far more enthusiastic, since from my wife's point of view my implant (inflatable silicone rubber cylinder), although it may feel mechanical and boring to me, works like a charm from her point of view, filling her with pleasure and excitement far beyond anything she has ever known.

My own satisfaction is not directly my own pleasure. It is more in the pleasure of observing the frustration of all those "associates" who called on my wife all the time. She has no need of them any longer. I thought our marriage was going to be very short-lived, and I saw myself half wiped out in a community property state. She'd have made a killing divorcing me. Dr. Emmer told me of several cases in which penile implant saved the marriage of men two and three times older than the young women they married without much assessment of the damage they were risking. She might find younger men, he said, but never longer lasting satisfaction. Surgery made her forget her "associates."

I am hoping to pay a visit one of these days to the campus at Tempe, where I spent happy years so many years ago. When you see my wife you will think she is my grand-daughter. People will think I am there to put my grand-daughter in school. Most of the buildings you have there now were scarcely even dreamed of when I was there. The women then dressed much more modestly than now, but whether we are better or worse for the change in costume I don't dare undertake to say.

I hope this information can be helpful to you in making your decision if you have not done so already. Have a good day.

Yours *collegially,*

March 4

Dear Dr. Youngdahl:

I am sorry if I astonished you or in any way rendered you angry. I would not have taken the coat if I had not heard that the weather here was to be so egregious. I would not have entered the house without your permission, but Saturday afternoon when I was making my last-minute arrangements for my journey you were not present. Your letter reflects some confusion about my riding in airplanes, asserting that certain "discrepancies" exist which I shall be able to explain. I shall certainly be happy to do so at an opportune moment.

Following your instructions, I have carried your greetings to the people you mentioned in your letter and to "Schiffy" and to other people you have mentioned to me by name. I find it difficult, however, and somewhat hypocritical to greet "other friends" unless you have specifically named them. Everybody says "O yes, he's a close friend of mine," but conversation reveals that he or she has not seen you or spoken to you or written you a letter or read any of your books for ten, fifteen, or twenty years, and it is hard for me to say to him or her that you instructed me to greet him or her for you.

This morning Abner instructed me that if I strolled by his office I could pick up my check for $10,000. It was all very casual.

You do not mention in your letter whether you have granted my request for a leave of absence from class in order to confer with my New York publisher and agent regarding my work, which was done as a student of that class. Frank Apthorp suggested that this trip to New York might be looked upon as a field trip for class. "Just as anthropologists or archaeologists or zoologists go to exotic places to study aspects of life and culture so have you come to New York to see the beasts and the ruins. It's only Sin City." I have certainly met a variety of people, all of them connected with

168/

publishing in one way or another. At Virgilia Suekuykeen's wedding I met many people whose names I have heard and whose books I have read. I have tramped the streets with "Schiffy" and found that my borrowed coat was welcome against the nippy winds sweeping down these streets. I will be happy to report to the class on these matters.

Very, very respectfully,

Dear Lee,

Point regarding courtesy questions. What do you hear from Beth on her worldwide tour? Congratulations to your son winning the election in Dallas, Texas.

Point regarding book with working title The Girl on the Diving Board and advance against royalties. Lee, you're the man that can do it if anybody can. I appreciate your setting it up with the promise and stages one through seven in Roman numerals, making it easy to follow for a person like me who by my own admission haven't got time to read things as carefully as I should. Your friend and pal Mariolena Sunwall criticizes me for criticizing books before I even unwrapped them from the wrapper, and she is right. It's the furious pace of life. When I started out in this business as a young man I read every book carefully, was never in a hurry, had no money. Now that I'm a millionaire I've got time for nothing and I'm a wreck. It was because of this insane pace that I thought you wrote incompetence when you wrote impotence. They were always hard words, as the following true story regarding impotence proves—

Point regarding impotence. Down in the deep South a country fellow was enjoying terrible difficulties relating to his wife. Her advice to him was to go up north to the highly intelligent doctors and find out what his trouble was. She said, "I believe you are im-*poe*-tent." He went away, traveling up north, where he visited the doctor. The doctor checked him over inside and out and upside and down and agreed with him that he was im-*poe*-tent. Therefore the country fellow went home. When he arrived home he was all dressed up in the classiest new suit ever seen this far south, he was wearing big thick eyeglasses, he had grown a mustache, he was carrying the latest copy of the dictionary under his arm, he was walking along sporting a cane, and in his mind he was even

170/

considering getting himself fitted for a hearing aid. "Well," said his wife, "what did the doctor tell you up there?" Her loving husband replied, "He tells me I am im-*poe*-tent, and by golly if I am im-*poe*-tent I am going to *look* im-*poe*-tent."

(Credit Don Nilsen.)

Continuing point regarding Girl on Diving Board and advance. Nothing is lost. I hashed over your promise on the phone with Frank. He and Francine immediately went for it in a big way, backing you as always with total enthusiasm, admiration and money. Talking with Francine, I pointed out that when you received your first advance from them it was $250, whereas Mariolena at the same age is receiving $10,000. At first Francine flew through the ceiling. "What are you saying? Are you saying Lee should receive forty times as much as she? Are you saying $200,000? You know that Lee doesn't write that kind of a shitty book." "Calm yourself, Francine. I'm not saying that at all. I'm saying the sum should be computed by age. Lee is 2.727272 times Mariolena's age, that's the way he's computing it. The sum we want is $27,272." "Isn't that a relief," she said, writing down the sum and looking at it. "Difficult bastards earn difficult sums," she said (I didn't say). "How old is Lee? That merest boy is sixty years old already?" she exclaimed in amazement.

Our pal Schiffy has a lot of material she is working on about impotence you can use as background for your book, and I am sure she will give you permission to quote her as freely as you want. She will do anything for you and possibly has. We had dinner with Mariolena the night she arrived. Both of them you sent to me and I am grateful for that. Now here's a chance for you to give her more good advice. She now has another book under way, moving up from sex in the sixth decade and after to sex between the 70's and 80's. I wonder where the audience is going to come from. People age 80 aren't exactly starting building their own personal libraries, and most people that age I see merely by looking out the window snoozing on the benches in the sun rather than pouring over books from cover to cover, and my guess is they have just about given up thoughts of sexual activities yet to come, although according to Schiffy I may be wrong.

But when I suggest to her keeping her audience in mind, possibly writing for a younger reader, I can see that she is politely turning me off. With Social Security going the way it is I don't see the government putting in a book allowance for the older folks, do you? Older folks these days feel lucky if they get a food allowance. Nobody wants to read about old people. Think about that girl on the diving board. Can you imagine a book with a woman between 70 and 80 on the diving board? Can you visualize the jacket of the book with a woman that age? Can you visualize Frank and Francine visualizing it? They would put ten toilets on the jacket first.

I don't know anything about impotence except what I hear from various men. Nobody gives it a thought until they've got it, which is the way with most diseases. But I'll keep inquiring. I am told that a sure cure for impotence is smoking marijuana, but I'm not speaking first hand. While everybody in New York was smoking marijuana I took the opportunity of staying sober and making my fortune.

If you don't mind a bit of personal opinion I always believed the chief cause of impotence was bicycle riding. I never rode one myself and was never impotent. You on the other hand are an incredible bicycle freak. You are the only man that ever met me at the airport on a bicycle. Out of my window I see these enthusiastic young males racing along on their bicycles, and as I watch them I can feel a severe pain creeping up on my testicles. When I see them bumping over the curb I wince. It shivers my timbers. The bicycle seat is a lethal dagger. One false move and your testicles are rolling down the street like marbles. Take a vacation from bicycle riding and see if it helps. This is the best advice I can give you.

You know that I am always anxious to pass along anything I possibly can to make life better for you and improve your working conditions. You are my bread and butter and my cocktail onion. I have made a lot of money from you over the years and a lot more from your various friends you sent me. He should have asked me for a finder's fee. Too late now. I shouldn't even suggest it. In the long run I made more money from my writers than any writer ever made for himself. I am at the age now when I am even making money from the dead. Some of my writers are making more money after death than before. Time flies if I say so myself.

For all we know Frank Apthorp may have had a touch of the

impotence himself. Some of the rumors suggested so. At Virgilia's wedding the biggest topic of conversation was still Frank and Francine's divorce. Francine said, "We miss each other." However, since it will take Frank two years to move out of the house, and since they are at the office every day, it's not what you'd call clear when they have any time alone to miss each other. Nothing changed. Except they now have two staffs of servants in the house. The latest rumor has it that now that they are no longer married they are liable to have an affair with each other, following their lifelong marriage pattern of fucking everybody but their own spouses.

Lee, believe me, I am totally relieved that we have worked out this new book with Frank and Francine and you are back again in the old writing swing. Your idea for The Girl on the Diving Board is awfully clever. I myself could never invent a story if my life depended on it. I need everything ready made.

In your premise I can especially identify with stage VI where "his never having approached her sexually has given her the impression he is sexually indifferent to her." Often a girl comes in from the hinterlands. Wherever they are. She is a small town girl accustomed to country boys. The biggest literary man in her life thus far was the editor of the junior college yearbook. She looks on me as too big a shot to be interested in her romantically. She knows I represent women of glamor in the literary field. I have got to make her see that I am interested in her all the same. She has plenty of glamor on her own. I advance in her direction slowly, little by little. I often relate anecdotes from my collection about book agents falling in love with women newly arriving in town. Some of these stories I might improve a little but they are all based on hearsay. I learned to keep exaggeration to a minimum. I blew it a few times before I got the hang of it. This is the same problem your man will be facing with The Girl on the Diving Board—how will she adjust to him when he turns the heat on? (Stage VI.) Thank God it's your problem, not mine. You solve it and we'll sell it.

Point regarding Virgilia's wedding to Sky King. It was beautiful. It was one of the great bashes of all time, living up to all expectations. Following your instructions I breathed your name to the bride beyond the hearing of Mr. Sky King. The bride stood there in her bridal gown, floral bouquet in her hand, looking as lovely as she ever looked in her life. With me were Dorothy and many more. For me the high point of the night was introducing Mariolena Sunwall to the bride. There stood Mariolena in her cowpunching hat straight off the ranch. The bride said, "So you're Lee's new cunt on the handlebars." Mariolena never blinked an eye. It was like she never heard her. She said, "I hope you will have the same good fortune in your marriage you have had in all your past marriages."

The wedded couple flew away for further portions of the ceremony in his home country, and then will fly around the world a few times by airplane and yacht before returning. It is wonderful to have a client so rich she will never retreat in her price. That way we have got a few of these bastard Publishers where we want them and wish all my writers were so successfully married.

Point Regarding Mariolena's Negotiations with Apthorp House. I was afraid you were sending her here with a chip on her shoulder ready to bite the hand that was feeding her. She is like many of the best writers I have known in the past, her private life is more sedate than the impression we gain from her writing. The wilder the writing the tamer the writer. Sometimes that's a truism. She writes everything down. She walked off the airplane scribbling in her school notebook. She couldn't believe she successfully completed her first airplane ride. She recognized me right away and said, "Dr. Youngdahl has told me so much about you I never doubted it was you." She never calls you anything but Dr. Youngdahl. She came to the office and prowled around among every loose paper she could lay her hands on and surveyed my bookshelves, taking out her hanky and dusting off your books, wearing her mother's mink coat.

All the main questions got settled with Frank and Francine in one long lunch. She agreed on the title *Lying in Bed*, understanding Frank and Francine's old fashioned feeling regarding putting toilet on the jacket. "Join us in this last stand for decency," pleaded Frank.

The second main question was stickier. I thought we were going to have real trouble, but Frank and Francine came prepared with their strategy, and poor little innocent Mariolena was not much of a match for them. She had many many thoughts about revision. She wanted to develop the professor further, bringing

174/

him into closer relationship with the locksmith. The girl was becoming more interested in the professor and less interested in young boys. She was beginning to realize how thin-headed the boys were when compared to the professor in all his sophistication. She is looking for someone substantial. She decides she wants a family. She recognizes that after so many boys in bed boy after boy she wants a full grown man. Time after time she quoted you, saying, "Dr. Youngdahl says this and Dr. Youngdahl says that," while Frank and Francine are saying, "All that is material for a future book, leave something for tomorrow, let a book go, don't polish this book out of existence, don't try and hitch a fourteen ton trailer to the back of your little Volkswagen."

She wanted to do revisions while Frank and Francine wanted the book as is. The problem was not settled when we got off on the question of her name. "This is the real issue," said Frank. "To say the least," said Francine. They are two criminals. They fought with Mariolena over the question of spelling her name Maria Lena or Elena Marie or Maria Lorna or a hundred other combinations of the same thing until I didn't know whether to laugh or scream because I knew they cared nothing at all about the name. Frank and Francine acted like they were losing their tempers. "We are drained from the struggle," Francine said. Mariolena began to feel sorry for them and said, "All right, then, if you give in on the name I will give in on the revisions." How we ever arrived there I do not know, but there we are. Mariolena will not revise as much as the tail of a comma in return for which she may spell her name any way she likes. Instead of revising she will go forward writing all her new ideas in new books such as a biography of you, which she seemed to think she can write in one year. Francine said, "I thought you were interested in a full grown man. You cannot write the biography of a full grown man in one year." All right, then, Mariolena decided she would write the biography of her baby instead, although even this was liable to take some time as she has written more than one hundred pages to date and the baby is not born yet.

After all the dust died down we were drinking a final drink. Frank said, "I don't mean to be personal but we have all heard about Virgilia's untoward remark to you at the wedding and we are wondering how you responded to it." "I responded to it with amusement," Mariolena responded. "Dr. Youngdahl and I are just good friends. At least I hope I can call him that. I am flattered that anybody can think I'm worthy to be chosen as his lover or companion, which was the implication of Virgilia's hint, but she must not know Dr. Youngdahl very well. He has a reputation of being a no nonsense teacher."

Teacher! Distinguished professor! Take my word for it, you can put her down right this minute for a grade of A and AA in your class, make it AAA, better still make it AAAA avoiding confusion with the automobile association. She turned out to be cooperative to the last degree. How many teachers' students sign up for a course in writing and by the end of the term receive an advance of $10,000? Point this out to those schmucks in your Department that are always downgrading your work. I know what a hard time they give you. Their reward to Mariolena for the great work she did in her writing course was expelling her from the dormitories with her baby. How many other students in the dormitories sold a book this term to Apthorp House or anybody else for $10,000? Not many.

Lee, forge ahead. I know that $27,272 is going to assist you in your enthusiasm for the new work at hand. The last thing Frank and Francine said to me on the street at parting was their expression of pleasure that you are breaking through with a new book at a time when many writers are hanging up the old eyeshade. Stay off the bicycle and live to 100. Mariolena tells me you are a common sight spinning along with your backpack on your back full of student manuscripts. I offered to walk her back to the Algonquin. "You needn't bother," she advised, "I know my way around town now." She gave me the warmest kiss on parting.

We have launched a new career. She is a beauty. I can understand now why professors put up with colleges.

Ever yours,

FROM: Earl Youngdahl, writer, Assistant
Professor of English, Western Kentucky
University, Bowling Green.

March 7

Dear Dad,

Loved your All Points with all its helpful information. I especially thank you for the account of the creation of your Calling Card. It was just the sort of information I was hoping for when I asked. A lot of my friends envy my hearing from you all the time. There's a wide variation in the way parents relate to their children, I must say. I have one friend, Gullick, who never hears from either of his parents and he's just as glad. I have another friend whose father writes *separately* to *each* of his *six* children at least once a week, very seldom duplicates anything he says, and never uses a Xerox or any other form of reproducer, not even carbon paper for his own records; to top it off, he burns their letters when he receives them and encourages them to burn his. (Notice how I'm learning to use the semi-colon; you were always a whiz with a semi-colon. Also, do you know that certain words you taught me to spell I now discover you taught me wrong? Examples upon request.) I have a friend who receives a postcard from one or the other of her parents about once a year from Paris or Cairo or somewhere. Either the handwriting is so small she can't read it or it's a big scrawl saying, "Mother will write you a letter," though mother never does and neither does father. Half a dozen words a year. (Pardon fragmentary sentence.)

Now, listen, the first chance I get I'm coming home to meet that Mariolena Sunwall, single mother of one. Please tell her to wait for me before she does anything rash. She sounds like the person I have been looking for for so long, the kind of person I'm just not finding in Kentucky, a completely literate person and yet a completely free spirit; above all, wholly committed to writing. That's where she must be exceptional. Your description of the way she has stuck at her writing is inspiring to me, how she sat crouched over her manuscript on the diving board, how she allows

/177

accident to mingle with purpose for best results. Last night I discovered this quotation in a preface to one of her plays by Enid Bagnold, which says it just as you have so often said it: "There is something lucky that happens to writers—a mixture of invention and memory that runs down the arm."

I am well into a novel which is keeping me absorbed. Mother read it when she was here and had some enormously helpful things to say about it. We had a little spat about it, however, before we arrived at agreement, and I could remember her speaking to you in the same way. MOTHER: Lee, you're being defensive. FATHER: You're reading it too subjectively. MOTHER: You're resisting what I'm saying. And then, some time after the fact, I might hear you say, "You were right, Beth, I'm glad you made me do it."

I feel that way about her now, but she was hard on me when she was here. Our conversation was slightly strained between here and Bernique's.

It took us two days to get Thornton on the phone to congratulate him. He said, "It was the mothers' vote that put me over."

I trust you don't think I'm admiring Mariolena Sunwall simply because she has received a $10,000 advance from Apthorp House. I don't care anything about how much money a woman has. You know I went with a woman whose family owns many racehorses and who herself personally owns Pejorative and Subordinate Clause, but it could not make the difference for me; we broke up, horses or not. We just weren't making it together any more. I still see her around town, and it's weird seeing somebody you were formerly so close to; yet now when you pass you barely nod or raise your hand a little. (Sorry about that construction: you . . . you . . . your . . . buffering pain with impersonal pronouns; bad writing, I'll admit, but the pain is still so awfully real.)

Please tell Mariolena I'm prepared to clear the decks and take off for Arizona on short notice. I'm ready to take off any minute, as a matter of fact. I can let this novel cool awhile. A little purposeful neglect will do it good. Right at the moment I'm blocked, and a trip will do me some good.

But isn't she awfully young? You don't precisely say in your letter how old she is. You say she "has been" a student of yours.

178/

Is she an older student, I trust, or did she come to college directly from high school? True, she is a mother (one gets an instant image of a slightly older woman), but mothers are often extremely young these days. How much have you told her about me? Does she know that I too am a writer?

As you make clear in your All Points, mother is worried about your possible infidelities with Mariolena. I tried to ease her mind, although logical or rational progress may have been difficult in view of the hard news she seemed to have received from Penny Drew. I can understand how misunderstandings might occur. Women are crazy about writers. Even when I mention that my work thus far is mainly unpublished women's eyes light up as if I might be someone special.

When your All Points arrived it seemed to me at first to be fairly convincing. However, at some points your logic leaves a good deal to be desired. You decline "at this time to assert or deny anything in general." Here you are avoiding the question. Your "at this time" promises or implies that at *some other time* you will assert the truth; but if you are intent upon telling the truth, why not tell it now? You are in any case deferring an answer to a question you have not been asked: mother has not challenged your behavior "in general." Rather, she is intent upon the particular case; now; not the case in time but in the moment; and you have dodged.

Then, in denying "*this particular case*" (underlining yours), you clearly wish to have your readers conclude that the particular exemplifies the whole, which, in turn, guarantees the particular— a veritable dizzying solipsistic cycle: *i. e.*, because I am innocent of this particular I am innocent of the general, which proves that I am innocent of this (or every other) particular.

Apart from logic there exists circumstance. The particular instance may be atypical in view of your claim for momentary impotence. The present, particular claim now neither represents the whole logically nor circumstantially. It is a deviant case; it is as if a man who has recently broken his leg denies all his life's running on the grounds that he cannot now run.

Finally, surely you cannot expect either mother with her precious stake in the matter or me as the rational semantic critic of your "affidavit," to feel satisfied in our curiosity by your assurance that you will measure up morally well enough in the general light of "humankind and its moral achievement." We will some time at some future day "decide which things matter greatly, and which do not." For mother, the thing that matters is neither the past nor the moral tomorrow, but the question whether you have been carrying on with Mariolena Sunwall, rich and talented daughter of ranchers boasting either 63,000 or 36,000 acres. You who have always taught us moral absolutism suddenly plead moral relativism, wherefore one might say, "I don't know, dad, you're sounding somewhat guilty to me."

As I listened to her I came to understand that all mother is basically seeking is her peace of mind and social ease: if you have been acting badly, stop. So she feels. She does not wish to be a leading item in Penny Drew's daily newscast. Never was mother's relativism more pronounced, and I must say I feel rather the same, as do Thornton and Bernique, to whom I have lately talked: dad should stop because it bothers mother. That's the reason everyone cares for.

Well, as I have heard you so often say, "I'm off to school, off to class, wish me luck." As a kid I never realized how much your classes were like mine—somebody standing in front of the room talking to the others sitting down. The boys and the girls were bigger, that was all.

Your loving son,

March 8
Dear Dad,

Ray and I enjoy your "all points bulletin" as always, but the most recent one was especially interesting and even a bit alarming. It came very much too close to comfort for me and reminded me of the time I was a senior in college and became confusingly involved with my professor of languages, one Dr. Pineda, whom you heard me mention often but never in the present connection. This is a first.

He was very taken with some poems I wrote in French and told me I had a great future writing poems in French, although now that I think back on it I wonder what he could have meant by that. It was just flattery to begin with. I don't think my poems were good in French or any other language, especially English, and I have destroyed them all, which Ray deplores.

I began going to his office occasionally after class. It smelled of wine. After a certain hour he would say, "My office hour has ended," and turn a switch which turned off the bright lights and turned on a low lamp, and he brought out the wine and we drank some. He was at that time trying to quit smoking, as was I. Since he was then 51 years old I, from the point of view of someone 22, was at a loss to understand why he worried about smoking any more, since a person that age was at death's door (so I considered). We talked in French and German and whenever someone else joined us Dr. Pineda talked in the language of whoever came along. He spoke Islamic languages and Hebrew, Japanese, various Chinese languages, and Russian, and he'd have occasion to say such things as, "Oh, I must confess I'm no good in Icelandic— oh, I can get *around* in it, I can have a decent polite conversation in it, but I can't be very philosophical in it," and that sort of thing. God, was I impressed.

We fell into the habit of going for a ride in his car over in those little towns on the north side of the river, and up into the hills and we'd sit in the car and talk, or sometimes in town we went to taverns or little restaurants in ethnic neighborhoods where he liked to listen to people talk and tell me what they were saying. He'd give me a word by word account of other people's conversations. They were all about love. Most of the conversations he reported followed the same line. It seemed that this was all people talked about in foreign languages in the Pittsburgh area, lovemaking and their troubles with their husbands and wives. I felt sophisticated listening to such things in the company of a learned professor whom I admired and respected, and I was amazed that he knew so much about love (sex) because I didn't know old men knew such things. I knew *you* knew such things, but that was because the boys were always talking dirty.

Dr. Pineda had a wife about whom he always spoke with affection. He was so attuned to his wife that I never imagined he might have eyes for any other woman. He was a distinguished scholar. I am sure it was naive of me but there it was. I never seemed to wonder why a man so devoted to his wife and children spent so many hours with me in ethnic taverns. I confessed many things to him within reason. I became very dependent on telling him everything, I brought all my problems and dilemmas to him, and I had many of those at that time, if you will remember. I often called home and cried for half an hour on the phone, but Dr. Pineda took over as listener and I called home less and cried less and drank wine more.

One day in the spring of my last year he asked me if I would care to accompany him and his "helper" to his summer cabin and help him fix things up a bit for his family's vacation. I remember phoning you or writing you telling you I was going to Dr. Pineda's cabin with him and neither of you said anything indicating you had any doubts about my doing so. That was the answer I wanted from you, and the reason I got it was that I hadn't told you the straight story. I had hedged. I had given you the idea that a whole gang of us was going.

I can smell the wine of his office yet. I was gone on smells. Do you know what I did once? I bought the shaving lotion he used and sniffed it so I could carry his smell with me, and he used to clean his eyeglasses with a little drug store spray, and I bought that, too, and sniffed it.

To tell you something I have never told you. I see now that this is becoming a letter Ray will never see. I was not a virgin at that time. I ceased to be a virgin when I was a senior in high school with the Cardiff brothers if you must know the truth and with several boys in Pittsburgh and with one of the younger professors there, too, so it wasn't as if I didn't know anything about sexual drive in the male. But I never thought of Dr. Pineda that way in spite of the million clues he tossed in my direction, most of which did not dawn on me until years later. Some of them right this minute. If only I could write! I see now that my mind was absolutely frozen shut.

Once I answered the telephone in his office. It was Mrs. Pineda, who spoke many languages herself. She asked me very angrily (in English), "Who is this? Where is Dr. Pineda?" and I for the first and last time in my life acted quick wittedly. I said, "There is no Dr. Pineda here. Please look up your number again and dial correctly." One minute later she called back and Dr. Pineda answered and he looked at me appreciatively. Although he and I had been going off together for some weeks on these little eating and drinking and driving excursions of ours it was only when the telephone rang for the second time that I knew something. I knew that Mrs. Pineda knew nothing of my existence. My opinion of him lowered. My opinion of myself lowered. But I went right on sniffing the shaving cream nevertheless.

When the day came for our little summer cabin trip we drove off. The "helper" who was going to help us fix things up in the cabin never arrived, and the people who were supposed to be already at work at the cabin were not there. It wasn't Dr. Pineda's cabin in the first place, but a borrowed cabin stocked with the things he liked and I was learning to—wine and low lights. I saw what was coming. "About time," you will say.

He had been so pure and so scholarly and I had concluded such reassuring things from all the family photographs in his office. When we entered the cabin he smiled at me in a way he had never smiled at me. It was not lewd or anything like that. It was only different and seemed to reveal a different side of him from the side I had always seen. In the weeks gone by when we innocently (?) touched, every part of me turned to warm liquid, but now in the cabin when he took me in his arms all the warm liquid turned sour. I said I was not expecting this. He said, "Then why did you conceal your identity to my wife on the telephone?" It was nothing I could explain. It had nothing to do with making love. Her voice on the phone simply frightened me, that was all.

I know that this must be where Mariolena Sunwall is (your writing student who has sold a book to Apthorp). If she were approached she would panic. At least I did. He had been laughing, but when I slipped away from him he stopped laughing and I began to be afraid of him. I wanted out of there. We were deep in the woods somewhere off the Turnpike halfway to Johnstown. You would have been frightened for me had you known. I made it clear I did not mind being here with him, even without the helper and others, we were good friends, I supposed two adults (one of whom had just become an adult about three minutes before) could very well occupy the same premises together but I had not come prepared in mind or body for love.

I remember becoming angry, too, asking him why he had waited until so late in the school year, in two weeks I would be gone forever, if he had cared for a true love affair why hadn't he begun it in November or December. I accused him of not wanting a love affair, of wanting only a quickie affair. I asked him if he played this game with a different student every year.

He became extremely angry, mostly at himself, squirming in his chair, when suddenly his eyes lit up and he said, "Look at those cigarettes." A supply of cigarettes was stocked there and we began to smoke them. He had broken his smoking habit for a few weeks, but now he had fallen off the wagon. This saved him from himself and saved me from him. As we talked on into the night (you can guess what we talked about, we talked about the same thing everybody in every ethnic tavern talked about, or so Dr. Pineda translated: making love, that was the only conversation) it began to seem that his sorrow at not making love to me transferred over and became his sorrow at having started smoking again. He drank some wine and delivered monologues and soliloquies in several languages.

I had the presence of mind to go easy on the wine. He cooked a lovely dinner, but it would have been better if he had not drunk so much wine ahead of time. It was midnight and I was exhausted and frightened, and I was afraid of him because of some of the things he was saying. He was in pitiful ragged shape. It was not the same distinguished man who could speak many languages in the past but one who could barely mumble intelligibly in any. He kept belching and I was afraid he was going to do something terribly embarrassing. He sat in a chair with a spatula in his hand, dozing off slightly, and I simply on an instinct stepped out of that cabin, which could have been so idyllic if only I had known better how to handle it. But I was a shocked fool and my mind was frozen and I could handle boys O.K. but I couldn't handle distinguished professors yet.

I had no idea where I was. The road was dark in both directions. Luckily I walked the right way and luckily the right person came along driving a big truck bound to Pittsburgh. I did not attend Dr. Pineda's class during the final weeks and I did not take his final exam. He gave me an A for the course nevertheless and I never saw him again. The last I saw of him he was sitting in a chair with a spatula in his hand dozing off slightly.

I bet you never expected this from your never-writing daughter. Ray and the children are fine. Mother has arrived.

With all love,

FROM: Halina Schiff, Ph. D., C. C. P., and
R. D., writer, New York City.

March 8

Dear Lee,

I have your letter and thanks. I'm sorry to hear you say you're
no better than you were. I'd have thought things would have
broken through for you by now. I'm convinced it's psychological,
not organic. "It's a prick, it's got to work." I never met a man
whose didn't. I have some ideas on the subject.

1. *You must not keep arguing yourself out of seeing Haddock
Hooper.* People all over the world are borrowing and stealing
money to go to Haddock's for his cure. You aren't compelled to
kiss him if you don't care to. Shake hands, that's enough. Maybe
afterward you'll be grateful enough to embrace him mildly. You
needn't call him by his first name, either, if doing so threatens
your need for formality. Just call him Mr. or Master or His High-
ness or Wonder Worker of the World. He doesn't really care what
you call him as long as it makes you feel better and doesn't hurt
somebody else. I hope you received a copy of his book I sent—
Any Cure is the Right Cure.

Your account of the swimming with the sharks stirred up
some memories for me of a comparable occasion with Haddock.
I went with him and many other people on a Swim With the
Crocodiles in the Florida Everglades. Once we arrived there we
found out they weren't crocodiles but alligators (or the other way
around) so we had to repaint all our signs and revise all our
slogans and rewrite all our songs. But we made our point, I am
sure.

After I'd read *Fire in the Toilet* (title now changed to something else) I knew I'd love that Mariolena and I did. While she
was here she said a few things that made me want to read her
book again keeping my eye out for you. Possibly you didn't notice
yourself—all your moral glory, your passionate heroism, your de-
tached Olympian purity, your financial generosity—and you can't

186/

be blamed if you missed yourself because it wasn't quite you in reality. It was only you as Mariolena saw you at a moment of a kind of innocence she now wishes to correct by revising her book, making you less heroic and more—well, more *you*. This dismays Frank and Francine, who don't want to allow a single word to be changed except the word "Mariolena," which they will permit the author to spell any way she sees fit except "Toilet."

Well, they settled everything as they went. Her adored (but more authentic) professor she will save for the next book, which is to be a biography of her baby, about whom she has already written two spiral notebooks' worth, and more to come. Frank and Francine are going to advertise this Sin City book as a second *Klutz in Love* complete with a big blurb on the jacket from the author of the first. God knows I am glad to give it.

I wonder if you remember that in early drafts of *A Klutz in Love* Klutzy was in love with her professor, her hero, her mentor, her intermediary between a little bit of recognition and total obscurity. There she was—there she is, Mariolena, not long in civilization after that isolated ranch. Until she met you she had never met a live creature committed to those books, those objects she had been devouring with hot-blooded devotion since childhood, halfway up her shins, as she tells it, in steershit, fighting off the persecution of her parents, who must be, from her tales of them, quite impossibly brutal and depraved. You created her. You threw (like the fellow in her book) a life-preserver into the desert, where it drifted on the sand. You have given her belief in herself. She has risen from nowhere up to somewhere, and you are the god who made it happen. You will remember I used to think so, too, and you warned me repeatedly I mustn't underestimate myself, not that you did it for me but that we did it together. After awhile it dawned on me that you were a big part of it, but not all of it, and I am sure it will dawn on Mariolena, too, who is after all nothing if not open to dawnings.

This is not to say that she loves you less, but that she loves you better. To be perfectly blunt about it, if she is nothing else she is the sure cure for your impotence. You have hesitated to move in on her because you have been under the impression you are impotent. Something is blocking your way. You may feel guilty about playing while Beth's away. But why permit your silly psyche to deprive you of good healthy fun? You do not stop *biking* while Beth's away. You feel that you must get into your new book before you can be sinful, or God will give you writer's block to go with cock-block. Now, Lee, you and I know God doesn't clutter Her mind with little things.

You complain that you throb but Mariolena does not throb back. She'll throb back at the grandest levels if only you'll throb first. You fear you can't. You fear what the trade calls "performance failure." But you!? Performance failure you? Performance failure is for people who have been accustomed from infancy to failing performing. You have performed—college degrees, family, books, swimming with sharks, all you have tried you have performed. Mariolena is so far smitten with you that her lip quivers when she mentions your name. In the hotel she sat on her bed talking about you, bouncing up and down like a little kid in town for Radio City.

I'm not so sure you correctly interpret her sense of those chaste grandfatherly touchings. What makes you think grandfathers are so grandfatherly? You should read some of my interviews with grandfathers lots older than you. She was only returning gesture for gesture. You are the teacher. It is you out of your experience who must make clear to her who you are and what you are about. The burden of knowledge is upon you. Your grandfatherly shuffling around in your antique swimming trunks is only some kind of cover-up. I'm surprised at you. Tighten up those trunks. Show her what you've got. You have so much more to offer her than even the University Housing Counselor. Approach her nakedly (boldly, frankly). Do unto her as you did unto me. Move in.

Her new view of you will take hold instantly. Your new character has been establishing itself in her mind. That was why she wished to revise her book. She has already received teacherly love from you, and what she wants now is the complete figure, not the idealized man of her early drafts. Her excitement will rise at the slightest provocation, she will leap upon you, she will transmit from her body to yours such currents and emanations of desire and enthusiasm that your impotence will vanish in the instant, your blood will course through your system in an oceanic and titanic wave mightier than any you have ever known, and you and

188/

that woman will be lovers for twenty years or more, as you and I were and I hope still are when you come to New York, and you will say in the first moment of your decompression thereafter, "Mariolena, my dear, why in the world did I wait so long?"

Your pump will be primed forever again, electrical charges will have recharged your battery forever. Remember the battle cry: "One time proves it."

How lucky you are to have me around to make this analysis for you. She made you feel noble. Her looking upon you as a god aloof made you *feel* like a god aloof. You played the part so well your well-traveled cock co-operated to the limits, pretending to die on you. What a role! Ladies and gentlemen, a round of applause for old cock. An Academy performance. An Oscar for Peter. *But now get up and get back to real life.*

Think things through and pick exactly the right day and the right hour and the right circumstances. Smoke a little pot before-hand. (Ask a graduate student to purchase you some.) Getting older, you may have been returning to your Mormon Puritanism, your old beginnings, back to that age when you thought it was possible to separate body from spirit. Poor Mariolena didn't know how to help you. She, too, was a victim of the same idea. From you she expected only mind. Body she expected only from boys in cut-off jeans tramping through the dorms and the little box houses of Sin City and swimming through infected pools.

She was afraid to have you read her manuscript in the first place. She thought you'd disapprove, you'd write her parents what a bad girl they had produced. You were authority, and all authority stood together against freedom. Imagine the author of *Boswell's Manhattan Journal* or *Robert Burns's Indiscretions* or *A Snow Job* or *The Telephone Tree* taking the part of parents against their independent child. But she had not yet begun to understand the way in which an author is connected to her/his work. (Of course she is not yet fully connected to her own. Abner wisely remarked to me, "She may be exuding more sex than she actually exudes.")

2. What was 2? I forget.

We went to Virgilia MacGregor's wedding—now Virgilia *etc. etc.* Suekuykeen—and saw many people I haven't seen in ages. There was one moment, believe me. Abner said, "This is Mariolena Sunwall of Arizona, she's here on a book." Virgilia's mind processed the data. I could see that she didn't want to do it—it was spoiling her evening—but she couldn't help herself. She said, "Lee's new cunt he rides on the cross-bars of his bicycle." Mariolena turned a little red and said, "I am sure your marriage will last as long as your others."

Go for it, Lee. Do you remember that boy in her book always tying up his bathrobe? Get yourself into that bathrobe, playing with the cord as you go. Sack out the baby. Light up a joint poolside. Say, "Mariolena, let's take a break from our writing now."

Your student forever,

TO: Mr. Abner Klang, literary agent, New York City.

March 8

Dear Abner,

What (you ask) do I hear from Beth on her worldwide tour. She wrote me a sweet letter from Earl's followed a couple of days later by a brief unhappy note fearing that I was scandalously carrying on with your client Mariolena, which I was not; not because I mightn't if I could but I can't; for what reason I do not know, but I don't believe it's the bicycle. It's something else. Yes, I'm in touch with Schiffy, who is giving me free (the freest) advice based on her research gleaned from her many interviews with dirty old men. I will follow her advice within the next few days and see what happens, or doesn't happen. At any rate, Beth is presumably at Bernique's now, fourth visit of seven projected.

I tremendously appreciate your concluding the matter of *The Girl on the Diving Board* with Frank and Francine, and their generosity in recognizing the justice of the sum $27,272. I appreciate as well your report on Mariolena's triumphal trip to New York, and I hope to hear additional details from her, perhaps later today. She is asleep in the guest house. And of course I appreciate the gossip of the wedding to which I was not invited, though I'd have well-behaved myself, for God sake, I wouldn't want to harm her marriage in any way, I'm a big boy now and she is above all by this time of our lives not so much a lover as a friend. He may turn out to be a genius of a husband, providing exactly the ballast she needs in a way no husband has provided for her. Years of managerial skill, years of union negotiations, years of dealing with governments and rivals and multinational gangsters may by now have given him just the talent for accommodating Virgilia heretofore too complex for lesser men. Does she continue to keep all the other names and just tack this one on, or do you suppose she might start cutting for space? You know that she becomes angry if you don't put all her names on her envelope. We'll see, won't we? You as agent she adores and behaves reasonably for. Did Suekuykeen inquire of you for some of your secrets?

Now Mariolena. You won't believe me. Well, maybe you will. Your having seen her and touched her and broken bread with her at The Two Fishes so dear and mouthwatering to me makes me feel you will believe things of her I would somehow not expect you to believe had you not seen her touched her broken bread and so forth.

She arrived at Phoenix airport a few hours ago *par avion* as she *will* say, dragging Beth's mink coat (*not* Mariolena's mother's mink coat) down the concourse, Spiral Binder clutched to her breast, quite asleep on her feet. She is asleep in the guest house now and has been so for some hours. She had been too excited to sleep on the plane, too speeded up from the whole New York experience, specifically from having sat talking excitedly all last night with Schiffy in the Algonquin lobby. Schiffy's old charity— sitting up all night with people on the verge. That much I suppose you can believe all right. But there's more.

This morning some hours before I was to set off for the airport (by car, old friend, not bike; that bike-ride to the airport was a one-time thing) to pick her up I received a phone call from a man speaking low, a little breathless, nervous, dry, unsure how to go about talking to someone as exalted as I—how shall he address me? It was her father. I had never heard his voice and I would not have guessed this to be the voice of a tough, violent, meaty, spurred, diamond-weighted pornographic rancher bloody to the elbows, as in fact it was not: it was the voice of one who is a postal clerk in Phoenix (main branch). He is a slender man, faintly pouched at the middle, who leans back on his heels to keep from falling forward, and prefers to sit down anyhow: perfect and ab- solute identical model or image of the mailman you will remember from Mariolena's book, who carried contraceptives in his hat, trying to conceal them from the postmaster. "Dr. Youngdahl," he said, "I hope I'm not interrupting something but the wife and I have a real question here we thought you might give us the answer."

"Try me."

"Was it you or us supposed to pick up Mariolena at the airport?"

"I've been planning to," I said.

"We didn't know," he said.

"She wanted me to," I said, "because it would be an awfully long trip in for you."

"Sir," he said, "it's not. We live right under the airport."

"Ah, you're at the town house," I said, "not at the ranch."

"The ranch?"

"Mariolena felt you'd want to be at the ranch all weekend," I said.

He inquired a second time, "What ranch?"

"Your ranch," I said. "The ranch. Green Osage Ranch or something like that in Tonopah."

"We have no green ranch," he said, "or any other."

"You know," I said, "in view of what you say I'm wondering if I might not have received a certain amount of misformation about you."

"From Mariolena?" he asked. "You might have. She's been known to misinform."

"You know," I said, "I'd love to get together and chat with you."

"Oh, but you're too busy for that," he said. "A busy man like you is much too busy."

"Mr. Sunwall," I said, "I'm not a busy man, I'm an organized man."

"She says you're night and day at the machine cranking out your writing like a factory," he said. "But if you got your routine under your belt for today we could do it. Did you also mean the Mrs.?"

"Of course."

"Where?" he asked.

"Right here at my house," I said. "I insist. I just brought home a bag of bagels."

"On your bicycle?" he asked. He laughed a little now. He was looser with me. "Just kidding. Maybe you don't ride a bicycle. Maybe she was making that up, too. We'll bring something ourselves," he said, "if you direct me how to reach there."

After awhile they arrived, Mr. and Mrs. Sunwall and—to my great surprise—the baby himself, the biographical subject. He made straight for the diving board. The reason for my surprise was that Mariolena had told me she'd be leaving her baby, as she often did (or as she *said* she often did, I now must qualify), here and there roundabout with friends in Sin City, whose names she might or might not know, who passed Mr. Baby about from person to person and house to house and fed him the best Pizza Neatsa. She had not done this at all. No, she had left baby instead with Grandma and Grandpa in their modest little house in Phoenix in which Mariolena herself had been raised and where her old room awaited her now whenever she cared to return, filled with the tokens and trophies and valued objects of her childhood, especially hundreds of books she had treasured and hundreds of others she had written. "Written *hundreds*?" I asked.

"Some of them were small," said Mrs. Sunwall, herself a long-time postal worker. Mrs. Sunwall's relationship to Mariolena's writing had from the beginning been intimate enough; she was her typist; had always been; Mariolena at six or seven spoke little "books" to her mother, who typed them as Mariolena spoke them, and whose role became more and more complicated and time-consuming as Mariolena's books became bigger and bigger and more and more intricate and more and more subject to her insistence upon rewriting and revising manuscripts which appeared to her mother to have been quite perfectly done at an early stage. "You bet I know those Spiral Binders," mother said, for it was she to whom Mariolena had all along been taking her manuscript for typing (as she was taking her baby for care), who typed each manuscript and each manuscript's many revisions. Mariolena had told me that her typist was a young man in Sin City who was "into" her for obligations never made explicit, but Mrs. Sunwall said no, no, I must have misunderstood something, "sometimes Mariolena mumbles."

She has a pleasant round face. I gain from her a sense of openness. They didn't seem to me repressive types—not literary, perhaps, but not the blackhearted censors, certainly, Mariolena said they were, self-indulgent smut merchants on one hand, punitive moralists on the other. No, said mother, she had never censored a word of Mariolena's writing nor ever really criticized her for language or theme. "I'm a man of the world," Mr. Sunwall said, "you've got to be ready for anything at the post-office."

They had brought a bottle of wine. It was inexpensive wine, not very good, I thought. Bagels and cheese and wine in plastic wine glasses (we never carry true glass to the pool deck; house rule), and surprise after surprise unfolding for me. For example, Mariolena has two brothers, one older and one younger than she, and close to her age, although she had presented herself so winningly to me as a child alone, solitary, inward, drowned by the silences of the vast family ranch. "Oh, no, no, no, no," her mother said, "she had a million playmates and her brothers, too. She was always busy."

If my impression of them was now undergoing radical correction so, of course, was theirs of me. They had had, for example, an idea that my house and grounds were much more expansive than they actually are. They thought I owned many animals, since it was their impression that Mariolena had been engaged by me to care for my animals in exchange for free rent; I more or less owned a ranch, a zoo, a herd, and poor Mariolena was to be more or less a shepherdess roaming my acres. (We have never rented the guest house. Actually, Mariolena has offered to pay rent, but she has never gone so far as to try to pay it. Instead, she has borrowed from me and from our bottle of money long kept by the front door as a kind of burglar alarm. Her parents tell me that they have helped her generously with money as their circumstances have allowed, and somehow I believe them, although she once told me they have made her life a "raging inferno.")

We toured my estate, where a subtle duel took place between her father and me and produced at the last a startling outcome. Plastic wine glasses in hand, we sauntered from the pool deck through Beth's flower garden, ending before the guest house. Here her father turned to gain a view of the route we had come. I think I knew what he was looking for, although I may of course be wrong: had it been my daughter I might have looked for the same thing myself. He was tracing in his mind my probable course from my house to Mariolena's. I could stroll at night through the flower garden, and swim the pool to her. I could also walk around the pool. She and I could also, of course, rendezvous night or day in the house or poolside or anywhere our hearts desired; we were consenting adults. Or Mr. Sunwall may have been thinking nothing at all. He may have been courteously admiring my house and garden, though I projected something more: seeing in him the protective, worried father, my sympathies rallied to his cause. A revelation sprang from me like the loud infernal banging of the

/195

poor fellow's tell-tale heart in Poe's story. Consenting adult I was, morally right, legally clear, ethically my own man, nevertheless I was unable to resist clarifying for Mr. Sunwall the question he may or may not have been asking in his mind. "Mr. Sunwall," I said—quite blurted, I think— "I am impotent."

I think they received my admission gratefully. At any rate my effect was as magical as I could have hoped. Our relationship instantly altered. They relaxed. We were now equals as we had not been a moment before. I was no longer the lecherous professor scheming to seduce their child, but, simply put, a nice old grandfather several times over. "As who isn't?" Mrs. Sunwall said, accepting my assertion as my guarantee not only that I had not slept with their daughter but that I did not intend to try. Nothing could have punctuated my thought better than their turning as one body from the guest house now that their question had been answered.

For better or for worse, then, no new grandchild soon to care for, although it was a task they seemed to enjoy. I easily saw how secure the child felt himself in their safe world. Where was the father Mariolena had told me about, who parked his children in the fiery sun while he browsed in porno shops? We strolled back through the garden as we had come.

What about their Mariolena? Did she really have a professional talent? What about the financial arrangements of book publishing? My opinion was something they very much desired, and in which they now placed a clear trust in view of my now being, as I was, freed of the taint of carnal interest. Was she a good student? How might she earn a living while awaiting the fame and wealth of her writing? Was there, in my opinion, something at all *sick* about a person who invented stories for a living—who, so to speak, lied for a living? Would her expulsion from the dormitory remain as a black mark against her on her record all her life?

"All right then," said Mr. Sunwall at last, "have we answered the main question?"

"Which was what?" I inquired.

"Who's supposed to pick her up at the airport?"

"I will," I volunteered.

I badly wanted to. This would be the new Mariolena I'd pick up, not alone the young woman who'd been to New York and back but the young woman transformed from cattle-thieving pornographic ranchers' daughter to the child of Mr. and Mrs. Sunwall, postal clerks.

To the airport. There she was, the new Mariolena, Spiral Binder clasped to her breast, and Beth's coat slung across her shoulder. I was glad to see that coat again. Affectionately she kissed me, licking her lips as she came, so that it was a wet kiss on my lips, and a very good kiss, too. We had never kissed before. "Look at this dump," she said. "How can they keep me in Phoenix after I've been to New York?"

"You'll settle in," I said.

Waiting for her bag, she seemed to sleep on her feet. I felt that I had her at a disadvantage. I knew a great deal about her now that she did not know I knew, and I was somehow hoping she'd not betray herself further, dig herself deeper into her own lies. Mariolena, however, has yet to learn to dare modestly, subtly. "God Almighty," she said, "I wonder where I'll ever locate my baby."

"Sleep first," I said. "That's what I'd suggest."

"Schiffy kept me up all night," she said, "telling me her troubles. I'm sure I'll be able to locate my baby if I wait and start out fresh."

"You really feel he's lost," I said.

"Not really lost," she said, "only I can't remember the names of the kids I left him with."

"If he were my child," I said, "I know I'd never forget the names of the people I left him with."

"You were another generation," she said, resting her forehead on my shoulder as we waited for her bag. When we arrived here we sat poolside a few minutes, nibbling bagel and cheese. She examined the label of the bottle of wine her parents had brought, and it seemed to ring some sort of bell in her head, but she was too tired to think it through; too tired to finish her bagel. She took herself to bed.

I have hung Beth's coat in the closet. I don't know if I've hung it in its correct place on the correct rack. The odds are against my having done so, and Beth will notice its being out of order, and I dread her noticing, I'll keep passing off the matter with little weak witticisms, and eventually she will dismiss it without forgetting it. If by chance I should receive, before she returns, my Apthorp check for $27,272 (less agency commission) she might be diverted by the thought that her husband must have been up to something genuine, after all, during her absence.

Whether Mariolena will be embarrassed to be caught in lies I cannot say. She'll explain it away somehow, like fire in the toilet, like the baby among the rushing bulls, she's quick, and her head is abundant with alternatives: her mother says she's written hundreds of books and "never got stuck yet."

But of course I'm happy it all went so well in New York, apart from whatever might go wrong or right here. Greetings to Mrs. Mannerly, who has written me four thousand letters—and I have never answered one. Kisses to Dorothy. I may be gone for a few days, off into the desert to visit Haddock Hooper, of whom you have heard Schiffy speak. You have certainly heard of his book, *Any Cure is the Right Cure*, which has sold millions of copies and cured everybody of everything. I just might give him a try. Might not. We'll see. If you have a message for me please leave it on my answering machine.

Yours,

March 12

Dear darling Schiff,

I haven't gone to Haddock Hooper because I thought I could solve things by following your advice to confront Mariolena so very frontally, but that has failed and I may go to Haddock Hooper yet. Today is three months and two days since my last erection, achieved by bicycle between the postal kiosk and the dormitory, a gloomy anniversary. Yes, thank you for *Any Cure is the Right Cure*, which the mailman threw into the pool. I appreciate your intention to support Mariolena's book with a blurb on the jacket by the author of *A Klutz in Love*. I am writing along on my own book with the bad title *The Girl on the Diving Board*. The model for the girl has disappeared from my view, but the general bleakness and loneliness and futility of it all was somewhat relieved this morning when I received not only your letter but Abner's check for my advance from Apthorp House for said book about said girl on said diving board. It lightens my heart without solving any problems.

Schiffy dear, I love you, you're wonderful, you're infinitely dear, you're funny, you're the most brilliantly homogenized writer half-scholar half-humorist there ever was, you're a grand genius of psychological counseling and I'm sure people come from all over the world to sit at your feetsies, just as you say people come from all over the world to fry in the desert with Haddock Hooper, but in the present immediate crucial heart-rending matter of my relationship with Mariolena Sunwall you were just plumb wrong incorrect and full of shit. I have been her hero, you say, her mentor, her creator, her god and her salvation, she throbs for me with electrical titanic oceanic tidal excitement, together we shall make an immensity of waves. Would that it were so. *Go for it, go for it,* you say. But how can I go for it when it has gone?

I followed your suggestions as well as I could, choosing my

/199

day and my hour. Maybe I miscalculated. I don't know. Fifteen minutes sooner and things might have gone differently. Something I did wrong, and as a result I never had the chance to give her a chance to start up my battery forevermore, to prime my pump, or to accomplish any of those feats of *rapport* promised by you experts in the sexual-renaissance business. I'm not criticizing you. I'm sure you did your best. You suggested a course of procedure and it most miserably failed.

Mariolena arrived home Sunday afternoon and went to bed in our guest house and slept until dawn. At dawn she parked herself on the diving board with her Spiral Binder and resumed writing her biography of her baby. Tuesday she returned to class and told us all about her trip to New York. (She described her flight to New York as "one of my first airplane flights." I seem to have boxed her in a pointless lie there, about which she feels sheepish.) She described you very well in great detail, Abner and his agency, Frank and Francine and their enterprise, and Virgilia's nuptials. Since she had not been to class for some time, she said, she was anxious to report usefully as well as vividly on her journey, so that she might maintain her grade by appearing valuable to the eye of the professor. In the course of that digression she touched upon the serious financial reprisals exacted against her by her family. I knew this to be another lie. She did not know I knew this to be a lie. I think it was my finally finding out about her lies that caused her to flee me.

She lied on. She had been telling me for two days that her baby was somewhere "lost" in Sin City. I knew that her baby was not lost but was as safe and happy as he could possibly be, at home in the little old family house in Phoenix, and I very badly wanted to sit down with Mariolena and tell her everything I knew, but somehow the moment to sit never came, and she was lost to me.

I thought that Wednesday night—last night—would be a good time for us. It seemed right. Mariolena would be well-rested from New York. I went off to school Wednesday morning, not because I had anything to do there but because I guessed she'd be more seducible in the evening after a day's writing, all guilt dissipated by a good day's work. I had turned up the heat in the pool. I had brought in good food and champagne, though I also had in mind an alternate plan—going out to dinner to a restaurant as nearly as possible resembling The Two Fishes where she went with you and the Klangs. Thus I could go either way, home or out, and whichever it was it would be as elegant as I could make it. No Pizza Neatsa for us. I was feeling very affluent and guiltless, too, knowing there was big money in the mail from Abner: I wasn't going to feel so awfully guilty wining and dining Mariolena.

My theory is that I shouldn't have gone to school yesterday. I have no Wednesday class. I pushed a bit of paper across my desk. I chatted with people in the halls. I went to a meeting. In the middle of the meeting I began to feel faint genital stirrings unlike anything I have felt in three months and two days, which, I can assure you, were induced neither by the exciting agenda of the meeting nor by the glamor of the speakers rising on either side of the question. No, it was my cerebral self rediscovered, coming home, even as the books of your trade have explained it to me. I who had suffered "fantasy failure" and "performance failure" was coming up now out of failure into revival. I left the meeting as gracefully as I could. I was confident. I knew it was going to work. In my mind I praised you and formed the letter I would write you to tell you how well you had advised me. I felt all life coming back into focus for me. I felt Beth restored to me, everything once again as it had always been between us, even with its disadvantages—my restlessness. But my restlessness was a part of me I could not simply will away.

I was like a hot-blooded boy again. At the airport Sunday Mariolena had kissed me a greeting, not passion especially, but not quite neutrality, either, and I was eager for another as I have not for a long time been eager for so small a thing as a kiss. Soon after I left the meeting I was overcome by another old familiar feeling: impatience, irritation, somebody agonizingly impeding me on my way to a tryst. I had made a quick stop at my office. Outside my door I was detained by a student who hadn't had the least plan to speak to me until he saw me, but now that he saw me he thought he might put his idle time to use. "I've just been wondering—" Well, we know what he was wondering, he was wondering what sort of grade he was earning in class. I told him he was earning nothing, he had not been there often, he had not read the readings, he had not read the work of the other students, and when he had appeared at class he had been on one occasion wrong and on the other occasion discourteous. "Yeah, well," said he, "a lot of us have been thinking not everybody is there all the time . . ." Like whom? Like Mariolena Sunwall, for example. What a hard time I'd have explaining to an uncomprehending world that I'd be giving *A* to Mariolena and as little as possible to that young man. The world would interpret things all wrong. What would that young man say if he knew she had lived on the professor's diving board while the professor's wife had gone touring distant states and foreign countries? I might write a splendid thoughtful essay *Reflections on the System of Letter-Grading in Higher Education.*

Thinking back, I think if I had *told* her to be there she'd have been there when I returned from school. I think if she had known my trouble she'd have helped me out; been delighted to do it, as a matter of fact. I think that everything you and Abner may have said about me in New York had brought me into range for her—it was what I think I felt in her kiss at the airport, she was seeing me anew. I should have said right off to her, "Mariolena, let's take a break this evening, the champagne is cool, the pool is warm, our day's writing is done." I think she'd have been there when I came home.

I must have missed her by fifteen minutes. If only I hadn't stopped to argue with that abominable lazy young fellow. She had phoned home about fifteen minutes before I arrived, and she heard from her mother that the Sunwalls, "lost" baby and all, had been to visit me. So I knew what a liar she was. So she fled, cleared out, packed up and was gone.

She left the world's briefest note on the hall table near our front door beside our little bottle full of money (empty now) which we have for years kept there on the advice of our security-alarm people. The idea is that if you walk into the house and see the bottle gone you'll know that a rude, grasping thief has been there; worse still, he may still be. So you back out fast and run up the hill to the Goldwaters' and call the police. Her little note said two words only: "Animals fed."

I telephoned her home and spoke to her mother. Mariolena was on the way home—home to her, to mother; she had just this minute phoned to say so. Had mother told Mariolena of our visit Sunday? Yes, just now told her, many many thanks again for the bagels and cheese, feel free to drink up the rest of the wine. I asked if she'd please ask Mariolena to call me, and she said she would and I'm sure she did, but another twenty-fours have passed and she has not phoned and I don't expect she will. She was absent from class today.

You see that she's not been the "sure cure" for my impotence. I am as impotent as ever. Yesterday's little stirring of the genitals is but a memory. The whole thing has been as clear a failure as anyone in the depths of pessimism might have predicted. I had had high hopes. I know that you know your business, that your insight into the problems of young women is keen and renowned; and I know you are a student of men of my decade. I must be a tough case.

I'm really fearfully depressed. If I didn't have this novel flying down the track under a full head of steam I'd be sunk and no mistake. It comforts me to feel my impotence dissolving at least at the literary level. But why not at every level? Is it too much to ask to be able to write and fuck both? So many folk do. How can I explain this unopened champagne to Beth? I think I'd go off somewhere if only I could locate the neighbor boy who feeds our animals when we're away.

I am sorry it has turned out this way. I know you are as disappointed as I. I'll tell you more if more occurs.

My love to you always,

March 12

Dear Dr. Youngdahl:

O God I have seen everything now!! Life wasn't hard enough for me—you had to call my parents in on it. Spilling everything to the parents the minute he feels that he has been done out of something. This is not the maverick professor, friend of students, friend of young writers, saboteur of the murdering Establishment. Not at all, this is professor Youngdahl as he truly is.

God knows what you feel you've been done out of. You are what is known as a dirty old professor, fit subject for a bit of writing I might yet insert into a book called—a book, I should say, no longer to be entitled *Lying in Bed*. O God how many times have I heard you mutter and mention, "I like that title . . . thought it up myself." You'll be going to your grave telling everybody the title of my book was really yours. And I'll be dancing on it. Maybe you wrote the whole book, too, like Scott Fitzgerald stealing Zelda's work and calling it his own. That will be next, although there the analogy ends: God knows I'm not your wife and pity her who is. Take back your fucking title. Here. Who needs it? Use it yourself. I wouldn't use it if it were the last title in the world and have so advised Frank and Francine by Mailgram.

Maybe they will threaten to withhold my check from me. You hastened to tell my parents that I had money coming from Apthorp House. You invited them to your house to tell them that, to squirm the truth about me. I can't believe it. It is inconceivable. It was not that I intended to keep it a secret from them or that I intended to conceal my wealth from them. I was saving it as a surprise for them, and you gave it away with your mouth. You have spoiled their surprise for them. You have left nothing for anybody.

The sum itself has been a lie all along. I am now given to understand that the supposed sum of $10,000 will be but a shrunken remnant of itself by the time it reaches me. It comes with $1,000 lopped right off the top by your conniving associate Abner Klang, leaving $9,000. And what is that sum but an *advance against royalties*? Far from earning money with the sale of the first copy of my book I must wait until sales have earned $10,000 before I begin to earn money. None of this was explained to me although you were in a position to do it. For what service does Abner Klang receive his cut? He is to receive $1,000 for walking down the street with a package of manuscript one block and a half. United Parcel delivered the package 2,400 miles for three dollars; Abner Klang delivered it one block and a half for $1,000. How much does he kick back to you on these lucrative deals?

Next, you will reclaim the sum of $515. You are in terrible haste for that sum, of which $400 is rent for ten nights at the most during which I dwelled in your guest house. You need $515 from me like you need cyanide in your swimming pool, which you rake and care for night and day keeping the holywater clean. Add $515 to $1,000 and you find me with a net gross of $8,485 of the original $10,000, and I a mother alone with a child to feed. How you are crowding me, demanding your money for your little bottle for the burglar at the door. You got your mink coat with a little honorable New York dust on it, didn't you? You'll get all the rest. You'll get everything that's coming to you (I hope). "How will I explain this to Beth . . . ?" But when you offered me residence in your guest house in your treacherous letter of invitation (now in my possession) you said nothing about the fact that your wife would be away. I was left to discover that fact for myself.

Here is the great mind at work, feeding upon the tiniest details. Cats must be fed thus and so. Dogs must be fed thus and so. We must be careful not to starve the dogs and cats. How many dogs and cats starve beneath the wheels of the Porsches and Jaguars and Mercedeses of Paradise Valley—you who are protected by your own personal United States Senator up the hill from whom you borrow as needed whatever you need, and run to use their telephone when yours breaks down, and he a known fascist, a known tool of the industrial-military complex, a known Air Force puppet. Yet you live in juxtaposition to him proudly. O but what a show of conspicuous consumption that is: your own personal United States Senator whose house you point to with pride for anyone who will listen while, in the same breath, you tell your captive listener how much you disapprove of the *policies* of your very own neighbor-United States Senator whose property so contiguously kisses yours and yours his.

I wonder now how I could ever have thought of writing your biography, to have thought such a petty mind was "a gem of purest ray serene." You are obsessed not by fine thoughts but by your property. You boast of your Mormon heritage but you have inherited from them only their infallible bookkeeping system for which they are justly famous. The keys to your property are numerous. They jangle as you stride. In front of your office you require ages to find the right key on your ring while education seekers snigger behind you. You take half an hour to lock your house when you depart. You live in fear that your dogs will drown in your pool. Do you think that a dog falling into a pool develops amnesia and forgets to climb out? You are obsessed. "Mariolena, was it or was it not your first airplane flight?" The never-ending interrogation never ended. Must I be expected to remember everything? Am I a woman or a data bank?

Dr. Youngdahl, I will tell you who is not "your" property. I am not your property. That should be clear to you by now, and if it is not clear let me make it clear in writing herewith. Following my return from New York I saw something frightening beginning to happen between us. Emanations drifted my way from you. Certainly not the reverse. From long and painful experience I began to know what I thought it was. I am sure now. You bastard. You asshole. You fuckoff. You jackoff. Never did I write a letter with such pleasure or say things with such pleasure as I am saying these. Never was justice so well-served as I am serving it now.

I had thought to myself, "How very lucky I am to have found a patron who invited me into his house—to his guest house, to be precise—and to believe that he was supportive of my steady daily progress at my work; who took such pride in me that he announced to all and sundry and caused to be inserted in the student newspaper news of his wonderful student writer whose novel was to be published by Apthorp House." (Not mentioned in the student newspaper was the fact that Apthorp House is run by two of the greatest raving perverts in the history of literature.)

Not that the professor himself is not more than a little bit along those lines himself. I felt you closing in on me, trapping me.

> Like cat down cellar wit' nohole mouse.
> Like cat down cellar wit' nohole mouse.

—lines 17–18, Scottsboro,
Anonymous, 1936

I had no escape. Hadn't I had enough of that sort of thing from the men of Sin City? I could have remained in Sin City if all I wanted from life was men pouncing upon me with their determined erections. Couldn't you, as a professor paid by the State to encourage student writing, have maintained at least the decency to allow me to plunge undeterred and undistracted into my own newest book, my biography of my baby, *Life Seen by the Eye of an Orange Bug* (a title at last whose creation you dare not claim), rather than sabotaging me with your carnal lascivious lechery? It is a shock from which I shall be a long time recovering. Though your house may be grander you were finally nothing but a boy from Sin City. But you had not even the honesty of a boy from Sin City who, rather than lurch and lurk behind his window blind, calls cheerfully out, "Hey, Mariolena [tentative spelling], I don't have a class until one-forty let's fuck."

If you had been at least that honest I might have retained in my soul some slightest iota of respect for you, but you are not that honest. You are a horny old professor. Schiffy's studies confirm what you are. It was all you ever wanted of me. Your interest in my writing was a deception. And you were mighty feebly slow getting at it—luckily for me, who had time to flee.

At first your shelter was a blissful retreat for me from the ardent, impulsive, incessant, daylong, relentless, crude, loathsome, disgusting bestiality of the college boys. I generalize. You teach us not to generalize. You taught me to string adjectives together like that, too, and then go back and pick out one or two just right. Go back and pick out your own adjectives. I rewrite nothing for you any longer ever. At last I am free of you, free to live my own life once again, free of your grammatical and syntactical structural anxieties.

Abner Klang put me wise to all that. You were suffocating me with your demands. Develop my characters, go deeper, ap-

/207

proach climaxes more slowly. But when my work was received in no place less than New York by nobody less than Apthorp House they rejected your pedantic ideas and welcomed my novel as was. Francine Apthorp said, "Lee's fatal flaw is his perfectionism, I faint away." Frank said, "I too faint." Abner warned me that I should resist your making me self-conscious about my style. Mrs. Mannerly agreed. "Schiffy" cautioned me about your fanaticism regarding commas and semi-colons. Wherever the Apthorps thought the writing was the worst it was worst because you had made it bad with your advice, and wherever it was good it was good because I had resisted you.

I shall mail this letter at the mail kiosk on campus where, as I was waiting for the tram one day not long ago, along you came with your offer of bicycle transportation. With many misgivings I permitted you to carry me to my destination. I was nervous, uneasy, and uncomfortable, but you had entreatied me energetically and I in my stupidity obliged. Very soon, of course, I perceived the reason for your entreaty. When by chance my eye involuntarily traveled below to nether regions I saw that you were elongated in heat like every male for miles around—many of whom have the decency to wear long trousers in preference to child-like shorts. Erection on a bicycle!! Imagine what would happen on a horse!! When I alighted I fled in mortification. Was that all you had ever really wanted from me?

I guess I should have seen it coming. Those few hours after my return from New York I should have seen that something was up (but not up *me*, Professor) when you marched home with Liquor Barn bags groaning with champagne and wine. You hinted we would "knock off" writing one night and talk. What would we talk about? Would we talk about all the money you loaned me and all the titles you have given me for my book? Inadvertently my eye fell on the truly decadent material you receive from Orgy Farm in the desert. So that was what you meant by "desert"—you were thinking of a few days in the desert. Not with me! At Orgy Farm the featured perversion is "a program of instruction" in masturbation, wherein one might engage in "therapeutic" masturbation among friends or in a group or alone with a "partner observer." Let me out. I can hardly speak of it. It was the end. It was the pits. It was Rome. We have descended to the gates of Hell. I could

208/

see it now. I have heard of such things from women of my acquaintance: along comes the dancing old reprobate with his pitch to the woman, "Jerk me off on doctor's orders."

I enclose herewith a stamped, self-addressed envelope, with official University form, upon which, if you will, you may issue instructions to the Registrar to permit me to withdraw from your class without penalty ("W"). I enclose in addition my key to your residence in Paradise Valley. You may of course give me a grade of Failing ("F") if you think I deserve it. I have recently absented myself from your class and do not intend to attend any class of yours in the future. If you fail me for the course I will pick up the necessary credit elsewhere. Never fear. The world will be interested to know, however, that grades of "A" and "B" were merrily distributed to all your students except that one student who published her class writings in New York. I do not have a stamp. I cannot find the key.

Your former student,

March 13

Dear Reverend Hooper:

I hope you don't mind my formal salutation. I'm not yet one of those people capable of entering abruptly into a first-name relationship. Maybe I'd be better off if I were.

You were referred to me, so to speak, by Halina Schiff, whom you and I share as one of our star students of the past; and by my physician, A. Whalen Drew. Recently I followed with much interest your struggle to retain your ministry: I cheered your victory and your vindication. I am pleased that you remember my role in the Swim With the Sharks, especially my slogan "Nobody Wins a Race." I suffer an ambivalence about slogans. I can write good ones, but I must say of myself with Donald Wetzel, "I could not chant the most wonderful slogan in the world." (Incidentally, the Scotch military fellows, their English antagonists, and the peacemaking policemen were actually actors in my play. Many people seem to remember them who can remember nothing else of my play.)

You will recall, of course, that you wrote me 27 February in connection with my condition, which I think of as "impotence," a reality you deny. Nomenclature aside, it feels like impotence to me. I become increasingly concerned about it with every passing day. The edge and the savor have gone from my life.

Schiffy's prescription for my recovery called for the loveliest of medicines: I was to pursue a love affair with a certain young woman of our acquaintance, whose alleged passion for me would so abundantly supply my own that my problem soon would solve itself forever. "One time proves it." However, as I worked toward my goal events intervened, the relationship collapsed: I had stocked my shelves and refrigerator with superb refreshment, only to find, when I returned home on the day my imagination had named,

210/

that my friend had fled from my guest house, and with her $115 which I had loaned her.

I want you to understand that my interest in Learning Together West is medical only. I do not seek the desert in search of fun and games. When you have solved my "problem" I shall be in the mood again for recreation (indeed, this is the point of the quest). This matter springs to mind as I consider your chapter "Group Play" in *Any Cure is the Right Cure*. That's not what I want; not what I would be going to you for. I want to be cured. I have no moral scruples against practices however bizarre between (or among) consenting adults, but the pleasure I seek now is simple recovery.

I am hoping you can help me. I have tried all the things the books suggest. I've popped the zinc. I've had two testosterone shots. In my gloom and desperation I went to Los Angeles to a surgeon specializing in penile implants, whose eagerness to operate on me aroused my suspicion. Your bloodless program sounds far more agreeable, but I have hesitations about abandoning accredited medical advice for yours. I recall controversies during which your medical qualification has been challenged.

Now, Sir, let's talk money for a moment. In your letter you say charges are "optional." However, I like to settle on a price beforehand. I hate to raise this question because I am aware how selflessly you have gone about so many crusades for mankind and the community over the years, both medical and spiritual. Nor does the world reward its saviors with economic security. Quite the opposite. I have admired your work for many years—not always uncritically, to be sure. I know several individuals whom you have helped at critical moments of their lives, and I have heard of many others. You advocate peace, openness, charity, imagination, and mercy. For that reason I feel somewhat crass bringing up the question of money.

Please tell me how we proceed from this point. Can you convert my "problem" to "opportunity."

In a recent letter Schiffy reminded me of your Swim With the Crocodiles (Alligators?) in Florida, and when I went to the *Encyclopedia* to read about crocodiles vs. alligators I came upon an account of Ponce de Leon's search for the "Fountain of Youth," which led him to the discovery of Florida. For years and years I have uncritically accepted the legend of Ponce de Leon as an elderly gentleman hoping to remain young. My recent experience leads me to believe he was probably less interested in the undifferentiated abstraction Youth than in the particular malady he was probably suffering: impotence. Out of the depths of my own case I redefine the past and instruct the present: round and round the world he sailed at enormous risk to the lives of many men, to find the place to prime his pump. The symbol of the "fountain" was sufficiently apt, an erection spouting.

Yours very truly,

P. S. I thank you so much for your sending me *Any Cure is the Right Cure*. I send you in exchange a copy of my own *When Your Bicycle Tires*. Please enjoy it. Schiffy reminded me in a recent letter that *Sex In the Seventh Decade (And After)* is dedicated to you. You may recall that *A Klutz in Love* was dedicated to me.

L. Y.

March 13

Dear Earl,

I am delighted you are learning to appreciate the semi-colon.
A handy fellow. Now on to the colon:

My dear boy, I admire you endlessly for your attack on my
logic, my reasoning, my question-begging, my descent into sol-
ipsisms, my flabby way in general of arguing my case for my own
virtue. I know that beneath it all the thing you care for is not my
strengthening my logic but my reassuring mother that everything
between us (between her and me) is as fine and as well as it ever
was or could ever be, and so it will be forever. You have stated it
perfectly— "the thing that matters [to mother] is neither the past
nor the moral tomorrow, but the question whether [father has]
been carrying on with Mariolena Sunwall . . ."

You are the best boy in the world to try to make me shape
up, to try to shame me into doing right (if right it is), and I thank
you. I am certain mother thanked you for herself while she was
with you. Your support will have cheered her and comforted her.
I must also comment on how well-composed your letter is, sen-
sible and sensitive and eloquent and gentle; a fine analysis. I thank
you also for being so hospitable to mother. She enjoyed your
hospitality, the frankness of your friends and the uninhibited qual-
ity of the talk she heard beneath your roof. Her observation of
your literary fertility—the way you weave your thinking back and
forth between your writing and your classroom—reminds her of
the ways in which you and I may be alike as writers and as
teachers.

Maybe we are also romantically alike. Like you, I suffered the
pain of love affairs with young ladies rich or poor, with or without
racehorses, nor did love affairs go away simply because I married.
When you marry—if you marry—you will be in a better position
as time passes to tell me whether it is perfectly simple for a man,

no matter how long he is married, no matter how deep his family commitment, entirely to resist beautiful women with whom he comes face to face every day.

Of course I will be delighted to have you visit here if and when you care to come. You can meet my classes and lecture to them. We can ride bikes and talk ourselves dry. You will want to bear in mind, however, that no matter how far you go or how long you stay the same problems always await you back at your own machine. The vacation crew never does a thing. On one hand you tell me you are "well into a novel which is keeping me absorbed." Mother's "enormously helpful" criticism inspired you to continue confidently. Four paragraphs later, however, you appear to feel your novel will benefit by your absence, you find yourself "blocked," a trip to Arizona will "do me some good." Some of this sounds as illogical and paradoxical as some of the things your devoted father wrote in his desperate defense of his behavior during his wife's absence.

Since your primary object in coming to Arizona was to present yourself to Mariolena Sunwall I suspect you of mingling romantic pursuit with the idea of creative blockage. Writing doesn't unblock itself when the author goes somewhere else. Hemingway speaks to the point in his preface to a book of stories we're reading in class. He tells of writing in Michigan, Paris, Barcelona, Madrid, Montana, Kansas City, Key West, Chicago, Toronto, and Havana; just as he begins to fall into the trap of ranking places according to their hospitality to the creative spirit he catches himself; he knows it isn't the place that matters, it's whether you stick to your last while you're there. See how well he says it: "Some other places were not so good but maybe we were not so good when we were in them."

You remember those ladies in Chekhov always going to Moscow where everything would be better. The moral was, don't blame it on Kentucky. Writing blocks are in the writers' minds. There's really no such thing. The writer moaning to all his friends and lovers and associates and far-flung family complaining that the Muse has run off with another man basically only wants everyone to come and kiss him and say, "Oh, you poor dear, it's no wonder you're exhausted." Kisses I can send you, and encouragement of every kind.

214/

But I also want to keep us all honest. Are you really fighting block or are you really coming here to meet that wonderful Mariolena who, for all you know, might not be so wonderful in the flesh as in your father's bubbling prose? In any case she seems to have fled. I have not seen her in two days. She and her Spiral Binders have disappeared. I don't know where she has gone—home, I assume, to her parents, whom I described in my last All Points less than accurately. Mariolena invented them, cast them as bloody shoot-'em-up ranchers when they are mild supportive postal workers, and my having penetrated by chance her myth, her legend of herself, has made her very angry at me. She was absent from class yesterday.

You ask how old she is She is twenty-two. You apparently received the impression from me that you'd find her "a completely free spirit," but that may not be the case. She may be just a writer whose spirit soars only so long as her butt stays put. Does my telling you this bleak news turn you back toward your work? I'm sorry for the news but consoled if some good can come of it. I, too, hurt. (How's that for a punctuated sentence?) Her disappearance is painful to me, even as you are pained by your break with your lady friend who owns the horses with the literary names.

Let's look upon our problems as opportunities. Sometimes when ladies make our choices they release us from distraction. I send you all my love all the time.

Your father,

March 12

Dear Dr. Youngdahl:

Your medical colleague, Dr. Barnabus Emmer, has assured me you will be able to be informative to me in a matter of some delicacy. You have recently undergone surgery for "penile implant." Dr. Emmer was your surgeon.

Alack! it has become necessary that I, too, undergo surgery of the same nature for the same purpose. Little consolation to me to know that this affliction strikes down seventy percent of all normal males and no alternative treatment exists. I am specially interested in your reaction because you are the only physician on Dr. Emmer's list.

I am of course particularly interested in knowing whether the operation was attended with much pain. I have never enjoyed pain. Please be assured that I will retain your reply in the strictest confidence. If you should wish to phone me rather than putting information of such delicacy into a written letter please feel free to do so "person to person collect" at the number shown on this stationery. These days you will find me almost always at home, if I may make a bitter joke. Would that it were otherwise as it was not always thus. Hopefully it shall return.

Thanking you in advance for your courteous reply, I remain,

Yours sincerely,

216/

March 14

Dear Mr. Skagg:

I hasten to inform you that I would give you my opinion on the "penile implant" work of Dr. Emmer if I could. I have not yet undergone surgery for penile implant and may indeed finally decide against doing so.

I am wondering about your belief that "no alternative treatment exists." You may be correct. For three months many people have been assuring me that my impotence is all in my head—that I am only for the moment blocked, that I'll come round right away, and so forth. The good breakthrough has not occurred, and I have come to the conclusion that people's generosity with their encouragement may be proportionate to their ignorance of the malady.

I am not a physician. I am a professor and a writer. Please see my "Calling Card" enclosed.

I send you my best wishes for your early recovery. I regret that I have probably not been helpful to you.

Yours very cordially,

March 16

Dear Lee Youngdahl:

I'll be a little more formal though formality comes hard to me.
I deeply appreciate your letter and I want to speak to the questions
raised. They are natural questions.

Let me try to put to rest those questions you may have about
our "medical qualifications" here at Learning Together West. We
are not in any sense a "medical" center giving "medical" treat-
ments of any kind, although we like to think we are much more
effective than so-called "medical" establishments in treating people in "medical" matters. You and I and most of us were raised
to believe in the "medical" sciences, and we at Learning Together
West have never denied that certain organic diseases may be real
and may be best attended by members of the "medical" profession.

We began in Arizona as an educational institution, but after
some struggle we were denied accreditation as such by the Department of Public Instruction and became an institute of creative
therapy and healing. As we grew and flourished we may have
threatened certain "medical" interests in the state, and we were
denied the right to licensing, just as we had been denied educational accreditation. Rather than fight against the state depart-
ments of education or health we simply, following principles of
passive resistance, re-organized ourselves on paper without sac-
rificing a single principle and declared ourselves to be a religious
institution. As such we merely continue to do as we have always
done, but with the added prestige of our having been declared by
the U. S. Supreme Court to be well within our Constitutional
rights. The Court decision may be that struggle to retain my ministry, of which you speak.

In medical terms so-called "impotence," which is your present complaint, may usually be cured by modern methods long in
use at Learning Together West, Learning Together East, and else-

where throughout the United States and the world wherever creative healing is practiced. Right now we are finding tremendous help available for cases of so-called "impotence" by use of the following methods and combinations thereof:

1. Program of talk, discussion, counseling, and co-counseling, including nightly Round Table conversation— "where there is no head of the table."

2. Program of massage.

3. Program of pool bathing and Hot Tub bathing.

4. Program of readings and study in erotic literature, illustration, Film Viewing and studies in world culture and history. For example, I am fascinated by your remarks about the famous explorer, Ponce de Leon, discoverer of Florida and immediately receptive to the idea of discussing him as a pioneer of the search for a cure for "impotence." What a commentary it is on the nature of man that one man will risk the lives of others for his own advantage. I am ordering books on Ponce de Leon for our library.

5. Program of masturbation. One of the latest discoveries of the healing arts is masturbation. All studies show that one of the most effective ways of restoring men and women to active sexual life is by instituting exercises which, by producing orgasms, convince the "patient" that he/she still has powers he thought were lost. "One time proves it" is a common slogan of our profession.

6. Program of hypnosis.

7. Program of meditation. Our Meditation Spaces, our Dwelling Rooms and our "Moonlight Trail of Rocks" are central sites for everyone who comes to Shoestring Ranch. In a world filled with many noises, not all of them agreeable, silence may at some moments be appreciated as the most interesting of all sounds. Yesterday a woman said to me, "Haddock, I walked last night on 'The Moonlight Trail of Rocks,' and when I stepped from the last rock of the brilliant path I stepped into a new life. Some of my 'problems' just drifted into the night, becoming lost among the stars."

Our seven-fold program requires the participant's belief in its workability. You as a famous teacher of writing know the value of the method of support and encouragement as being superior to the method of technique-teaching. In many "medical" areas even so-called scientists tell us that patients must have faith.

"Mind over matter." Freud was a physician as well as a healer in the tradition of Learning Together West.

You, as you tell me, have actually had the experience of contemplating surgery for your so-called "impotence," but you have rejected it as appropriate procedure. You are already somewhat skeptical of "medical" authority and are glancing our way as millions are doing every year.

In reply to your comments, I understand very well your attitude toward "fun and games." Our programs follow the lines of your ultimate objective. But recreational pleasure and relaxation often follow the actual healing treatment. No laws of God or Arizona prohibit us from mixing healing with pleasure, for when we are cured of our afflictions we may then be most in the mood for games and love. At such times our recuperative baths may become our pleasure baths. Our mind-sets have changed. We have crossed at Learning Together West from the society of fierce competition, selling, stress, war and destruction, self-advancement and nuclear hatred into our enviroment of loving oneness and openness. Many men and women have come to us paralyzed by tension and anxious living, thinking themselves "impotent," only to be amazed by their swift recovery.

Let me tell you a tale I will admit I have told before. A man of our acquaintance entered a hospital in a major city for a penile implant of the kind you mention. He was a man of science, a hard-headed industrialist who had amassed a fortune in the aerospace industry, accumulated doubts about the morality of bomber building, and joined us at Learning Together West for prayer and discussion. The day of his operation approached. As preparations went forward he began to think back on conversations he had had at our Round Table. At first he had thought we were "quacks." He now decided, however, to give us a chance to assist him on the medical side as we had assisted him spiritually. After all, what could he lose? If the program here failed to cure him of his "impotence" he could always return to the hospital for surgery, but once he had undergone surgery he could not undo it. Therefore he announced to his surgeon that he had decided to postpone his penile implant operation. His surgeon replied, "You can't do that. We have already reserved the O. R. (Operating Room) and made all related arrangements." "What! Just because we have made arrangements are you telling me I must go through with this? I have made my will, too, but I am not obliged to die. Unheard of." At this point a nurse standing by, having become embarrassed by the dispute, queried the surgeon, asking, "What shall we do, doctor?" The doctor was heard to reply, "Chloroform the bastard." The nurse and various members of the hospital staff and even the surgeon himself set upon our acquaintance and forcibly subdued him on the bed and disconnected his telephone. The surgeon, becoming angrier by the minute, seeing ahead the dissipation of his $50,000 fee, was heard to shout, "Stick it in him." Seeing that the "medical" staff was trying to knock him out with an injection my acquaintance with the strength born of desperation began to scream and protest in such a loud and lusty manner that his stentorian shouts managed to produce a favorable outcome. Certain persons of the hospital staff, joined by strolling visitors in the hallways, hearing the screams and shouts of struggling and scuffling, were attracted to the scene, entered my acquaintance's room, and rescued him from his plight. Suffice to say he was released from the hospital promptly, and came directly here to Learning Together West, where in a short period of time he was rescued from his "impotence" by our program. Through our follow-up program we have learned that he has ever since enjoyed ideal sexual relationships with various partners, including his wife of many years. For us he has become much more than a mere acquaintance. He is a magnanimous contributor to The Learning Together East-Learning Together West Foundation and has recruited to our cause other men of his stature. The generosity of wealthy contributors has made Learning Together West available to less affluent people. Contributions are tax deductible.

In your letter you raise the question of the cost to you. Our charges are optional—from each person according to their evaluation of us. To start with it will cost you a quantity of gasoline from your house to ours. Even in this day of expensive gasoline the cost is very little, isn't it, when measured against the satisfying prospect of *the full recovery of your potency*. Will you invest in a few gallons of gasoline to restore your sexual powers? I must tell you of an unforgettable statement made in my presence not long ago. A man who came to Learning Together West to be cured of "impotence" was restored *overnight*. After remaining among us

/221

for several days he decided to take his leave. He contributed a generous sum to the Learning Together East-Learning Together West Foundation, for which I was duly grateful, you may be sure. "Haddock," he said, "you don't seem to appreciate the bargain you have made available to me. When I arrived here several days ago no woman was possible for me. But today every woman in the world is possible."

That is your initial investment. You pay your own gas. But let us go beyond that into a "double or nothing" gamble. Here are the conditions of my gamble. *You will pay nothing unless you are cured. Then you will pay a reasonable sum.* Let me give you a suggested figure. Your letter tells of the woman you sought as partner on the advice of our mutual friend Dr. Schiff. Your partner fled, taking with her $115 belonging to you. Let us double the figure and think of it as a daily rate. If you are cured at Learning Together West you will contribute $230 per day to our Foundation for each day of your residence with us. If you are not cured you pay nothing. Of course you may exceed $230 per day as you see fit.

Let me suggest that when you come to Shoestring Ranch you bring with you to share with us some of that good refreshment you had stocked for the disappointing lady. As your treatment progresses you will be more and more in a celebrating mood as you perceive us achieving goals we have identified as objectives. Please bring linen and a pillow (we supply blankets).

I send you my best personal and professional regards. I hope you have not found me too informal. I have tried to be "strictly business." Please extend my greetings to our wonderful Dr. Schiff if you should be in touch with her, as I know you have recently been.

Welcome,

March 16

Dear Lee,

Passed over you. Looked down on you to see if you were behaving yourself. I'm on the beach. It isn't that I'm trying to be tricky like the President's missiles. I waited until the last minute to find out where the sun was before deciding which end of California to go to. I don't write out my travel route or where I'm going to be every day because I'm never guilty about where I am. Writing out the names and phone numbers of all your hotels never meant a great deal to me because often you weren't there when you said you would. After some years I stopped counting on it.

I hope your student is very successful in New York and remains. There will be another where that one came from, I'm sure. These little writing girls pop out of the bushes at a moment's notice. None of your denials persuade me of anything. I trust my vibrations to the final inch. In spite of what you say I don't know what she looks like because I never asked anyone to point her out to me at Bob's Tavern or anywhere else. I remember the occasion but I do not remember the girl. She must not have made much impression on me. Also to set the record straight I didn't think her book was as marvelous as you report in your letter. You report with honesty my *smiling,* but I do not remember *erupting* and I do not think I did. I don't think it's right to go back over someone's letter and hold him responsible for all his words and phrases. Yet I was not unhappy to read Earl's reply to you. He caught you up logically.

But even then, I stick with vibrations over logic. I don't care how talented someone is, how deserving of sympathy and understanding and recognition, it is my diving board. If her parents are cruel to her let her find other fathers than you. When I left home I imagined you would be busy with your writing, trying to get into a new book beyond your being blocked, and you insisted that I go on this tour in spite of everything literary or medical. I made every possible provision for your being comfortable while I was gone. I am above arguing small points. Nothing matters less than whether it was a bikini or shorts and halter. Say shorts and halter and give you the point. The question is bigger.

I remember writing you from Earl's, urging you to go to Haddock Hooper, all else having failed. Tetsey tells me people go from Montreal all the way to Haddock Hooper and his name is mentioned in superlatives in books on the subject. But Tetsey herself has doubts about him and believes him to be somewhat of a fake. A fraud. A slick operator you can't dislike. I hope you have solved the problem by now, for your sake and mine, but if you have not solved it by now we shall solve it soon. We have solved all our problems.

This has been a glorious trip for me in spite of anything. I suppose a day or two less at each port of call may have been just right. It is already a part of memory, as if it is over, and yet it's still happening. Tetsey says she believes we sometimes do these things not for the things themselves but for the memory we'll have after. And she noticed me "spacing out." My mind will wander. She pressed me to tell her where I was wandering. I was only keeping my numbers straight, uncontrollably counting everything up, how many days I have been gone, how many places, how many airplanes, how many beds I have slept in, how many restaurants, how many automobiles I have ridden in (impossible to calculate) and how many mule-drawn buses through the mud (one). How many credit-card vouchers? A terrible lot. I'll phone you my arrival time.

I am hoping the boxes arrived from Lucien's and were not hurled over the fence. I hope you found the Roll-a-dex.

With love,

FROM: Halina Schiff, Ph. D., C. C. P., and R. D., writer, New York City.

March 17

Dear Lee,

I'm just so crushed. In my head I was reading the letter you were planning in your head telling me how perfectly everything went with Mariolena. To be honest, my pride lay not in its going well so much as in its going well *by my advice.* But instead of your letter of success, congratulating me on my professional insight, I have here your baffling letter of failure. I had so much wanted my advice to be good for you. I don't think I now dare give you any more.

When she was here she was so eager and obvious about you. When anybody mentioned your name she sat upright and saluted. She carries your Calling Card. My first thought is that you are right—yes, your catching her in lies made her sheepish and therefore angry. What kind of lies were these? You mention an airplane lie and then a family lie. Did you go around as a detective trying to find out things about her? Surely that would make her angry, to be snooped on. If you have discovered weaknesses in her character you put her at a competitive disadvantage. In her eyes you have been the perfect and admirable man, and now your virtue escalates in proportion to her moral decline. If she believes you are too good for her she must tell herself she doesn't want you, anyway, although knowing herself to be a liar she won't believe herself unless she really carries it out. Ergo, you are rejected, to prove to herself that she does not want you.

It is commonplace in my trade to say, "When a relationship goes bad look for a failed love affair." To that I add, "When a love affair goes bad look for money." Mariolena and I talked a great deal when she was here. Several times she mentioned money in a way that made me feel it complicated her relationship with you. She was chagrined for having borrowed from you. Nevertheless she was looking for a reason for not repaying you. "He's very rich

/225

and he doesn't really need it." Yes, Mariolena, but you *borrowed* it with the *understanding* that you'd repay it. Response: "He owns classy cars, classy bicycles, two of everything." Yes, Mariolena, but no friendship can survive broken promises.

You are truthful and she is a liar. You are rich and she is poor. In every department you are humiliatingly superior to her. Yet I don't think she really objects to being thought of as a liar. She has been chastised for lying ever since first grade, but her lies win her applause in school and $10,000 from Apthorp House and might before long make her even richer. When lies turn to money they must be true. She's a big wheeler-dealer like her violent father, whom she hates for his mercilessness and inhumanity.

If only some emergency threatened you she could go to your assistance. She would then be seen as much different from her heedless father, although I think that the more I trip along here the more confused I become. Scratch it all. My eye catches your statement that her baby was at home "in the little old family house" all "safe and happy." I may have missed something. If only she knew that you were dying—I don't know. If only some emergency were bringing you down . . . if only some irate student were to rush to the front of the classroom and attack you she could rescue you . . . you see me "floundering through the streets" at a loss.

Can't you *demand* that she appear before you? Can't you as her teacher and Advisor and what-not send her a stern official communication on the crispest possible university stationery informing her that unless she reports to you she will fail the course, fail to graduate? No, you wouldn't do a thing like that. Forgive me. I just don't know. It is true, as you guess, that I am as disappointed as you. If I have a decent thought I'll be in touch with you immediately. I so badly want things to go happily and healthily for my friends.

Your old friend,

FROM: Ms. Mariolena Sunwall, student, c/o Mr. and Mrs. Sanford Sunwall, Phoenix, Arizona.

March 18

Dear Dr. Youngdahl:

O what an insensitive person I have been and what a lesson I have learned!! You should have told me the situation. You should have spoken. I assumed too many things I had no right to assume. My inexperience got the better of me. I assumed you had invited my parents to your house, conspiring to consult about me, comparing notes. But that was true only in a technical sense. It was my father who phoned you—he who made the overture; it was *they*, really, for when my father makes a telephone call you may be sure my mother's standing by. Not that he was unwilling. He'll go anywhere on Sunday. They went to you of their own accord. From the time I was a girl they had the habit of prowling around to see what my friends looked like, especially if they were male friends, as they commonly were. They phoned you on a pretext: they knew perfectly well I did not expect them to pick me up at the airport.

You put me through the wringer of love. I had no idea what the true problem was. Then at last my mother revealed it with a chance remark. I had assumed you were finished with love. You had so kindly invited me and I had so eagerly gone, but in the days that followed you made no significant move in my direction even as I lounged in my bikini on your poolside diving board (where else a diving board? in the garage? swinging from the chimney? I too am a soldier in the war against redundance) exhibiting myself all but naked to the world, jumping and springing and leaping and tumbling and flying my ass through the air from sunup to sundown in the hope of attracting your attention.

All the time you were riveted up there at your typewriter!! It shamed me that I, by contrast, was so easily diverted from my work. I saw in you the powerful concentration required by a true

/227

writer, and I increasingly despaired to see how weak and strengthless I was when compared to you at your lofty window.

And in all your remarks you referred endlessly to your wife, who seemed to be, from your remarks, everything to you. I am not necessarily daunted by impossible undertakings, but forty years of marriage looked like a rather high hurdle to clear. After a time I became convinced I hadn't a chance, and my bitterness gathered, as you may have detected from my recent correspondence to you. You made me in my desperation turn all truth inside out. It was not that I objected to your emanations: it was the question *where were they?* I sent you every message short of words.

Now after discussion with my open-minded parents the missing clue has been luckily supplied. I resort now to words, and I shall persist until my words have reached you, nor will they be subtle and indirect or coquettish or blushing. I have telephoned you and left hourly messages on your machine. I will persist. I will wear your machine out. I hope you are still impotent because I crave the pleasure of revitalizing you. There I was, and now I will be there again, especially if I can locate you. I will do everything to make you whole again. Do you remember one recent day, when I was waiting for the tram at the kiosk, you offered me a ride on your bicycle? Your bare legs shone. The hairs of your calves glistened in the Arizona winter sunshine. It was the thrill of my life. I was hoping the whole vehicle might collapse under us and we would sprawl on the ground violently smashed up against one another. My eye caught your erection. Hope sprang to my breast. But what then is impotence? I'm really not that clear on the subject. The young men of Sin City are vague. I get the idea you can't fuck. Sir, never. Can't-fuck time has come to an end, dear darling Dr. Youngdahl, accept this prophesy or prediction from your affectionate friend, mistress, companion, one-time bicyclist.

Star student, too. I hope you have not issued premature instructions to the Registrar regarding my grade for the course. However, fail me if you will. I have not fulfilled your requirements as you outlined them to us on Day One. I have sometimes been absent from class, thereby failing my fellow-students whose work

228/

I was morally contracted to critique as generously as they had critiqued mine. I would have fulfilled my obligation had I not been called away to New York. I am now hopeful that instead of your giving me a failing grade, or my withdrawing, you can give me at least a grade of "C" as if to honor my good intentions, so that I might receive credit for the course and graduate in May, an event to which my parents have looked forward for many years, and for which they have generously and self-abnegatingly sacrificed to support my development as a writer and as a student: if you have been my spiritual pillar they have been my first line of material defense.

Perhaps you have simply forgotten to switch off your machine. Your house is tight closed. When I tried to unlock the front door alarms sounded and I fled. I will find where you are and be there. I recognized from my New York experience how you take mistresses from your class. I suspect by the scintillation of her eyes that "Schiffy" is known to you, and Virgilia Magoogoo Kamoomoo Makaka Suekuykeen. As I began to divine the drift of history I felt myself left out, for I had thought of you as my own, my mentor, my Advisor, my shelterer and my harborer, everything but my lover. But when I found out that for others it had been possible to be lover, too, I interrogated myself, "Why not me?" My expectations rose. Some months ago when I was very low you said to me, "O well, that's what we writers have to put up with." You were saying that I, too, was a writer, and so saying you sent my confidence to the sky. Confidence breeds confidence. If I am a writer and share your agent and your publisher and your intimate friend "Schiffy" and your guest house and diving board then why not share your soul as well?

I was shocked and confused that you invited me to your private grounds but not farther. I searched myself relentlessly to learn what was wrong with me that you had invited me so far— then drawn the line. One week ago you abandoned me. You left. You went to school, though you had no class, no business known to me. How had I offended you? By now my self-doubt was spun tighter than I could bear. I left that place as fast as I could.

My mother was kind enough to give me the medical news. Bad as it sounded I rejoiced to think the deficiency lay not in me but elsewhere, and her information inspired me also with a determination to assist you in your difficulty. I was at the end of my selfishness.

With difficulty, I have been re-reading my manuscript. It doesn't sound good to me any more. I have grown and matured. Abner's fear has been justified that you will "sophisticate" me, spoil me, render me as worthless in the market as a cow-shit-eating chicken. Whatever you make me that's what I want to be.

Your devoted student,

March 21

Dear darling Schiff,

I have had many things to thank you for over the years, and
now again. Things at Haddock Hooper's retreat in the desert went
well; indeed, better than I had expected or even hoped; indeed
perfectly; and I am home again a new man, enjoying and expe-
riencing erection after erection at the slightest provocation. I don't
know why I was so skeptical, or why I so long put off going. It's
an old stubbornness with me, the constant feeling that I can help
myself without the intervention of any man, especially so un-
literary a man as Haddock Hooper. He has certainly not read me
"thoroughly," as you promised, or read me at all, or read anybody's
work thoroughly or otherwise, although he has certainly read
everybody's slogans and mottos; he knows everybody *reductio*,
familiar fragments from Mark Twain, Emerson, Thoreau, leaping
then into the idiotic self-help literature of the present age, especially *Any Cure is the Right Cure*, a copy of which may be found
in every Meditation Space and Dwelling Room at Shoestring Ranch
like Bibles in hotels. Haddock claims to have "read Marx," but
he has read the Manifesto only. He's wild about the American
Constitution but he really hasn't read anything in it except here
and there a favorite Bill of Right, which he quotes at intervals to
uphold an idea which may by chance be passing through his head
at a given moment.

He's an actor. At dinner the first night I was there, at the
wonderful vast Round Table—headless; except that wherever
Haddock sits there's the head—he placed his fingertips to his
temples, summoning from dusty memory this lost wisdom presumably, "I think I recall Santayana's saying, 'Those who cannot
remember the past are condemned to repeat it.' " Some years ago,
when I first heard some politician quote that sentence, I was
wonderfully cheered to think that anybody in public office had

/231

read anything of Santayana. I rejoiced at our amplified possibilities. But soon I heard another politician quote Santayana. The same sentence. Then another politician. Same sentence every time. And then one day as I was traveling through Washington I saw in an airport building that very sentence painted across the wall a mile high, and I realized with disappointment that politicians had not taken to reading Santayana, only to reading walls. So I didn't get off to such a hot start with Hooper. "I think I recall . . ." he'd say. Jesus, once an hour he'd think he was recalling something, dredging up some old pickled sentence from the literature of the past he's never in the least cared for.

I was embarrassed to arrive. It wasn't that he seized me and wrapped his arms about me but that he called out over my shoulder, "Everybody, this is professor Lee Youngdahl, author of two dozen books, world expert on Ponce de Leon who discovered Florida"—about a dozen books more than I have written; as for Ponce de Leon, whom I had mentioned to Haddock in a letter, I have read three or four paragraphs about him in the *Encyclopedia*. I wriggled out of his arms before he could kiss me.

I had arrived with linens and a pillow and my bathing trunks. I thought I'd take a swim, arriving at the pool only to find that everyone there was nude. I wasn't quite ready for that. I returned to my Dwelling Room and relaxed on my bed thinking things over. Soon a stunning nude woman came along carrying her bathing cap and a package of cigarettes. This is the kind of thing you fantasize—you check in to a room and the next thing you know— Well, she explained, Haddock was hoping to make a little twosome of us. Her vice was smoking. She had come to Learning Together West to stop smoking, which wasn't my problem at all; my problem was impotence, which wasn't her problem at all. I was to rescue her from tobacco. "Whenever you see me take a cigarette smack it out of my hand," she instructed me. "Destroy my cigarettes. Hide them. Shred them up. Bury them in the desert sand, if you will be so kind," and off she walked, lighting a cigarette. I leaped up and ran after her and knocked the cigarette out of her hand. "O. K.," she said, "we're on the way."

I had been hoping people would dress for dinner, and indeed they did. They dressed very well, some in comfortable togas, most of us in sports clothes. These are affluent people, as I am sure you know. Haddock in principle welcomes poor people, but I don't think he actively recruits them. My arrival was formally announced at dinner by Haddock, who rose at his place, tapping his glass with a spoon, like any Rotarian. He urged me to tell everyone why I was there and what I hoped to accomplish: I was there for my impotence and hoped to cure it. Haddock assured me that although no such thing exists as "impotence" I had come to the right place to cure it. Many of the guests at table assured me that this was so, that I should solve my problem and have fun in the doing. Some of my fellow-guests had once been impotent. Others suffered various mental blocks and vices which we were even then discussing at our headless table as part of the seven-fold program upon which we were embarked. Everything pleasurable anyone did could be seen as one phase or another of the seven-fold program.

After dinner my smoking lady and I walked out into the desert along the Moonlight Trail of Rocks. You too have walked the Moonlight Trail of Rocks, Haddock tells me. So you know how impressive it is in its spaciousness and its silence. I felt that I was walking on the moon without all those moon-like disadvantages. My smoking friend kept lighting cigarettes as we walked, and I kept knocking them out of her hands. I was awfully sorry for her. Had she really come to the right place? Yes, she said, Haddock has stopped many people from smoking, he's a miracle man, it was all a matter of matching the right smoker with the right mate, they'd cure each other of whatever they wanted to be cured of by focusing totally on each other's need. We walked into the desert, quite beyond the end of the trail of rocks, leaving behind, however, a moonlight trail of cigarettes smoking themselves to death in the sand. When we retraced our steps she retrieved them from the desert floor. As quick as she picked them up I slapped them from her hands, she resisted me, we struggled. "You've got to care," she said, "or it's no good," but I was caring, I really do care; you know how I hate smoking and all such suicidal vices. "I mean you've got to care for me," she said, "like a lover, to get you over the problem and have some fun besides," but none of our tussling and grappling either animated my genitalia or cured her of smoking. When we stopped to rest she lit up another. We went to pools and hot tubs (part of the program), no sooner set-

/233

tling into the water for play and relaxation, thinking positive thoughts, defying "performance failure," than up she'd leap and run away dripping in search of tobacco. Wherever she went I pursued her dripping, she'd hide and I'd seek her and wrest her cigarettes from her. I seemed to take a humane satisfaction in confiscating and destroying her cigarettes until at last she had none, but I could feel within myself not a quiver of sexual emotion; not so many months ago I'd have played such a game with all the laughing tumescent enthusiasm of the boy I was at sixteen, the boy I have been ever since, except during this recent impotent period.

The next morning the hypnotist came to me. She was a lovely woman with a soothing, melodious voice who has never failed through hypnotism to produce erections in subject-men. She has also produced poetry in poets, inventiveness in inventors, memory in forgetters, and relief from aches and pains whenever they are associated with tension and the psyche. I was her first failure. I could see by her face when I awoke that I had disappointed her, betrayed her, hurt her. "You are a strong-willed man," she said. Maybe she was a weak-willed hypnotist. "This was all you kept saying," she said, showing me a seven-digit telephone number I had repetitively shouted out from the deep. It was the telephone of the neighbor boy who feeds our animals when we are gone.

You know, the smile never departs from Haddock's face, but he had a hard time maintaining it by the end of my first twenty-four hours. He likes to win. He doesn't like to think there's a weakness in his system. New people started arriving, and those who were leaving felt themselves cured or assisted along the way. He urged me not to give up so soon. We had a good little talk over lunch. "It does not exist," he kept emphatically saying.

"Then what have I got?" I challenged him. Challenge—you know what I mean. One challenges Haddock in a low voice. Nobody raises voices. I like that. "You may not want to give it a name," I said, "but it's something."

"There's no synonym for it," he said, "it does not exist."

"There's no synonym for *wheelbarrow*," I said. "Everything has failed."

"Never say that," he said. "You'll depress everybody."

I was tired of this place. I would go home. We had tried

everything I had cared to try. I had come from zinc and testosterone to the program of talk discussion counseling and co-counseling around the old Round Table, through pools and hot tubs and hypnosis. "I've about had it," I said.

"You haven't tried everything," he said. True, I had massage, pornography, masturbation and meditation yet to go. During the afternoon a nice lady came to me and gave me a nice massage. I lay inert, I was a disappointment to her, as I had been to my hypnotist. Hypnotist, masseuse, and my smoking lady were all at dinner, all surrounding me, tending me, as Haddock, I think, had urged them to, or in his mild tones ordered them to. He had taken my failure very personally and talked me up all over the place, so that at dinner I was the center of attention. My past was revealed, my credentials were known. As a one-time Mormon I was expected to answer questions about polygamy. Haddock asked me for a lecture on Ponce de Leon.

"Now?"

"Why not? We're all eager."

"Because I don't know anything about him," I said. "In any case he didn't find what he was looking for," I said. "His mission failed. And I am really and truly sorry to say that this mission has failed for me, too. It's awfully nice and noble, and I want you all to go on having a good time, but I really must be leaving."

Haddock, at his place at table, bowed his head respectfully. After a moment, however, he jerked it erect when the door opened and in walked Mariolena.

She was awed. To a young woman who has lived all her life in a little crowded house in Phoenix the splendor of Shoestring Ranch equalled even the splendor of the Algonquin. She told me afterward that she had felt badly dressed. I hadn't noticed. She wore the Wire Brim cowboy hat she'd worn to Virgilia's wedding. I was amazed and delighted to see her. I had thought she was gone from me forever. People made a place for her at table and she sat. "What's happening?" she asked.

"We are counseling one another," Haddock said.

"Have they cured you?" she asked me.

"Of what?" I didn't know she knew.

"I know," she said. She had written me a letter I had not received. I hadn't been home.

"Are you the person Schiffy recommended?" Haddock asked her.

"Did Schiffy recommend me?" Mariolena asked. "That was smart of her. She saw right through me in a minute. What have you tried?" she asked, addressing everyone. She was the doctor and she had arrived.

"Almost everything," I said, "and nothing works."

"What do we do now then?" she asked.

"We thought we would embark on a program of masturbation," said Haddock Hooper. "It's the latest discovery."

"How late?" she asked. "It took a long time to get from Phoenix to Carefree. When I was a child I was told that my hands would fall off if I masturbated, and I supposed it was true since so many people said so. Then one day I looked around school and I said to myself, 'Hey, I just *know* that a lot of these kids masturbate because they've told me so, and the boys have told my brothers, and I don't see a single kid with fallen-off hands,' and I began to whack away on my own and enjoyed every orgiastic minute of it. Sometimes I think it's almost as much fun as writing." Everyone at table applauded. "How's your manuscript coming?" she asked me.

"Breaking through," I said.

"Are you a writer?" Haddock asked her.

"Am I a writer?" she asked me.

"She's on the way," I said. "She's just sold a book to Apthorp House." Once more everyone at table applauded.

"I love this," she said.

"It's obvious you care a great deal for him," said Haddock Hooper.

"He's my teacher," she said.

Mariolena and I walked out along the Moonlight Trail of Rocks—"tinted by moonlight." So she put it. There was almost no moon at all. She asked me what her grade would be for the course if she were to return. Had I been talking with the Registrar? Wasn't it possible for me to see her trip to New York as part of her classwork? "Abner recommends a quadruple-A," I said, "and I usually do what my agent says." She threw her arms about me. Then we walked on. "The woman I walked out with this way last night," I said, "has the most awful smoking problem. Haddock thought I might help her but I couldn't."

"You can only help writers," she said. "You can't help anybody else."

"Look how she littered the desert floor with cigarette butts," I said.

"The first writing prize I ever won," she said, "was for writing an essay against littering Grand Canyon. The bottom of Grand Canyon is covered with little yellow film boxes. It's a crime."

"Where's your baby?" I asked.

"At my folks'."

"You didn't just dump him somewhere in Sin City with somebody whose name you sort of know."

"I don't do that any more," she said. "How much is this costing you?"

"Let's see," I said. "I think I have it right. I'm to pay him two hundred and thirty dollars a day if his cure works, nothing if it doesn't."

"You got a good deal," she said. "How will he know if it works or not?"

"I'm on the honor system," I said.

"I owe you five hundred and fifteen dollars," she said, once again throwing her arms about me, quite climbing up me as if I were a tree, kissing me, while her tears ran, and now for the first time in more than three months—since that day at the kiosk on campus—I began to become erect; indeed, became stalwartly, brilliantly, hugely, dazzlingly erect—for a moment not realizing that it had happened at last, it was such an old familiar memory, after all—but there I was again, as in the days of my past, flowing, throbbing, bursting, hot as iron, and I was with lover again—and my organ in turmoil and joy and commotion ran wet, and her eyes and nose ran wet, too, with crying and relief, and she said, "You said you wouldn't take rent so it's only one hundred and fifteen."

"That's my calculation, too," I said.

"You don't have to tell him," she said.

"Tell who?"

"Haddock Hooper."

"Tell him what?"

"That he's cured you," she said.

"Oh, I've got to tell him," I said, "it's what we agreed. It's the honor system."

"God what fun we'll have," she said, "now that you're in business. Where's your room?"

"Not far. Dwelling Room we call it."

"A pleasure to think of it," she said. "Farewell to Sin City. Farewell to hard floors. No more inside my VW bug. No more roommates barging back in any minute. No more on a pile of laundry in the laundry room. Hold out until your Dwelling Room. Think of the postal kiosk. Think of the smell of bicycle tires. Think of the shape of handlebar grips."

"That's all right," I said. "I'm there. I'll last now. Don't worry about me."

"One time proves it," she said. "It's over. You've broken through. No more block. But I'm just wondering if you really do think it's necessary for me, a poor, single mother, a struggling undergraduate, to pay you back one hundred and fifteen dollars. You owe Hooper four hundred and sixty dollars. You owe him nothing if you want to. You choose to pay him. I don't think a man who can afford the honor system four hundred dollars' worth really needs a hundred and fifteen dollars from me." We strolled the Moonlight Trail of Rocks, but a little more swiftly now, as if we had a destination. I was breathing hard, as if I had ridden my bicycle fast a good distance. We were hand in hand, tinted by moonlight. Schiff old girl, there it was, the melting of the block, the thawing of the bay, the happy vessels sailing through. I don't know if anyone has ever written of the good cheer of this particular deliverance. You sexual scientists have written about causes and cures, but you haven't sufficiently celebrated the new life which begins when one is enabled to return to the old, as he was, good as new, when all the familiar lifelong motives and incentives fall into place again, and the writing won't stop because at the end of the writing lies love. "Because I'm so damn broke," she continued. "If you were to forgive me the one hundred and fifteen dollars I could start all over fresh again with a clean slate."

"A poet once said, 'A stiff prick has no conscience,' " I said.

"If a poet hadn't said it you'd have said it," she said.

"Call it fifty," I said.

"That's fair," she said, though I think she was a bit disappointed. "I expect my check from Abner any day."

So much for the local news. When will I ever see you again? When will you come west? Or I go east? You'll see I've got the old crotch back now. I'm so happy I can't tell you. I thank you again and again for your persistence in making me go to Haddock Hooper and for *Sex In the Seventh Decade (And After)*, especially your chapter "Getting Going Again." You saved my life. Not that alone: as you can see I'm in good spirits, home again, and Beth will be home in a few days from her tour of seven children in two foreign countries and three American states. She will rejoice in her husband's return to health. She will accept Haddock Hooper as wonder-worker.

I'll write again soon. I'll try to be in touch better. I should not write you only when I need you. I send you as always my love and affection and greetings and medical history and hopes and best wishes for your health and prosperity and the continued success of your valuable health-giving research. Kisses.

As ever yours, your professor,

FROM: Ms. *Virgilia MacGregor Kuhmerker*
McDevitt Suekuykeen, writer, New York City.

March 19

Dear Lee,

I wish you had come to the wedding. You could have made it if you tried. All along I thought you would try. We have just returned from our little trip and everything is going very well. Life doesn't seem to be different at all, it's the old routine. Things are in the groove. Do you remember "In the Groove"? I remember all the music of the '40s and not a note since. After the wedding we went overseas and were married again there and now he arises in the morning and goes to the office like any other man, and I go to my typewriter.

You must not destroy my letters. I trust you to know better than to do everything I told you to do. My friend Sid gave me my letters back to be destroyed, and after I destroyed them I was mournful for days. I have felt very angry at him for doing as I asked. Through all the excitement I carried in my head (the letter itself I have hidden away) your letter about your visit to the urologist (I almost said chiropodist) regarding your impotence. I hate to tell you that I recently met a man who has been impotent for many years and has never been able to find any help for himself though he has traveled for reputed cures to every corner of the world.

Come to town when you can. There can't be any harm, can there, in an occasional meeting? Write or Telegraph. Send me a funny postcard.

Always affectionately,

240/

                                                    March 20
Dear Lee,

   Point regarding possible article re impotence. Lunching with
a Reader's Digest editor the subject of impotence came up. She
is interested in a good article on the subject paying in the neighborhood of $15–$20,000, not too bad. For years I could never
place you in the Digest. I look on it as a challenge. Leafing back
in my mind I began thinking of this as a spin off from your novel
re the girl on the diving board. Why not take a break from the
novel and write this article on impotence covering such questions
as first signs and symptoms of the disease coming on, possible
embarrassment in telling members of the family, especially wife,
first visits to the physicians and what kind of physicians you go
to, discussions pro and con regarding surgery or not, psychological factors or not, questions of adjusting and resigning to the
situation if necessary, various medicines or other treatments a
man takes, and every other aspect of the topic, covering all moral
and religious aspects of the matter as well, might quote from Bible
where feasible. Explain how patients seek religious help and guid-
ance, consultation and research with clergymen, maybe weaving
your own experience into it all, showing how God helped you
overcome your impotence. If not, accept it as one of the acts of
God, etc., whichever way you go follow a line and stick to it. Who
am I telling you?

   If you're interested in going ahead with this idea notify me
right away and I'll put you in touch with the editor, an aggressive
and up and coming young girl who has read all your books and
is dying to get you in the magazine.

   I am glad *The Girl on the Diving Board* is going well. Don't
let anything interrupt you.

   I am glad to hear that Beth is coming along on her worldwide
tour and has reached Earl's. I hope Earl is working ahead on his

novel without interruption and will send it along to me soon. I'm not as worried about the fur coat in the closet as you are. It's easy to explain you saw a rat run in the closet, you plunged in after the rat, all the coats on the rack fell down, you picked everything up and put them all back the best you could, nobody's perfect. Everything you tell me about meeting her parents and the revelations of lies come as no surprise to me after forty years dealing with writers. You're lucky you got the coat back at all. She left it in four different restaurants. Dorothy said if you're going to wear rags to New York you're lucky you've got a mink coat to hide them under. I was also excited to hear that Mariolena has written many other books. Small or not I'm going to ask her to send them along, as we are getting very enthusiastic reactions to early readings on her book.

Point regarding further difficulties with Mariolena. She changed her mind about the title, and then she changed it back again. I sent her a check but it did not go through the bank as she did not endorse it correctly. She did not like the way I spelled her name, returned it to me, and I sent her another made out to the name she preferred. I hope it lasts.

Point Regarding Ending Your Book. It's always hard to end a book. There was a certain author hanging by his thumbs at the crossroads of his career. He had a book in the works that would make him or break him. All his friends were behind him. All his enemies were against him. Too bad he couldn't tell which was which.

Naturally his loyal and fun-loving agent cheered him on through all his agonies. Month after month the author slaved at his labor, suffering loss of appetite, loss of hair, loss of wife, he chewed his fingernails to the bone, and his ulcers flared away. Soon he came to the end of the book, working at it night and day against the most overpowering exhaustion any man ever knew. At last he could do nothing more. He polished up every tail of every comma. Off he sent the book by United Parcel to his faithful agent, who loved it and immediately ran it across the street to the famous publishing house of Hooker & Crooker. Hooker had promised the author if this book was half as good as Hooker & Crooker hoped they would pay him twice the money of his dreams. Crooker concurred. Our author would be sitting pretty. His troubles would be over. His hair would grow back and his wife would return from her exile.

Now day after day our author waited for word from his agent. No word came. At last word came. On the telephone was the agent. "Tell me the news," screamed the author, "what's the verdict from Hooker & Crooker, I can't wait, don't keep me hanging."

"A little suspense is always fun," said his fun-loving agent. "I've got a little bit of bad news mixed in with a lot of good news, so tell me which one you want first, the bad or the good."

"How can you do this to me?" the author asked. "However, I suppose you must do it your way, so go ahead and tell me the little bit of bad news you got mixed in with the good."

"Which first?"

"The bad."

"The little bit of bad news is that Hooker & Crooker unanimously with one voice supported by every associate and every junior editor in the house say they would go out and dig ditches before they would publish your novel, which they consider the stinkeroo of the 20th Century, the work of a madman. They have mentioned their opinion throughout the trade. Your chances of finding another publisher are reduced to sub-zero. You are ruined. Don't call me back."

Our author sank to his knees. It was like he was felled. He clutched the telephone line. His brain ached. He quoted aloud, "Death, where is thy sting?"

"What's that?" said his agent. "Speak up. There's something wrong with the line since the AT & T divestiture."

Like every drowning man, our author reached out for some last bit of floating material. His mind remembered his agent's opening remarks. He said, "You mentioned there was a lot of good news mixed in with this little bit of bad news. Now tell me the good news."

"Oh, yes," exclaimed his agent. "On to the good news. Do you remember that attractive woman employed by me in my office for several years? Well, last night I finally seduced her."

(Credit Irving Park.)

Ever yours,

THE END

ABOUT THE AUTHOR

MARK HARRIS is probably best known for the Henry Wiggen Series, *Bang the Drum Slowly*, *A Ticket for a Seamstitch*, *The Southpaw*, and *It Looked Like For Ever*. His book *The Heart of Boswell* (McGraw-Hill) is a reader abridging the private papers of James Boswell. Mark Harris lives in Tempe, Arizona.